Also by Jeremy Akerman

and available from Moose House Publications

Memoir
Outsider

Politics
What Have You Done for Me Lately? - revised edition

The Marc LeBlanc Mysteries
Holy Grail, Sacred Gold
Unspeakable Evil
The Plot to Kill the Premier
Best Served Cold
My Brother's Keeper

Fiction
Black Around the Eyes – revised edition
The Affair at Lime Hill
The Premier's Daughter
In Search of Dr. Dee
Explosion
Come From Away: a Cape Breton Odyssey (due in 2025)

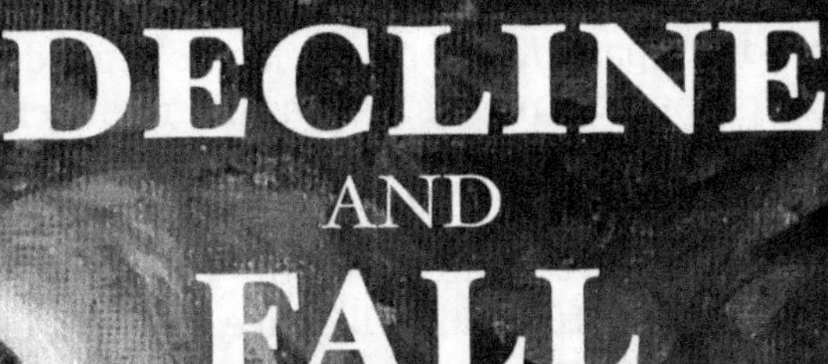

DECLINE
AND
FALL

PROCTOR UNVEILS RADICAL PRO
remier declares "War on Wo
WIN WITH WENDELL
THE MAN OF THE MOMENT
PROCTOR FOR PREMIER

OLVED that the caucus ask
e party to hold a leadership
review as soon as possible
THOSE IN FAVOUR
THOSE OPPOSED

JEREMY AKERMAN

Cover illustration and other images by the author
Cover design: Rebekah Wetmore
Editor: Andrew Wetmore

ISBN: 978-1-998149-85-8
First edition May, 2025

Moose House Publications
2475 Perotte Road
Annapolis County, NS B0S 1A0
moosehousepress.com
info@moosehousepress.com

Moose House Publications recognizes the support of the Province of Nova Scotia. We are pleased to work in partnership with the Department of Communities, Culture and Heritage to develop and promote our cultural resources for all Nova Scotians.

We live and work in Mi'kma'ki, the ancestral and unceded territory of the Mi'kmaw people. This territory is covered by the "Treaties of Peace and Friendship" which Mi'kmaw and Wolastoqiyik (Maliseet) people first signed with the British Crown in 1725. The treaties did not deal with surrender of lands and resources but in fact recognized Mi'kmaq and Wolastoqiyik (Maliseet) title and established the rules for what was to be an ongoing relationship between nations. We are all Treaty people.

This book is dedicated to my friend Vince MacLean,
who would have been a good premier
if his own troops had not brought him down.

This is a work of fiction. The author has created the characters, conversations, interactions, and events; and any resemblance of any character to any real person is coincidental.

Decline and Fall

Decline and Fall

1

For some time, I had known that Ray Bland was interested in and had some connection with politics because the premier of Nova Scotia, Wendell Proctor, was a guest at his and Rachel's wedding. That occasion was my introduction to Proctor and it led, eventually, to my being engaged by him to conduct investigations into threats he had been receiving. In turn, that gave rise to a friendship, though not perhaps a deep one, between the premier, his wife, Cynthia, and my wife and me.

My name Marc LeBlanc, and I live with my wife, Rosalie, in what most people would regard as luxury, in Grand Pre, at the beginning of Nova Scotia's Annapolis Valley. I consider myself a lucky man, not only because Rosalie is a beautiful, loving woman, but due to the fact that, through speculation and inheritance, I am a wealthy man. Ours is a large, well-situated property with a spectacular view across the Minas Basin, famous for recording the world's highest tides.

Rosalie teaches history at Acadia University, in nearby Wolfville, while I am licensed to conduct private investigations into matters which intrigue me or appeal to my sense of injustice. I have recorded accounts of these investigations in five books: *Holy Grail, Sacred Gold; Unspeakable Evil; The Plot to Kill the Premier; Best Served Cold;* and *My Brother's Keeper.*

The most conspicuous manifestation of my wealth is my pride and joy, a car like no other in the world, the Bugatti L'Or Blanc. It is white, with cobalt-blue lines artistically painted around the body, has a top speed of around 407 kilometres per hour and can accelerate from 0 to 60 in 2.5 seconds.

It is extraordinary for a number of other reasons, not least of which is that the exterior of this 1,001-horsepower vehicle is surfaced in a mix of aluminum and carbon fibre, but has been painted using the same patterns and techniques employed by the artisans at German porcelain designer Königliche Porzellan-Manufatur Berlin. Many of the finer details, such as the wheel centerecaps, fuel filler cap and interior trim pieces, were all fashioned from porcelain, most of it by hand. It is a masterpiece.

Ostensibly, the Bugatti was a gift from my friend Sheikh Abdul Aziz, for whom it was originally made, but I strongly suspect it was purchased from him by a man who is supposed to be dead.

Despite Ray and Rachel having become among the very best friends that my wife, Rosalie, and I had, we had never talked about politics. Certainly, I had often discussed Middle Eastern affairs with Rachel, who was a strong partisan of Israel, but I could recall no conversation with Ray which had anything to do with either local or federal politics. I realized that I had not even inquired how he knew the premier, or how close was their relationship.

I am about the least political person you could wish to meet. I have voted in most elections, but in a desultory manner, and by no means always for the same party. My interests are in wine, cooking, cars, and my work as a private investigator. If you put a gun to my head, I suppose I would describe myself as a liberal, but not one that any modern liberal would recognize.

I think I broadly believe in civil liberties under the rule of law, individual autonomy in so far as that is possible, free market and laissez-faire economics if fairly and reciprocally applied, limited government, as much economic freedom as is consonant with a civilized society, political freedom and, above all, freedom of speech. In saying that, I am aware that I am in a very distinct minority in a society where most people are branded by their opponents as "the lunatic left", "the far right fascists" or the "indifferent, ignorant masses."

However, under no circumstances could I imagine myself rising up or going to the barricades for my beliefs. Rather shamefacedly, I recognized that if John Stuart Mill was right when he said, "Let not any one pacify his conscience by the delusion that he can do no harm if he takes no part, and forms no opinion. Bad men need nothing more to compass their ends, than that good men should look on and do nothing," then I would generally qualify as an unwilling enabler of bad things.

So it was that, when I was in Wolfville one day and my lawyer, Walter Bryson, told me that Ray was seeking one of the party nominations for the forthcoming provincial election, I was surprised only because he was a very busy man with a thriving auto sales business in New Minas and political life would take him away from that in a very significant way. But I was very surprised when, subsequently, Ray called me and asked me if I would help him in his endeavours.

I told him that, while I would very much like to assist him, my knowledge of partisan politics and the necessary machinations attendant upon their practice was extremely limited. He said that my lack of experience did not matter, and that the first thing I had to do was to sign myself and Rosalie up as members of his party, go to the nominating convention and vote for him. If he was successful, he told me, there would doubtless be other ways in which I could contribute.

"Ahah! You want money?" I said with a laugh.

"Well, yes. We'll need money to finance the campaign. But I also want people to know that solid citizens like you and Rosalie are on my side."

"I've never been described as 'solid' before, and before you ask, I would be no good going door to door—"

"Why not? You do a lot of that in your work as a private investigator."

"That's why I shouldn't do it. I'd come across as an interrogator, rather than a persuader. But Rosalie would be very good at it and I think she would love doing it."

"I'd better give her a call."

"No, why don't you and Rachel come to dinner? We can discuss it thoroughly then."

"Good idea. When?"

"No time like the present. How about tonight?"

"I'll check with Rachel and get back to you."

It turned out that both Rachel and Rosalie were agreeable, so I went shopping to see what I could find for dinner.

My surly butcher, whose bark is far worse than his bite, said I could have a large piece of beef tenderloin if he approved of the way I would cook it. I told him I would make a beef Wellington with a Madeira sauce and serve it with small roast onions and asparagus. He grudgingly gave his consent and handed me the prize, wrapped in brown paper, over the counter.

I then directed my attention to the other courses and, seeing some good-looking rhubarb and some half decent strawberries, decided that a pie would be nice for dessert. At the fish counter I noticed some very fine salmon so I thought that, for a starter, I would poach the fillets and serve them cold with a dill and cucumber dressing.

Our house always sticks out like a sore thumb because it is the only ultra-modern edifice in the neighborhood, all others, except the winery which is hidden by trees, being typical large, old Annapolis Valley houses, mostly white with green or black trim.

Ours was built by a millionaire who spared no expense on the house and its airstrip, but sadly then went bankrupt. It was mostly glass, which had the advantage of providing plenty of light, but the drawback of creating the feeling that the occupants were under constant surveillance. But it was amazingly well equipped, with superb appliances and an airy cellar for my wine.

I am a bit of an eccentric when it comes to wine, and have one of the best cellars in eastern Canada, containing hundreds of bottles, many of them old and very rare. Rosalie says I am a snob, but I am a rich man, and if indulging myself in this way makes me one, so be it.

Since Rachel and Ray are very special friends, I decided on this occasion to select some really fine wines to match the food. For the cold salmon I chose *Château Haut Brion Blanc* 2006, for the main course, the red from the same property of the 1989 vintage, and for dessert *Château Rieussec* 2001.

I made and rolled out the pastry, made duxelles by cooking mushrooms in Kosher butter, hammered out some chicken breasts until they were paper-thin then wrapped them around the tenderloin, which I had previously seared until brown all over and smeared with English mustard. Then I covered the chicken with the mushrooms and wrapped the whole assemblage in pastry, and put it in the larder until ready to cook. Normally I would have employed regular butter and prosciutto, but I knew Rachel was an observant Jew.

Then I made the strawberry and rhubarb pie and poached the salmon fillets in water acidulated with lemon juice and seasoned with dill, salt and pepper.

In the event, all the food turned out well and was appreciated by our guests, but it was the wine which stole the show. The white *Chateau Haut Brion* was incredibly rich and complex but while perhaps a little past its prime, it complimented the salmon perfectly. The red Haut Brion was breathtaking, being a sensuous blend of leather, truffles, blackcurrants and spices. For a thirty-six year old wine it was still vigorous and full of life. The Rieussec was a stunning wine, presenting sensations of honey-soaked apricots and nectarines with vanilla and caramel overtones.

"Why do you want to do this, Ray?" Rosalie asked when we were at the table. "You're successful, you're quite wealthy. You have a beautiful wife. Why would you want to spend several months stuck in the House of Assembly in Halifax, and the rest of the year being pestered by people wanting jobs, pensions, and complaining about dogs knocking over garbage cans?"

"That's exactly what I have been asking him, Rosalie," said Rachel, "especially the part about his beautiful wife."

"My business took a lot of work and time building up, but now it can run itself with the right manager," Ray replied in his rich bass voice, "and I feel I should give something back to the community."

"If you don't mind my saying so, Ray," I said, "That sounds like a cliché. I think there are other reasons. Out with them."

"Well," Ray cleared his throat. "You're quite right, Marc. There are two other reasons."

"You're not the only one who'll be interested to hear this!" Rachel declared.

"The first is rather petty, I know, and you'll probably be ashamed of me Rachel, but Sean O'Leary is also looking for the nomination and I despise the son of a bitch with every fibre of my being."

"I understand," Rosalie said, nodding fiercely. "I know Sean O'Leary and he is one of the slimiest men I know."

"Ughh. Rosalie is right. But even so, Raymond, it is not a good enough reason to do it." Rachel sounded disappointed.

"What's the other reason?" I asked, "I expect this is the kicker."

"Right again. It's that Wendell has asked me to do it. Says he wants me in his cabinet if I get elected."

"You should have told me, darling."

"I was going to."

"If the premier wants you, why do you have to contest the nomination?" Rosalie asked. "Can't he just say: Ray Bland is my man'?"

"In the old days, the premier could impose candidates on constituencies, but they are long gone," Ray explained. "Now if the members thought that he was trying to interfere, it would work against the person he wanted. That's why this has to stay in this room."

"There will be no leaks from here," I said seriously.

"No indeed," Rosalie agreed. "So, sign us up and tell us what to do."

"Many thanks." said Ray, taking party membership forms from his pocket and pushing them across the table. "Here you go. Just sign."

We all signed, including Rachel, which surprised me as I thought she would already be a member, and I wondered why he had not involved her more in his plans.

"Marc," said Rosalie to me. "Open some Champagne. We must drink to Ray's future success."

2

After we had dinner and moved back into the lounge, Ray and Rachel explained the background to Ray's decision. Some of what they told me I already knew, but most was news to me. I realized that I was quite ignorant about public affairs and that, as a citizen, I had been negligent in my duty.

I understood that the election was about to take place because the premier had decided he needed a "fresh mandate" from the people. This would be the second election in which Wendell Proctor would lead his party. The first had happened four years ago, shortly after he had acceded to the party leadership. I remembered that the leadership had become vacant when the previous premier, Brenton Granger, died in a tragic drowning accident. The ensuing leadership contest, according to Ray, had been an exciting and surprising one in which Wendell had beaten the favourite, Angus MacKinnon, after a number of ballots.[1]

Ray told me that he was seeking the party's nomination in the Kings South constituency on this occasion because the sitting MLA, old Dr. Kimble, had decided to retire. The process to replace him, Ray explained, entailed the party members within the constituency gathering at a convention and voting for whom they preferred to be their candidate.

"How many members are there?" I asked.

"At last count there were three hundred and sixty-two." Ray said.

"What do you mean: 'at last count'?"

"The deadline is Friday for new members to be signed up. Everybody who has a membership by that date can vote at the nominating convention. As you can imagine, the total is growing fast because each

---

1 As described in *The Premier's Daughter,* also published by Moose House.

of the contenders is signing up as many people as he or she can."

"You said 'she'. Is there a female seeking the nomination?" Rosalie asked.

"Yes, Agnes Howie."

"The woman who has the store on Main Street?"

"That's her. She has quite a following."

"I can't think why," said Rachel. "She's not very bright. And she wears that awful purple shawl everywhere she goes."

"But I hear she has a large family."

"There's just the three of you running?" I asked.

"That's right. Agnes, me and Sean O'Leary."

"How strong is his support?"

"I'd say he was the front-runner at the moment."

"Where are you?"

"Running second, I think. With Agnes bringing up the rear."

"I suppose that means all the friends, relatives and neighbours will be signing up for something they know very little about?" Rosalie asked, rather tartly.

"Anybody and everybody."

"But don't the members have to be supporters of the party?"

"No, not really. They have to sign the form—as you've just done—saying you believe in the principles of the party."

"What are they?"

"What are what?"

"The party principles. What are they? Can you tell us what we signed up to?"

"Er...not really."

"Ray! Even you don't know what principles you're seeking to represent." Rosalie was indignant.

"Well, I know we're better than the other guys," Ray said. "And I know Wendell's by far the best leader."

"This would be funny if it wasn't so sad, darling," said Rachel, laughing.

"That doesn't make a lot of sense to me either," I said.

"It's ridiculous, I know." Ray shook his head. "The parties use these events to raise money. And they hope that those who signed up will stay with them throughout the election."

"So, a person could be chosen as the candidate even if the people he signed up were supporters of the other side?" Rosalie asked in-credulously.

"Yes."

"That's crazy!" Rachel said.

"It also means that someone who doesn't support the party could actually end up being the party's candidate," I protested. "In theory, that person could be a staunch member of an opposing party!"

"In theory, yes." Ray said, "I know it's nuts, but all the parties do it, and if you want to play, you have to play by those rules."

"How many members have you signed up, Ray?" Rosalie asked.

"Personally, forty—forty two with yours—but my supporters have signed up another ninety. Most of our mutual friends have obliged."

"Really?"

"Walter and Joyce signed yesterday."

"*Walter Bryson*?"

"Sure."

"But he's a rock-ribbed member of the opposition. I think he's even on the executive committee of the other side!"

"He said he'd do it as a personal favour, but he said he couldn't vote for me in the election if I got to be the candidate."

"That's insane," said Rosalie.

"Well, you're doing pretty much the same thing," said Ray. "You've joined as a personal favour."

"I suppose that's true, although we know and like Wendell so we would be voting for his candidate anyway."

"Even if it was Sean O'Leary?" Rachel grinned.

"No, if it was him I wouldn't vote at all," Rosalie said.

"I think I'd have to," I said. "Wendell is a good friend and I'd hate to see him lose. But let me ask you another question."

"Go ahead."

"What happens if nobody comes forward to seek a nomination?"

"Doesn't happen very often."

"But if it did?"

"I guess, the local committee would go to see prominent citizens—like the school principal, the mayor or a councillor—and try to per-suade them to come forward for the good of the community."

"And this prominent citizen may not have had any prior party alle-giance?"

"No. That's quite likely."

"Yet if they got elected and went up to Halifax, right away they would be partisan to hilt, cheering their troops and shouting down the other side?"

"Er...yes. I guess they would," he said sheepishly.

"Instant partisans! How stupid," Rosalie said.

"I didn't make the rules," Ray said, clearly resenting being subjected to our barrage of questions. "I can rip up those membership forms if you like."

"No, don't be silly." Rosalie grabbed him by the arm. "If you want to do this crazy thing, of course we're with you a hundred percent. When is the nominating convention?"

"On Monday evening at seven o'clock in the church hall."

"We'll be there."

3

When Ray had described the convention at which Wendell Proctor had become leader of his party, and consequently premier, we thought that the coming nominating convention in Kings South might be similar in flavour. Ray said that at the leadership convention some four years ago, the candidates and their supporters were decked out in different coloured costumes, waved bright banners and placards, and had bands playing their chosen theme songs. He said the atmosphere had been electric, particularly with the jockeying for position each time a contender with the lowest vote had to drop off the ballot.

There had been five candidates in the race, the powerful, silver-tongued Angus MacKinnon from Antigonish having led on all but the last ballot. Joan Howard, the beautiful former actress and now cabinet minister, had placed a surprising third on the penultimate ballot and, in a dramatic gesture, had swung her support to Wendell to put him over the top. Ray told us he would never forget the moment when all of Howard's supporters pulled off their red sweaters to reveal Wendell's blue ones underneath.

Throughout the weekend, therefore, rather than dreading the Monday meeting, Rosalie and I actually looked forward to an upbeat event which would be enlivening and entertaining. Neither of us had ever been involved in anything like this before, and we keenly anticipated broadening our horizons.

"Do you think we should make up signs which we can wave?" she asked.

"I expect Ray has taken care of all that and we'll be given them when we get there."

"How about badges?"

"Ray will have those, too. I wonder what they would say."

"They'll probably be a fair number of Baptists there, so it might be

'Pray for Ray'."

"That might suggest he's in need of divine intervention. I think we'd better wait and see."

In this frame of mind we went to the church hall on Monday evening, and were bitterly disappointed to find it unadorned with banners and minus a band or refreshments. True, there were a few people wearing homemade buttons, but beyond that very little outward indication of who was supporting whom.

As we filed in, we showed our party membership cards, and were each given two ballot papers. Looking around, I saw a number of people we knew, including, surprisingly, Gerald, the proprietor of the bookstore which had been owned by my father before his murder some years ago. You could hardly miss him, because he was ostentatiously dressed in a mauve jacket. I also noticed Walter Bryson, despite his obvious attempts to remain inconspicuous, and some of Rosalie's colleagues from the university.

At ten past seven, a portly man, whom I recognized as the owner of the local hardware store, mounted the stage and invited the three candidates to join him. After failing to get the microphone to work properly, he summoned someone called Archie to correct it and a young man dressed in overalls came up and fiddled with the instrument. He then tapped it, and despite it being clear that the trouble was already fixed, continued for several minutes to say: "Hello, hello. One, Two, Three, Four. Are you receiving me? Alpha, Bravo, Charlie, Delta, Echo, Foxtrot."

This performance brought gales of laughter from the audience, which reduced Archie to a deep redness of face, and he scuttled quickly off.

The chairman, who told us his name was Reg Harkness, called the meeting to order and read a section of the party's constitution relating to the selection of candidates. The audience, having warmed up on poor Archie, shouted, "Get on with it Reg," and, "We know all that!" and, "Let's hear from the rivals!"

Reg gabbled over the rest of the section and called for nominations.

Sean O'Leary was nominated by a local businessman who extolled the extensive virtues of his choice; and a long-winded, feminist professor described Mrs. Howie as "a woman of strength, courage and determination." They both said they would "like to place in nomination the name of..." while Ray's nominator, a county farmer, simply said, "I nominate Ray Bland," and promptly sat down.

Then the chairman said he had drawn names from a hat to decide the order in which the candidates would address the convention, and that accordingly Mrs. Howie would be the first, Ray the second and O'Leary the final speaker.

The speeches were inexpressibly repetitive and boring, although we thought Ray did reasonably well in his plain-speaking bass. Mrs. Howie was embarrassingly confused, calling the chairman "premier", referring to her opponent as "Mr. McCarthy", and several times mentioning "the honour of going to Ottawa." From the groans and chair scraping in the audience, it was clear that she would come a poor third.

When O'Leary rose he spoke clearly and articulately. He was impressive in a slick way, but he seemed to annoy many in the crowd when he harped on his academic qualifications and implied that being a lawyer made him a better choice than the others because he "was used to being on his feet" and they were not. Judging by the respective amount of applause I guess that O'Leary was slightly ahead.

The Chairman announced that balloting would begin and that we should proceed "in a speedy but orderly file" to where polling stations had been set up at the end of the hall.

"Quickly now," he said. "We don't want to be here all night!"

Whether because of his admonition or not, the voting was remarkably fast and, much to my surprise, was completed in less than twenty minutes. The chairman announced the result in, I thought, an unnecessarily pompous manner, commencing with "It is my duty to inform you that I have in my hand..."

Agnes Howie got 62 votes, for which accomplishment she received a thunderous round of applause. Now that there was no danger of her being the candidate, the crowd was magnanimous, shouting, "Good show, Agnes," and, "Well done, Agnes."

Ray received 144 votes, and Sean O'Leary 157. There was a collective roar at this news, each member rapidly talking to his or her neighbour, expressing surprise that the result was so close.

The Chairman said we would now proceed to the next ballot and, at this point O'Leary made a fatal mistake.

"Point of order, Mr. Chairman," he said, rising.

"What is it?"

"I think the candidates should be allowed to address the convention again."

A cacophony of competing shouts erupted from the floor, as Ray rose.

"Mr. Chairman, I think the members know who they want. They don't need to sit through more boring speeches."

At this there was wild cheering from all parts of the hall, which clearly impelled the chairman to say that there would be no more speeches and that they would vote again "forthwith."

Now, people were positively running to the polling stations, "like a stampede", as Walter Bryson later said to me. The result was that Ray won with 222 votes to 137. O'Leary had outsmarted himself, not only failing to gain any of Mrs. Howie's votes but losing many of his own. For reasons best known to themselves, a number of members had not voted.

I saw Ray looking at me with a huge grin and giving me the thumbs-up sign.

Having declared Ray to be the official candidate for the constituency, the chairman pointed to the back of the hall and announced to a delighted audience that the premier had just arrived.

As Wendell, as tall, handsome and black as I remembered, strode to the rostrum, the crowd cheered like mad. I was sitting in an aisle seat, and was surprised and overwhelmed when he recognized me and stopped.

"Marc! My God, what are you doing here?"

"Here to support Ray."

"Of course." He leaned over. "Is that you, Rosalie? How are you?"

"Fine, thanks, premier."

"Go," I said, seeing that his entourage were getting impatient over this unforeseen delay. "And give 'em hell!"

The audience had been enduring these hard seats for hours and had sat through many boring addresses, but Wendell brought them to their feet time after time. He was electrifying and, not for the first time, I considered myself privileged to call this man my friend. However, I knew that while I might see him occasionally, the times when circumstances had made us close were a thing of the past.

I could not have been more wrong.

4

The first indication I had that all was not well with Ray was when I visited him at his auto dealership in New Minas. I was in the area, and dropped in to invite him and Rachel to join us for dinner.

In the event, he said he had to decline because of his campaign schedule, but as I was entering his office, an elderly man I had never seen before was coming out. Assuming he was a customer, I gave him no further thought and took a chair across from Ray's desk.

Immediately I noticed that there were small beads of perspiration on his forehead and that he looked very worried.

"Hello, Ray." I learned forward. "Are you okay?"

"Oh. Hi, Marc." He mopped his brow with a handkerchief. "No, I'm not okay."

"What's up?"

"Bloody Willis Parker."

"Who's he?"

"My partner."

"I didn't know you had a partner."

"Yeah. More's the pity. He's not active in running the business, but he invested in it when I first started out years ago. Then it was literally a one-car lot."

"If that's true, you've come a long way since then. You have the biggest dealership outside of Halifax now."

"Maybe not for much longer," he mumbled.

"What are you saying?"

"I can't go into details, Marc. I may tell you about it someday, but right now I have a campaign meeting in Coldbrook."

Later, I mentioned this strange encounter to Rosalie, but she was also ignorant of Ray's having a partner or what his troubles might be.

"What was his name?" she asked.

"I think it was Willis Parker. Does the name mean anything to you?"

"I'm not sure. I think I may have heard it before, but I can't remember in what context."

"Hmm. Well, whatever the problem is, there's nothing we can do about it. I thought Ray was a little brusque in getting rid of me."

"That doesn't sound like Ray."

"No, it doesn't. That's why it upset me."

I pondered the problem for most of the rest of the day and even called Walter Bryson, my lawyer.

"Walter, this is not a legal inquiry," I said. "Just a friendly personal call."

"I get it." He laughed. "You don't want to be billed for my time!"

"If you did, I don't think the small claims court adjudicator would uphold it."

"You're probably right. Well, Marc, what can I do for you?"

"Have you heard of Willis Parker?"

"Sure."

"Who is he?"

"An old fellow who lives near Greenwich. I don't know a lot about him, except that he's been around for ages and seems to be quite wealthy."

"What's his profession?"

"I'm not sure he has one. At least, I've never known him to be in any profession."

"Thanks."

"Why do you want to know?"

Knowing that Walter was a staunch member of the opposite party from Ray, I hesitated before answering, in case whatever Willis was involved in could be used against Ray. I decided that, at least for the time being, discretion was the better part of valour.

"No particular reason. How's Jennifer doing at university?"

"Very well indeed. Her marks are terrific."

"I'm glad to hear that. Please give her our best wishes."

"I surely will. She calls home twice a week."

"Why don't you and Joyce come over for dinner soon?"

"That'd be nice. When would be convenient?"

"How about Saturday?"

"Fine."

"See you then. About six."

For several days other matters put Willis Parker from my mind. I had business to attend to in Halifax, and I had to help my partner, Louise, with stock-taking in the wine store we own on Main Street in Wolfville. It was not until some days later, when Rosalie and I turned on our television to get the news, that we were confounded by what we heard:

> In the election campaign, there is surprising news from the constituency of Kings South, where the government candidate, Ray Bland, has pulled out of the race only days before the official nomination day. Local party president Reg Harkness says the party is devastated by this development, but hopes to have a replacement for Bland before the deadline. Kings South has traditionally been a government party stronghold, but analysts say a change could now be on the cards.

"Holy cow! Did you know anything about this, Marc?"

"No, not a word," I replied. "How could he do this?"

"*Why* would he do it?"

"I can't think. Ray's one of our best friends. You'd think he would've told us."

"Especially considering that you're his biggest financial contributor."

"Maybe it has something to do with that fellow Willis Parker."

"I think you should call him now."

I hesitated before calling, but after thinking about it for a few seconds, I realized that it would be impossible for Rosalie and me to remain in suspense. If we did not know what had happened, it would haunt us for days.

Rachel answered the phone.

"Hi, Rachel, it's Marc."

"Hello, Marc. We've been expecting you to call."

"We were thunderstruck when we heard it on the news. Can I speak to Ray, please?"

"Ray's not speaking to anyone right now. He's in a pretty bad way, as you can imagine."

"Can you tell me what it's all about?"

"I'll try. You know about Ray's business partner?"

"Willis Parker?"

"Yes." I could hear her taking a deep breath. "He's been embezzling huge amounts over some years, apparently, and now the business faces bankruptcy. It could go into receivership."

"My God, how did that happen?"

"I don't know all the details, but it seems Ray has been far too trusting and, truth to tell, maybe a little negligent, too."

"I'm so sorry, Rachel. Is there anything we can do to help?"

"Just be understanding for the present." She sobbed. "There is no way he could carry on as the candidate. All his efforts must be directed to trying to save the business."

"Of course. I do understand. I won't bother you any more, Rachel, please tell Ray we're thinking of him."

No sooner had I explained to Rosalie what Rachel had told me that the phone rang.

"Mr. LeBlanc?"

"Yes."

"This is Reg Harkness, I am—"

"I know who you are, Mr. Harkness."

"You've heard the news?"

"Yes. I've just been talking to Ray's wife."

"Then you'll know the circumstances."

"Yes. I have to say that I think Ray made the right decision."

"As much as it pains me to say it, so do I."

"If he had stayed in, the opposition would have had a field day. Besides, he has to devote his energy to saving his business."

"I agree. Look, Mr. LeBlanc, could you come over to my house?"

"I could, but why?"

"To date, you've been our most generous contributor."

"So I gather, but that was because Ray is a close personal friend. I won't ask you to return the money, but it's not likely I would contribute to any other candidate."

"I understand that, but we'd like you to join us anyway."

"All right if you insist. When?"

"Now."

"Now?"

"Yes, please. Do you know where I live?"

"No, I don't."

"I'm on Pleasant Street. Do you know the big yellow house with the large bay windows?"

"Yes."

"We'll see you in—shall we say—twenty minutes?"

I was mystified as to why the party insiders would want to include me in their deliberations, but I felt I should oblige them in case there was some kind of attempt to help Ray.

"Please don't give them more money, Marc," Rosalie said. "Unless it is to go to Ray. After all it's not as if we're rock-rib party supporters."

"I'm just going to see what's on their minds. I have no intention of becoming embroiled in any political machinations."

"Good."

When I got to the house, I saw that there were already an assortment of vehicles parked in the yard and on the road. I put the Bugatti further up the street and walked back.

Harkness greeted me at the door and led me into his den.

In addition to the host, four men and two women were perched around the room on chairs, couches and ottomans. I was introduced to everyone, but could recall only a few of the names.

The two women, both in their sixties, were large and formidable, both with slightly bluish hair. Their names were Maude Taylor and Mary Driscoll, and it was clear from the outset that they carried a lot of weight, both in influence and avoirdupois. When some of the men spoke, often others would speak over them, but when Maude and Mary were speaking, there was a respectful hush.

"Come on, Reg," Mary barked, "let's get this show on the road."

"Alright," said Reg, looking for a place to sit and finally squeezing onto the corner of a pool table. "The question is very simple. What do we do now?"

"I don't know if there is any protocol or precedent," said Maud, "but with the official nomination deadline only two days away, there is certainly no time to hold another nomination meeting."

This was greeted by a general murmur of agreement.

"So Reg asked Mary and me to approach the contenders who were beaten by Ray at the previous meeting."

"What happened, Maude? How did you make out?" asked a little man with a moustache, whose name was Alfred.

"Sean O'Leary can't be found."

"What do you mean, can't be found?" several people demanded in unison.

"He's is somewhere in South America. Apparently, he was disgusted at not winning the nomination, so he and his wife took off on vacation for Trinidad. From there it would seem they went to see the Angel Falls in Venezuela."

"Where are they now?" asked a large black man whom everyone called Joe.

"Nobody knows. They can't be reached. And, no, we don't know the reason."

"Probably couldn't get back in time, even if we could reach them," said Albert, an old man who sat in the corner.

"Which brings us to Agnes Howie," said Reg, to a chorus of groans.

"No way will she do it," Mary said. "She was on her high horse when I went to see her. She said if she wasn't good enough for us before, she's not good enough for us now."

"In some ways, that's a relief," said Joe.

"But it leaves us without a candidate," Reg said. "Are we all agreed that we must run a candidate?"

There was no dissent from this, several of those present saying that never in the history of the constituency had the party not been on the ballot.

"So what do we do?" Reg said. "Is there anyone in this room who wants to do it?"

"How about yourself, Reg?" Alfred asked.

"You want to kill me? I've got a heart condition. A campaign would put me six feet under."

"What about you, Alfred?" Someone inquired with a laugh.

"Haha. I'll be eighty-five next birthday!'

"I think Mary would do a great job," said Joe.

"If you'd asked me twenty years ago I'd have jumped at the chance, but my Ernie's very sick and I have to put him first."

"What about you, Maud?" asked a man with an artificial leg and a speech impediment.

"I have peripheral arterial disease," she said sadly, "and they are going to operate on my legs in a week's time."

They all sat glumly looking at each other in silence. Suddenly the phone rang and Reg threaded his way to a desk at the back of the room to answer it.

"Oh, hello again," he said. "Yes….No, we've been through all the possibilities…no, nobody…no, nobody can contact him…no, she won't do it. She says she's been insulted…oh, the usual gang, and Marc LeBlanc…Yes, he's here. I asked him to join us…I don't know…I'll get him. Marc, phone for you!"

"For me?"

"Yes."

I elbowed my way to the desk, bumping into Reg on his way back into the room. I was pretty well bored with the evening so far and resolved that, as soon as I had taken the call, whoever it was from, I was going to make my excuses and leave.

"Hello."

"Marc?"

"Yes."

"It's Wendell."

"Jesus!"

"No, not Jesus. Just me. Marc, we have a problem."

"We?"

"Well, I have a problem."

"Yes?" I felt my blood getting cold.

"We're down to the wire and have no candidate in one of our strongest ridings."

"I know, I've heard nothing else for the last hour. Cut to the chase, Wendell."

At the sound of his name, a loud murmur ran through the assembled company.

"Okay. I want you to be our candidate in Kings South."

"Oh God, Wendell I'm no politician—"

"I'm asking for a personal favour to me."

"Can I have time to think about it?"

"No. I need you to do this for Cynthia and me." His throwing his lovely wife, a woman Rosalie and I adored, into the mix was a low blow.

"I can't even consult Rosalie?"

"Is she at home now?"

"Yes, she is."

"The minute you say 'yes', I'll call her and soften the blow."

I did not know what to do, say or think, but merely sat there, my head spinning. During the silence, which lasted a full two minutes, the room went totally quiet.

His patience exhausted, Wendell finally said, "Yes or no?"

"Alright, Wendell. As a personal favour, I'll do it. But if you don't square it with Rosalie I shall pull out immediately."

"Understood. Many thanks, Marc."

As I put the phone down I had a heavy, bilious feeling in my belly.

I dragged myself back into the gathering.

"It looks like you have a candidate," I told them.

The resounding cheers did nothing to restore my sense of well-being and, despite Wendell's assurances, I dreaded going home to Rosalie.

5

Having no experience of politics, I did not even know what had to be done to get my name on the ballot, or what running a campaign entailed. Following Wendell's phone call, I was mobbed by the group at Reg Harkness' house, heartily congratulated, and had my hand almost shaken off, but nobody told what had to come next. So, I had little choice but to wait until somebody told me what to do.

As soon news of my candidacy was disseminated throughout the constituency, I was besieged by calls, most of them looking for favours, jobs or promises that I would "take up" their pet projects if I was elected. A few friends called to wish me well, but did so in a rather patronizing manner which suggested either that they thought I had little chance of success, or that I had made a serious mistake.

Several callers, who wished to remain anonymous, averred that if only I had been nominated for a different party they would have been my biggest supporters. The rest were from various characters who claimed not to have made their minds up as to how they would vote and said that they had heard I "had a few bucks" and wondered if I could "help them out."

All of this bewildered me and filled me with trepidation, but my greatest fear, that Rosalie would violently berate me for my stupidity, did not materialize. Whatever Wendell had said to her in my absence I could only surmise, but he must have laid on the charm with a trowel, because she was very sweet about the whole thing.

I had parked the Bugatti, quietly let myself in and tentatively poked my head around the living room door.

"Is it safe to come in?"

"Of course it is," she said, running towards me. "See, the conquering hero comes!"

"I haven't conquered anything yet," I said timidly, "and it doesn't seem likely I will. Roe, I have no clue what to do."

"Why don't you ask someone? Wendell will know. Why don't you ask him?"

"I can't go running to Wendell every five minutes. He's the party leader in the middle of a campaign. It probably wouldn't be possible even if I wanted to talk to him."

"Well, we have the Brysons coming over for dinner tomorrow and you know Walter will tease you mercilessly, so you'd better find out what's what before they get here."

"It's late, so there's nothing I can do now. I guess I'll make some calls in the morning. Right now I think I'll have a stiff glass of Dalmore Sherry Cask scotch."

I did not get a great deal of decent sleep, because one of the few things about elections that I did know about was that the candidate was supposed to go door to door, asking for support, and I absolutely hated the idea of doing that. I tossed and turned, dreaming that doors collapsed upon my knocking them, people with shotguns appeared when they opened, and naked old women beckoned me into their houses.

When I got up in the morning, I felt as if I had been dragged through a hedge backwards. I staggered into the kitchen to make a pot of Jamaican Blue Mountain coffee, shoved some bread into the toaster and flopped down at the table.

The toast popped up at the same time as the phone rang. It was Reg Harkness.

"Good morning, Marc."

"Oh, hi, Reg. I'm so glad you called."

"Oh, why's that?"

"I don't know what I should be doing."

"What do you want to do?"

"How do I get myself nominated, for starters?"

"Don't worry about stuff like that. All I need is your signature on the papers."

"That's all?"

"Yes. We've got a certified cheque for $200, and we have six citizens who've signed your papers. When you've put your John Henry on them all I have to do is take them to Bill Haliburton."

"Who's he?"

"He's the Returning Officer. His office is on Front Street."

"What then?"

"How do you mean?"

"I mean, will you tell me what to do? Where I should go. That kind of thing."

"It's really up to you, Marc. Ray had Chester Beamish as his campaign manager, but of course he quit when Ray did."

"Do you have a replacement for him?"

"No, sorry, I don't. There's nobody on the committee who's up to the job, for one reason or another. If you had a campaign manager, he would tell you where to go, but without one, it's entirely up to you."

"But how would I know? I don't know anything about politics."

"Really? We kind of thought that you wouldn't have accepted the nomination if you didn't."

"Wait a minute, Reg. I accepted because you were desperate. I did you a favour!"

"Oh? I was under the impression that you were doing the favour for Wendell Proctor."

"Well, er..."

"Was that not the case?"

"Yes, I guess it was."

"There you go then. Anyway, we'll take care of the paperwork, like I said."

"What about poll workers? I assume we have to have someone in the polls."

"No worries, Maud and Mary will look after that."

"Oh, good."

"After that, if you take my advice, you'll be seen at all the malls every day, walk up and down Main Street, shaking hands and go to see Joe and Alfred for names of their contacts."

"Okay, thanks. I assume you'll be around if I have any questions?"

"For a couple of days I will. After that I'm going to see my sister in Winnipeg."

"I see. I hope you have a good time."

"Sure will. I usually have a blast when I visit her."

Feeling a little like an orphan in the storm, I finished my meagre breakfast and then set about preparing for dinner with the Brysons. For a change, I thought we would start with a delicate dish of shrimp, quartered hard-boiled eggs and a gentle cream curry sauce. For the main course I had a large, plump chicken from the farm up the road, which I intended to roast with slices of black truffle inserted under the skin. The French call this "Chicken in Half Mourning" and the addition of this extraordinary fungus turns the humble hen into an exquisite luxury.

For dessert I would make a simple tart, consisting of a pastry shell generously painted with Bon Maman apricot jam and covered with slices of ripe pear. This would be baked and served hot with English clotted cream.

I went down to the cellar and searched for appropriate wines for the meal, and decided upon a *Sauvignon-Chardonnay* 2020 from Domaine Saint-Lannes in Gascony, which would give the richness I wanted as well as a bright, grassy quality to complement the mild curry. To go with the chicken I chose a 2002 *Chambertin* from Domaine LeRoy, and for the dessert a 1989 *Château de Fargues*.

When Walter and Joyce arrived, they hugged Rosalie a little more tenderly than usual and regarded me as if I were a temperamental hospital patient. I knew the evening would be a disaster unless the air was cleared, so as soon as we settled around the lounge with glasses of *Cuvee de Winston Churchill* champagne, I introduced the subject immediately.

"Okay, let's get to it. You've heard the news. Who has anything to say?"

"Oh, Marc, you're so brave," said Joyce.

"Walter?"

"What could have possessed you?"

"I was asked personally by the premier if I would do it. Because he is a personal friend and we admire him, I felt I couldn't refuse him."

"I think I can understand that," Walter said thoughtfully. "It is has been so long—what is it now, twenty-four years?—since my party was in power here, so I wouldn't know what that feels like, but I imagine I would do the same."

"Thank you, Walter. That's very kind of you to say so," said Rosalie.

"Yes, thanks, Walter."

"Marc, may we speak in absolute confidence and with complete honesty?"

"Certainly."

"Even though Ray is a good friend of ours—"

"Oh yes," said Joyce.

"Thank you, darling. Please don't interrupt me."

"Okay, sweetheart."

"As I was saying, even though Ray is a good friend, a very good friend, of ours, I have known you, Marc, a lot longer."

"Yes."

"So, I couldn't find it in my heart to tell Ray that I would vote for him, but I can tell you—in strictest confidence—that I shall vote for *you*. Joyce, of course, has a mind of her own and can do what she likes."

"Naturally, I shall vote for you, Marc," Joyce said hastily.

"Thank you, Walter. And thank you, Joyce. I know it won't be easy for you."

"No, it won't," said Walter, "especially when a few votes here and there could make the difference in the result."

"Do you really believe it could be that close?" asked Rosalie.

"Let's look at the facts." Walter took a generous sip of his champagne. "This constituency has been with your party—"

"It's not really my party," I said.

"You're its candidate, so for the sake of the argument it is your party. It has been with your party for six elections. The majority in the last election was over 3,000 votes, but that was for Dr. Kimble, who was extremely popular. He took himself out of the picture and, from what I hear, will be dead within the year—"

"Oh no..."

"Joyce! Please let me finish."

"Sorry, Walter."

"Now, Ray is also very popular; not as popular as Kimble, but very popular."

"What's your point?" I interjected a little too harshly.

"The point is, Marc, that you are not popular. You have no following here and no family. You've only been back here five or six years—"

"Seven."

"Seven, then. People see you as disgustingly rich, aloof and hardly what you might call a man of the people."

"Aloof?"

"Darling, you know it's true," said Rosalie softly.

"So, what's the bottom line here?" I was getting tired of this and wanted to get it over with.

"Well, you agreed that I should be honest. I would say that Dr. Kimble's majority of 3,000 votes has pretty well been eaten up by Ray's shenanigans and your...well, lack of charisma...to the point where your chances of being elected are doubtful, to say the least."

"Thanks, Walter." I said, rising. "I think it would be a good thing if we had some food now."

6

People who have been politically active, whether as elected representatives or as volunteers, are intensely interested in all things political. However, the remainder of the population is either bored stiff
with political affairs or simply does not give a damn. Until my nomination, I was one such person, and the introduction into conversations
of political matters was guaranteed to produce a yawn.

That is why I intend to skip over the election campaign as quickly
as I can and move on to the main story, which is essentially about the
interaction of people, how their loyalties shift, how true to their word
they are, and how a man who is a hero today can be a liability tomorrow. That the setting for this story is a political one is incidental; a
similar account could be told about almost any organization, whether
a company, a charity, or even a church.

When I was nominated in Kings South, I was told by the older
members of the executive that religion and ethnicity played a large
role in elections. At one time these, considerations were paramount
and, while they had lessened over the years, they were still influential
with some voters. Maud and Mary, in particular, said that my being an
Acadian and a Catholic would be a huge drawback to success.

When I investigated the demographics of the riding, I found that
they might be right. Only 29% of the population was Catholic. The
rest were protestants, but not, as I had been informed, predominantly
Baptist. This misconception likely sprang from the fact that in 1828
the Baptists founded Horton Academy, which, after several transform-
ations, became Acadia University in 1891.

Mary and Maud were certainly correct in assuming that Acadians
were in a distinct minority, despite this area being the one in which
they were established in 1682 and multiplied to a population of some
15,000 by the time they were expelled by the British in 1755. Now, I

discovered that fewer than 1,200 identified as having French origins and only slightly more than the Chinese, Dutch and Germans in the riding used their mother tongue in their homes.

Pursuant to Reg's instructions, I started going to the mall in New Minas, but gave it up after several days because most people did not want to stop and talk to me, and the majority who did were from other constituencies. I tried politicking on Main Street in Wolfville, but, again, those I encountered were ill-inclined to interrupt their business. Either that, or they were embarrassed to tell me that they would not vote for me.

One morning, I was surprised to see a number of signs around town with my name on them, as I did not know who had authorized them or who had erected them. Similarly, Rosalie and I were taken aback to hear commercials advocating my election on local radio. These were not the only surprises during the three weeks between my nomination and Election Day.

The first occurred when I was walking down Main Street and was stopped by a very attractive woman in her mid thirties.

"Hello. Aren't you Marc LeBlanc?" she asked,

"Yes, I am."

"I thought so. How is your campaign progressing?"

"Oh, it's stumbling along. I'm awfully new at this game."

She was extremely polite and very pleasant and I took an instant liking to her. We talked for about ten minutes.

"Excuse me," I said. "I don't think we've met before. Do I know you?"

"You should," she said with a laugh. "I'm Kay Kinsman, your main opponent!"

As she made her way up the street, I felt heartened by the thought that, if I were to be defeated, I would not in the slightest resent her success.

I encountered another, rather jolting, surprise when I was doing some of my desultory door-knocking. I rang the bell at a house on Fairfield Street, and after a few seconds the door opened to reveal a totally naked young woman. Averting my eyes, I muttered an intro-duction and asked if I could count on her vote.

"I would, but I don't live here," she said, smiled and closed the door.

During the final week, I caught laryngitis and could only speak in a hoarse undertone. I had been directed by Joe to see a Marty Howell on Sherwood Drive, so I went there and knocked on the door to have it opened by a middle-aged woman.

"'Morning," I breathed. "Is your husband at home?"

"No," she whispered. "Come on in."

Those few weeks passed quickly without any scandals or controversies, and finally, and not a moment too soon for my liking, Election Day arrived.

I noted that, at the previous election four years ago, Dr. Kimble received 9,462 votes to his nearest opponent, who got 6,472. A third candidate brought up the rear with 2,168.

I knew that I could not hope to get anything like Dr. Kimble's tally and that I should be very lucky to receive the number his opponent netted. The mood in the headquarters that evening was subdued, which suggested that I was right to be pessimistic.

I confided my fears to Joe, who countered with his belief that Wendell had run an outstanding, charismatic campaign, that the Leader of the Opposition was not well liked and that our constituency had been a stronghold.

When the results came in, at first at a trickle, later like a torrent, there seemed to be equal support for Kay Kinsman and me, the polls alternating between us. The final result was:

Kinsman Kay	7,211
LeBlanc Marc	7,219
MacKay Rudolf	3,024

Rosalie kissed me and told me I was a wonder. My workers went wild, cheering, and pounding the tables. They mobbed me, telling me what a fine fellow I was, and saying that Wendell would be proud of me.

Around the province he had done exceptionally well, garnering 30 seats to the opposition parties' 15 and seven.

Around eleven o'clock, when most of us were half drunk on disgustingly cheap wine, I was called to the phone.

"Is that Landslide LeBlanc?"

"Wendell, is that you?"

"Yes. Congrats, but there'll almost certainly be a recount by a judge, so don't count your chickens until they're hatched."

"How long will that take?"

"Judicial recounts usually take place a month and a half after election day. I have to pick my cabinet right away, so that means you can't be in it."

"Ha! You weren't going to put me in your cabinet!"

"No, I wasn't. Gotta go. Talk in about forty-five days."

In the event, it was almost two months before the recount was held, and, after hours of agonizing suspense, I was formally announced the winner by the staggering total of three votes. For better or worse, I was now the MLA for Kings South.

7

Those who can remember the sensations associated with their first day at high school or college will appreciate how I felt on entering the Nova Scotia legislature. On second thoughts, it was more like the first day at primary school, when, being torn from the warm bosom of my mother, I was thrust into a totally alien land, full of unknown places, objects, rules and customs, and peopled by dozens of tiny, timorous creatures together with a few enormous, omnipotent, omnipresent, forbidding adults.

I had been in Province House several times before, when I was passing through from the parking lot to the premier's office across the street. I had also spent time in the galleries of the House of Assembly when my friend, Superintendent Patrick Kennedy of the RCMP, and I were keeping watch on the premier when he had received death threats[2].

However, not until now had I ever been on the floor of the House, even when it was out of session. The public is not allowed on the floor when the House is in session, although many years ago it was the custom to allow former Members to sit and observe proceedings from chairs on either side of the Speaker's throne.

Since my election had not been confirmed until two months after everyone else, I was the last Member to take the oath of allegiance to King Charles, which was administered by the Clerk of the House, Dudley Morton. He was an old, withered, Dickensian character who had held the job for years and who, I later learned, was, behind his back, widely known as "Fuddy Dudley."

I had gone to the Red Room at Province House, as directed by a phone call the previous day, and there I waited. I wandered around

---

2 That affair is described in my book *The Plot to Kill the Premier.*

the large chamber, admiring the huge portraits of various generals and officials of a bygone British Empire, and peering out of the tall windows at pedestrians in the street.

Some twenty minutes after the time indicated, Morton, dressed in a black gown, came scurrying in.

"Come on, come on!" he said curtly. "I've left my deputy in the House but I have to get back in. You're LeBlanc?"

"Yes. Mr...er..."

"Morton. Clerk of the Assembly. Now take this Bible—you're not a Muslim or an atheist, are you?"

"No."

"Alright, hold it and read the oath from this card. Hurry up!"

I did as I was told, whereupon he gathered up his gown and hurried out into the passage. "Follow me."

I followed him past several security guards, through two swinging doors into a kind of lobby. To the left was a lounge with armchairs, and to the right were toilets and a cloakroom. Then he flung open two more swinging doors and thrust me on to the floor of the Legislature.

Light streamed in through enormous windows. For a second I was like a rabbit caught in the headlights of a car. I froze, the noise of debate washing over me. Ahead I could see a raised throne occupied by The Speaker, also garbed in black robes.

"See that empty seat in the back corner over there?" Morton whispered and pointed to our left. "That's your desk. Go and sit at it."

I saw it was the nearest desk in the third row, against the wall, under a portrait of some as yet unidentified statesman from the mists of time.

I shuffled past the front row of desks, barely able to squeeze past one of the cabinet ministers, who looked up, obviously wondering who on earth I was. As I moved crabwise past the middle row of desks, the man closest to me scowled.

Attaining my desk, I quickly sat down and took a deep breath. Every sight and sound around me was an overwhelming novelty. It was, I reflected, *exactly* like the first day of school.

The next desk to mine was occupied by a rather bulky, middle-aged woman with dirty blonde hair. She looked at me and, not so much smiled as showed her teeth at me.

"You Marc?" she said, *sotto voce.*

"Yes."

"Shhh! You should have bowed."

"Pardon?"

"When you came in. I watched you. You should have bowed to the Speaker and then to the person who has the floor."

"Sorry. I didn't know."

"You'll learn," she said and allowed her not inconsiderable bulk to sink back into her swivel chair.

From her attitude and demeanour I gathered she was an old hand who had graced the government benches at least since Breton Granger's time. I later learned that, like me, she was newly elected, and had been an MLA for only a few months.

"I'm sorry, I don't know your name," I said as softly as I could.

"Zila Franks," she said, sounding surprised that anyone would not know who she was. "Hants East."

"Ah," I said, and foolishly added, "Is there a Hants West?"

"Yes, of course there is. Liam Hudson. He's that little snot in the middle of the back row across the way. Proper little prick."

I adjusted myself so I could see Hudson, and noticed a perfectly-normal looking man about my own age. I wondered what he could have done to poor Zila to deserve such contempt.

Looking around the chamber, I could only see three or four people who looked villainous, and two of them were on my own side. I found it difficult to identify the government supporters because there were many I had never seen before, and because I could see only the backs of their heads.

Wendell was easy to spot due to his height and handsome black-ness. I assumed the woman to his right was Joan Howard, the Deputy Premier and onetime glamorous movie star. Next to her, I thought I recognized Angus MacKinnon, who was so kind to me and with whom I had spent some time when I was investigating death threats against the premier.

The others on the front bench I could only guess at, but on the throne in the middle of the House was The Speaker, old Ernest Mad-dingly, whom I had got to know under very curious circumstances. He was now well into his eighties and was perched, bird-like, at his dais, looking rather as one imagined Wackford Squeers in *Nicholas Nick-elby*, except that instead of a cane he wielded a large gavel.

The Government

1 – Ernest Maddingly **Speaker**
2 – Leila Hendricks
3 – Bill Clark
4 – Stephanie Gilmour
5 – Angus MacKinnon
6 – Joan Howard
7 – Wendell Proctor **Premier**
8 – Chester MacCormack
9 – Angel Stairs
10 – Mark Gardiner
11 – Pierre Dorion
12 – Kesegoo'e Sillyboy
13 – Gloria Jones
14 – Harold MacDonald
15 – Delia Parish
16 – Daniel Nathanson
17 – Freeman Murphy
18 – Fred Askey
19 – Hector McNeil
20 – John Trevor
21 – Zandili Joseph
22 – Jill Rutledge
23 – Sean Leaman
24 – Alaric d'Entremont
25 – Arthur O'Sullivan
26 – Cullum MacPhee
27 – George Savory
28 – Jennie Chan
29 – Jeremy Reid
30 – Emma Mitchell
31 – Carol Walters
32 – Zila Franks
33 – Marc LeBlanc

The Nova Scotia

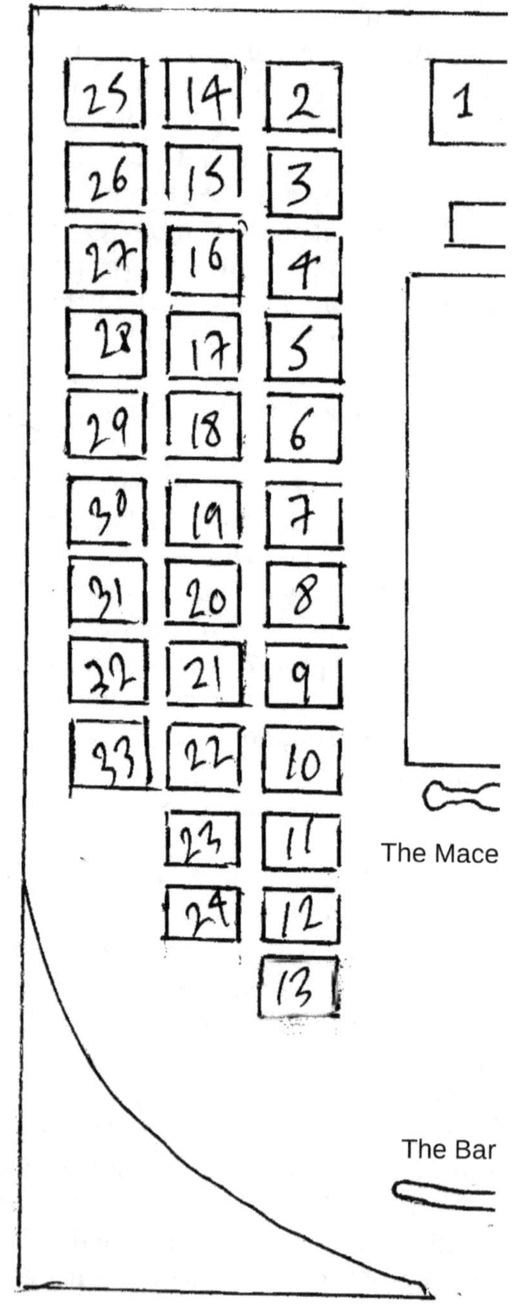

Legislature

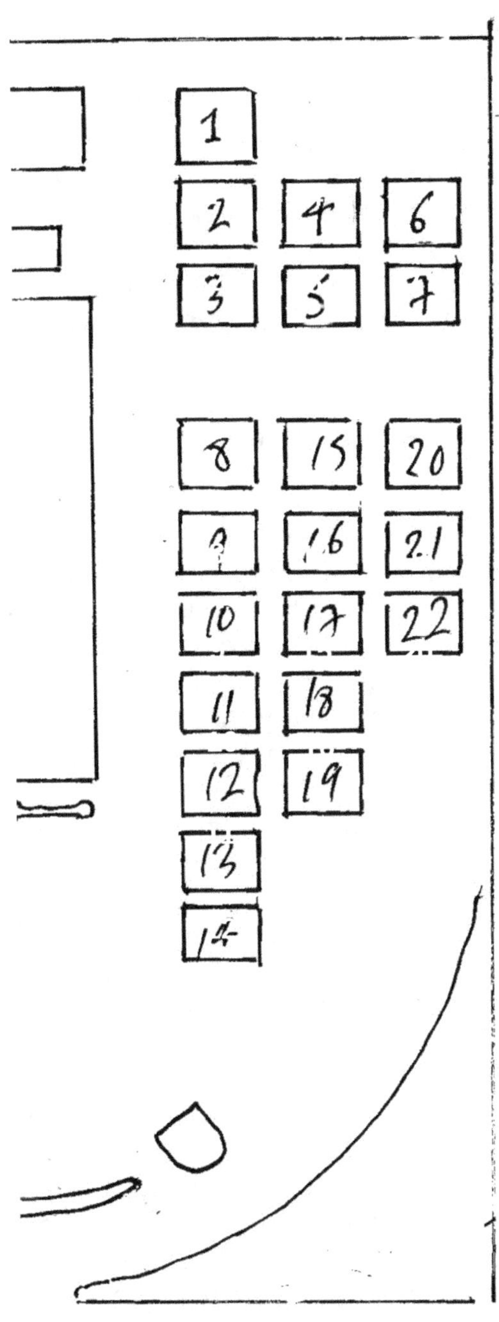

The Loyal Opposition

1 – Joyce Babin
2 – Alan Lau
3 – Dana Edwards
  party leader
4 – Andrew MacEachern
5 – Gerald Toole
6 – Phyllis Gordon
7 – Winnie Saccary

8 – Ellie MacLeod
9 – David Cohen
10 – Dayle Doucet
11 – John Wilkins
  Leader of the Opposition
12 – Eric Downey
13 – Celia MacArthur
14 – Eugene Comeau
15 – Bill Jenkins
16 – Cliff Wolf
17 – Dennis Macnamara
18 – Martha MacNaughton
19 – Sam Wong
20 – Ed Gallant
21 – Liam Hudson
22 – Michael Winters

I had reason to remember Old Ernie, as they called him, because I had gone to see him at Wendell's behest about the death threats. He was then Provincial Secretary, a somewhat outdated position with few responsibilities.

I went through a set of double doors into what seemed like another era. Apart from the intercom and a telephone, the office could have been something out of Dickens. Maddingly must have deliberately asked the Public Works Department to comb the cellars for old furniture and, it would seem, the older the better.

Had the minister been sporting a wing-tip collar, I would not have been surprised. Instead he wore a top-quality, dark gray suit, which I could see had been made many years ago.

He did not get up from the desk or offer me a seat, so I looked around and, spying an elegant Victorian chair, dragged it closer to the desk and sat down.

"Yes, what is it?" he asked in a pained manner.

Ernest Maddingly was thin, sallow and had a few bad teeth which made him appear more sinister than I suspected he really was. He constantly rubbed and fiddled with his very bony, white hands on which the veins stood out, reminding me of a relief map of the Andes.

He had been testy and unwelcoming until I mentioned his having been premier for a brief period. Suddenly, everything changed. His face lit up, he edged forward on his seat and actually smiled. When he spoke, his tone was entirely different.

"Ah, yes indeed," he said with a satisfied sigh, "and a very good premier I was, too, by all accounts. Of course I wasn't given the opportunity to occupy that office for long. Had I been treated properly—as I rightly deserved—and permitted a decent term, I'm confident I could have achieved much, much more. In fact, I think it's fair to say that I could have gone down in the history books as one of the best, if not *the* best, premiers in modern times."

I was astonished by this outburst and by its energy. Maddingly had become a different, rejuvenated man, his former listlessness transformed. I sat back and let him ramble on.

Proudly, he told me how his constituency had been re-electing him for nearly fifty years, how he had served in the cabinets of five premiers, and how honoured he had been to be able to contribute to the political life of the province over such a long time. He held the record, he repeated "the record", for service in the history of the legislature.

Then, just as suddenly as he had become young and spirited, he became harsh, bitter and sneering as he relayed the story of how, when a former premier had drowned and he had stepped into his shoes, 'they' conspired against him and denied him the chance to govern for what he called a 'decent length of time'.

He had never specified who 'they' were, but he had repeatedly referred to them as "a jumped-up cabal". No names were mentioned, but it was clear to me that he had felt 'they' had cheated him out of his rightful place.

On the other side, there was nobody I knew, although I had seen John Wilkins, the Leader of the Opposition, on television a few times. He sat flanked and backed by fourteen of his colleagues at the centre and right of that side of the House. Further down, closer to The Speaker, was a small cluster of seven members of the other party, most of them frowning and looking extremely earnest. Their leader was a grey-haired, elderly woman, whose name I had forgotten, who seemed perpetually aggrieved and squirmed in her seat as if she were afflicted by hemorrhoids.

"Here," Zila hissed at me, shoving a leaflet at me. "You'll need this."

"Thanks. What is it?"

"Look and see."

I did as she instructed and saw that it contained a plan of the house, with the names and constituencies of all the Members. I studied it eagerly and discovered that I had rightly identified Joan Howard and Angus MacKinnon, and that the hemorrhoidal lady was called Dana Edwards.

I looked at my corner of the plan and read:

Mark LeBlanc, Kings South

Damn. They had not even spelled my name correctly.

Whatever had been debated on the floor during this time was completely incomprehensible to me, although I had not been following closely, having been preoccupied with trying to accustom myself to this strange environment. I heard Wilkins demand to know why only amended bills had explanatory notes while new bills, which most needed them, had none. Some unseen person from my side accused

Wilkins of being "obsessed with minutiae", a phrase he liked so much, he repeated it several times. Mrs. Edwards intervened to protest the amount of time being wasted on mundane matters when those of life and death were being ignored.

As she was speaking, a man from the Official Opposition, whom I saw from the plan was Samuel Wong, shouted, "Rave on!" His seat-mate, Denis McNamara, bellowed, "Siddown!" to Mrs. Edwards, but she took no notice.

From time to time, old Maddingly croaked "Order! Order!" but I could not tell if anyone obeyed his commands.

Suddenly, Maddingly got up and left the chair and all around me people were rising from their desks. I sat there in a daze and let them go.

When most of them had filed out, a man I thought I had seen before, who had been sitting in the middle of the front row, came towards me.

"Marc LeBlanc."

"Yes, that's me."

He was a man in his fifties, tall, rangy and balding. He immediately struck me as a man who seldom smiled and had little pleasure in his life. "John Trevor."

"Ah yes," I said sticking out my hand, "You're from Kings County, too. I thought I had seen you somewhere."

"Kings West. Next to yours." He spoke brusquely, and did not take my hand. "My constituency begins on your side of Cambridge."

"I didn't know."

"You should know that. What you also should know is that I'm the government chief whip."

"Oh."

"Do you know what that means?"

"No. Sorry, I don't. You see I only got into this—"

"Shuddup. The Chief Whip is in charge of discipline. Understand me?"

"No."

"It means you do what you're told, keep your nose clean, don't do or say anything without clearing it with me. And, for God's sake, never, never vote against the party."

"Ah, I see."

"Do you?"

"In general terms, yes. But aren't I permitted to exercise my own judgment on anything?"

"No."

"Then why am I here?"

"Until such time as you might be promoted, which is highly unlikely, your job is to keep quiet, vote for government motions and legislation, and refer constituents' problems to the relevant minister."

"But surely, there'll be occasions on which I would be guided by my conscience, especially if it affects my constituency."

"No. Not if you want a future in politics."

"Well, if you really want to know, John"—My back was against the wall, literally, and I was getting annoyed—"I have no intention of having a future in politics."

"You're not going to run again?" He sounded astonished.

"No."

"Christ! Well, you'd better tell your association to start grooming the next candidate."

"Okay. I have no problem with doing that."

"Good. And don't think that because you're the premier's little dog you can break the rules, because you can't."

"I'm nobody's dog." I was seething now. "I got into this because I happen to be a personal friend of the premier."

"Yeah, well, we'll see how that goes."

"Can I go now, Mr. Trevor?"

"Yeah. But since you're late arriving you missed the orientation program for the new boys and girls, so you're going to have to see Ray Hutchinson at nine tomorrow morning."

"Who's Ray Hutchinson?"

"Caucus Office Manager. He'll show you the ropes, and tell you the dos and don'ts."

"Alright. I'll be there at nine. Where is it?"

"Where's what?"

"Where do I go to see this Hutchinson guy?"

"Caucus office. Seventh floor of the bank building on Hollis."

"Thanks."

"What hotel are you at?"

"The Muir."

"Fuck me! Are you a millionaire or something?"

"Yes, as a matter of fact, I am a millionaire."

"God help us. I guess you can stay wherever you like—"

"Thank you."

"But don't be socializing with the other side. No little drinkies after hours with the Opposition. No letting caucus secrets slip out over dinner."

"Whatever secrets there might be, I can promise you I won't reveal to our opponents, but if you think you can tell me who I should and should not meet with after work, you've got another think coming. Good night."

He glared at me for a few seconds and then stalked off muttering to himself. It sounded like, "Fucking freshmen. Always the same. Hawking their fucking consciences from pillar to post."

Cabinet in Order of Precedence

Wendell Proctor – Premier
Joan Howard – Deputy Premier, Minister for the Cabinet Office
Chester MacCormack – Finance
Angus MacKinnon – Economic Economic Development
Angela Stairs – Justice
STEPHANIE GILMOUR – Health
MARK GARDINER – Tourism and Culture
KESSEGOO'E SILLYBOY – Social Services & Native Affairs
BILL CLARK – Transport and Public Works
GLORIA JONES – Labour & Women
HAROLD MacDONALD – Energy & Mines
PIERRE DORION – Municipal & Intergovernmental Affairs
LEILA HENDRICKS – Education
HECTOR McNEIL – Agriculture and Fisheries
JILL RUTLEDGE – Environment
ZANDILI JOSEPH – Lands and Forests

ANDREW MacISSAC – Secretary to Cabinet
JOHN TREVOR – Government Chief Whip
TOM ALDRIDGE – Chief of Staff to the Premier

8

I was not sure what they would—or could—do to me if I was late for my appointment with Ray Hutchinson, but, with a sense of trepidation ridiculous in a man of my age, I arrived at the caucus office early.

When I pushed open the door, I expected to see a frenzy of activity and to be assailed by the sound of rattling printers and ringing phones, but the quiet was almost unearthly. The space was long, with a series of tiny cubicles on each side and what looked like a secretarial pool at the end.

I crept slowly along, peering into each cubicle, but few MLAs were at work. Those who were in their spaces—"offices" would be far too grand a word—barely gave me a second glance, had their feet up on their desks and were playing with their mobile phones.

As I approached the end of the room, I saw several secretarial people busy at their computers and an elderly battleaxe of a woman sitting in a commanding position, clearly overseeing the younger women. Behind them were three offices, one large and the other two smaller. These were real offices with doors which closed and glass separating them from the lesser world.

Tentatively, I edged up to the battleaxe. She looked up imperiously and regarded me suspiciously through glasses which were perched on the end of her nose.

"Yes?"

"Good morning. I'm here to see Mr. Hutchinson."

"He's not in yet. Do you have an appointment?"

"Yes, I do."

"Name?"

"My name's LeBlanc."

"LeBlanc?"

"Yes, Marc LeBlanc."

"Oh you're the newbie," she said, barely disguising how little respect she had for me. "You'll have to wait. Or come back."

"Can I just wander around Ms.—?"

"Sandy Fergusson." She sniffed. "I don't think it'd be a good idea to wander around. You might get lost."

"We wouldn't want that!" I laughed nervously. "Is there…do I have… er… an office?"

"An office? Oh, you mean a compartment?"

"Yes, I do."

"There are two empty on the left hand side there. You can have either of those. Just let me know which one you pick."

"Thank you. Is there a phone there?"

"Of course there is. Dial nine for an outside line. In theory, you can call where you like, but we keep a record each month and if we find you've been calling Hong Kong every day, Ray will have your guts for garters."

"How about correspondence? I assume I'll have some."

"If you have any letters to go out, let us have the draft and we'll send it."

"Does that mean you'll redraft it?"

"If it needs it."

"What about press releases?"

"What about them?"

"How do I go about putting one out?"

"You don't'!" She looked startled and stood up. "You won't be issuing any press releases unless Ray says you should, in which case he'll do it for you."

"Oh. What if I want to write a speech?"

"You won't."

"I beg your pardon?"

"You won't be making any speeches for a while yet. When you do, Hillary will write them for you."

"Who's Hillary?"

"Hillary Randolph. She's our research director."

"Where would I find her?"

"Office behind me, but she'll find you if she wants you."

"I see. Well, thank you, Ms. Fergusson. I think I'll just go to my off— my compartment and wait for Mr. Hutchinson."

Of the two available compartments, I chose the one furthest away from Ms. Fergusson. I sat at the small, utilitarian desk and looked at the wall, since there was no window.

Being an MLA was not at all what I had been expecting. The closest similitude which came to mind was that of a drone bee in a hive.

Just then a head appeared around the doorway. "How's she going b'y?"

I looked up and saw a jolly-looking, but rather dishevelled, man in his early 60s. He grinned and helped himself to the only other chair in the compartment.

"Good morning," I said, standing up. "Are you Mr. Hutchinson?"

"Lord, no! I'm Art Sullivan. I'm from the Pier, dear."

"I'm sorry, I don't understand."

"Cape Breton Centre and Whitney Pier is my constituency. You must be Marc LeBlanc," he said, except that he pronounced it "Lib-long."

"Yes."

"Welcome aboard. I meant to catch you yesterday when the House rose, but old Misery Guts had you cornered."

"You mean John Trevor?"

"Yeah." He wrinkled his nose. "Stay well away from him. He's one of those apple shiners."

"Apple shiners?"

"Yes, you know. Farm types from the Annapolis Vall—Oh, jeez, I just remembered. You're from there, too."

"I am." I laughed. "But I'm no apple shiner. I never worked a day on a farm in my life."

"No offense intended, b'y."

"None taken."

"If I were you, I'd spend time in Halifax only when Misery Guts orders you to be here, and spend as much of your expense money as you can in the constituency. Throwing money around down here won't buy you any votes."

"Have you been here long, Art?"

"Lemme see, it must be about thirteen years since I was first elected."

"Are you the most senior Member?"

"Lord, no. Ernie Maddingly—he's The Speaker—has been here

pretty near forty years, and George Savory was first elected about twenty-five years ago. Brent Granger was the premier when I first came up to Halifax."

"I've heard about him. What was he like?"

"None better."

"Better than Wendell?"

"I heard you were a friend of the boss so I better watch what I say."

"Wendell and I are friends, but I'm not his spy, Art."

"You'll have a hard time convincing the rest of the caucus of that."

"I can't help what they think. But I promise you anything you say to me will be kept in confidence."

"I believe you. But since you ask, the boss is good. He's strong, he's smart, he's a great speaker, and, best of all, he's a good voter getter."

"But...?"

"But he's arrogant, and this latest win will make him worse."

"Arrogant? I've never found him to be like that."

"That's because you know him from outside politics. To those of us on the inside—I guess that includes you, now—he's always right, always thinks he knows everything, and doesn't treat everyone the same."

"How do you mean?"

"If you can do something to help him, he'll be all over you like a dirty shirt. If you're just an ordinary schmo who only has one vote in the House, it's another matter."

"You surprise me."

"Well, that's the way it is. Have you had your lecture from the principal yet?"

"You mean Hutchinson? No, I was supposed to meet him at nine, but he still hasn't turned up."

"You'll get used to that treatment."

"Art, am I to understand that we report to him? That he's our boss?"

"Most of the time it'll be Missy Randolph, Misery Guts, and Lauren Oakley."

"Who's she?"

"She's Ray's assistant."

"Then who's Ray's boss? The Premier?"

"No, his boss is Tom Aldridge, the boss's Chief of Staff. I see from your face that you know him."

"Yes, I do. What do you think of him?"

"I don't see much of him. He doesn't speak to the likes of me."

"It's beginning to dawn on me that it doesn't count for much being chosen by the people. An unelected staff member seems to have more clout."

"Does have more clout. Don't you forget it!"

"Surely, that isn't how it's supposed to work."

"How what is supposed to work?" demanded a haughty voice from the doorway.

"Oh, it's you, Ray," said Art. "This here is Marc LeBlanc."

"Yes, I'd figured that out for myself. Now get lost, Art. I need to have a few words with young Mr. LeBlanc."

Art quickly exited the compartment, and Ray Hutchinson sprawled in the vacant chair and put his feet up on the desk. He was a small, slight man, obviously quite fit, who was approximately thirty, which, being several years younger than me, made his addressing me as "young Mr. LeBlanc" especially offensive.

He tilted his head and directed his remarks to the ceiling. "Now listen and don't speak until I'm finished. If I have left any points uncovered, which is unlikely, you can ask questions then.'

"Okay."

"What did I just say? Shut it."

I shut it and listened while he addressed me as if I were a public meeting. Most of what he had to say I had already heard from Trevor, Art and Zila, so I mentally turned off and shifted my thoughts first to Rosalie and home, and then back to the horrendous decision I had made when Wendell had pressured me.

I wondered how it could be right that the elected representatives of the people could be, in effect, subservient to civil servants, and how the MLAs could tolerate it. Then I answered my own question when it occurred to me that few of them could ever get re-elected without the party apparatus, and that equipage would not be available to any who did not toe the line. I also realized that Wendell must know all this and must have approved it, because the entire machinery was being operated in his service.

I did not know how long I could have hacked it in the absence of my loyalty to Wendell, and knew that, were it not for that fact, I would be in open rebellion and heading for an early resignation.

Hutchinson wound up his dissertation with a few pious homilies about good behaviour being rewarded and bad behaviour being punished. Then he rose and made for the door, but stopped, came back and sat down again. His supercilious, patronizing manner completely changed as he leaned across the desk in a positively loathsome, almost fawning fashion,

"Of course, Mark, I had to give you the lecture so the gang won't think I'm playing favourites, but between you and me, this has been a mere formality. So, when you're speaking to the Great One, I hope you'll make it clear that I wasn't too hard on you."

Then he made an exaggerated wink, which was almost too much to bear, before continuing. "I know you stay at his house, so you must have a lot to say to each other."

"I have stayed with the Proctors in the past," I said, referring to a period when I was investigating the threats, "but I thought that during the session it would be too much of a burden on Cynthia."

"Cynthia! Ah yes, Cynthia. That was very thoughtful of you. Well, I won't trouble you any longer."

"Well, goodbye."

"Oh, Marc?"

"Yes, Ray?"

"My door is always open." Then he added, "To you."

If my compartment had a window I would have opened it as wide as possible to clear the air of Ray's insufferable presence. Failing that, I lurched out into the passage and headed for the door.

Just as I was about to exit a rotund, old man came shambling in. "Ho! You're the one who just joined us yesterday?"

"For my sins, I am."

"Very pleased to meet you, sir. I'm George Savory, from the great county of Shelburne."

"My pleasure, George. May I call you George?"

"It's the name I was given by my parents back in nineteen hundred and forty eight, so you may as well use it." He laughed heartily as if he had cracked a huge joke.

"I hear you've been here a long time, George?"

"Twenty-eight years to be precise, sir." Of course the place has gone to the dogs since my day. Gone to the dogs."

"Who was premier when you were first elected?"

"Savage. Savage by name but not by nature. He spoke down to you, but then, which premier doesn't?"

"It would seem to go with the territory. Do you think this one is the same?"

"Hmmm." His eyes narrowed and he pursed his lips. "I heard you were cozy with him, but I won't be running again and I won't be getting back into the cabinet, so I don't give a damn. Tell you the truth, he is, sir. Not as bad as it has been in my day, but heading in that direction."

"I'm sorry to hear that."

"Look, what time is it?"

"Er...eleven thirty-two."

"Look, let's go and have a drink and a spot of lunch. Interested?"

"Yes, I guess, but ought we to be drinking? The House sits this afternoon, doesn't it?"

"You planning on giving a speech?"

"No."

"Neither am I, so who cares, eh? 'Course, in my day, fellows rolled in roaring drunk. But it's gone to the dogs now."

"I might be persuaded to have one drink if we're having food."

"Champion! I know a nice little place where you can get an eye-opening martini and a nice bit of fish. You like fish?"

"Yes. And martinis."

9

"Ahh!" George smacked his lips after sipping the martini. "Finest kind! That'll set you up for the day, Mr. Man."

As I listened, I became entranced with his lilting accent, somewhat similar to country dialects I had heard when I lived in Britain. I noticed that he did not roll his 'r's like most Nova Scotians, used curious expressions like "Mr. Man", "he turned to work", and "Finest kind", and that when he said "Shelburne" it became something approaching "Showbun."

"I've only been back in Nova Scotia for six years," I said.

"You were away?"

"I lived in England for almost seventeen years. And, to be frank, I don't know as much about Nova Scotia as I should. Shelburne is one of the poorer counties, isn't it?"

"You think? There are only six counties out of eighteen with a higher median income than Shelburne, and two of those are where all the federal and provincial civil servants on inflated government salaries live."

"I didn't know that. That surprises me."

"Sure, there are some poor people in Shelburne, like everywhere else, maybe Birchtown would be poorer than most, but, Mr. Man, if you want to see a lot of big shiny cars and huge 98-inch televisions, you come on down to Shelburne County!"

"Really? Is fishing the main industry?"

"Yes, fishing and fish processing. 'Course, the outlay can be huge."

"The outlay?"

"Your license and your boat are gonna cost you hundreds of thousands, but once you get those, if you own the boat, you could haul in over $200,000 in a season."

"Do lobster fishermen still collect Employment Insurance?"

"In my day it was called *Un*employment Insurance, which made much more sense, but, like everything else, the English language has gone to the dogs. I mean to say, you 'ent being insured against being employed are you? You're being insured against being out of work."

"Yes, I guess you're right."

"I know I'm right."

The waiter brought our food. George dived into his haddock with relish. and we ate in silence for a while.

"You were telling me about the fishermen collecting the benefits," I said at length.

"In my day it was based on the hours worked, but they wised up to that and now fishing benefits are based on earnings. Imagine making a good living lobstering, and then getting handouts from the government in the off season!"

"Weren't you in the cabinet at one time, George?"

"I was. For six years."

"What portfolio?"

"Minister of Fisheries, naturally. In my day Fisheries had its own department, but now it's been rolled into other departments. Gone to the dogs."

"What happened? Were you…er…demoted?"

"Not exactly. When Brent Granger was drownded and Mr. Proctor took over, he turned to work, made a new cabinet and included me out."

"So, what's it like being on the back benches after being a cabinet minister?"

"Like being sent back to school after graduating from college."

"That bad?"

"See, when your party is in government, it's like being on an ocean liner. There's first class, Second Class, Third class and Steerage. Being a backbencher is Steerage. People like John Trevor and Freeman Murphy—"

"Who's he?"

"He's the Caucus Chairman. They are in Third Class. Then there's members of the cabinet—they are Second Class, In First Class there's just the premier and his little circle—"

"Tom Aldridge?"

"That's the fellow."

"Anyone else in First Class, apart from him?"

"Joan."

"Joan Howard?"

"Yes. Now, she is good people, Mr. Man. Yes, I think she's in first class alright, sir. In every sense of the term."

"And like on the ocean liner, I guess there's not a lot of interaction between the classes."

"You got it. Almost none. Unless those above want something from those below. Then they'll turn to work and let you know how they've been your best friend all along."

"I got the impression it worked something like that."

"So what you've got, Marc, is four classes with the people in each class—except for First Class—all hoping, praying and angling to climb up into a higher class. You're new, so I guess you have hopes to climb the ladder yourself."

"Not me. This is it for me. After this session, I'm out. I never wanted to be a politician. I only became a candidate because they were stuck and because Wendell asked me to do it."

"My! I can see you're going to be quite a novelty around here. Someone who doesn't want to move up!"

"I guess that even some of those who do never make it to a higher class."

"Oh yes, quite a few."

"Is Art Sullivan one of them?"

"Yes, he's one. Poor old Art."

"I met him this morning. I quite liked him."

"Art's alright, but he's never going to get out of steerage."

"He doesn't seem to be that upset about it."

"What choice does he have? He's bluefin tuna in Whitney Pier, but an insignificant minnow here in Halifax."

"On that pleasant note, we'd better get over to the House. It meets in twenty minutes."

"Neither one of us is going to run again, so what can they do to us?"

We were late getting to the chamber, and when we entered (I remembered to bow), we got dirty looks from John Trevor and a man I later discovered from the floor plan was Freeman Murphy.

The debate was about some legislation relating to municipalities, the bill being piloted through the House by the minister. I took another look at the plan and saw that he was Pierre Dorion from Argyle, someone, I confess, I had never heard of.

He seemed to have some difficulty explaining a section in the bill and was being heckled from the Opposition benches by MacNamara, Wong and a woman I identified as Dayle Doucet.

I noticed that, apart from Angus MacKinnon and one other minister, the front bench was deserted. That was Angela Stairs, the Minister of Justice, whom I had seen once before when I was briefly admitted to the cabinet room two years ago at the premier's invitation.

I had never seen any person who looked more like the Ice Queen. She was as pale as she was haughty, her long, white neck supporting a close-cropped head which disdainfully surveyed what she undoubtedly regarded as a rowdy bunch of reprobates.

Just when Dorion seemed to be inextricably mired in his bill, the doors swung open and Wendell appeared and stood frowning at the Opposition, his very presence subduing their obstreperous antics. He bowed to The Speaker and strode to his desk.

It took him less than a minute to take in the situation. Then he rose and, I thought with unnecessary ruthlessness, proceeded to lash and slash the opposing benches with insults. They physically withered under his perfervid verbal barrage, while everyone on our side of the House cheered and thumped their desks.

Quickly, all empty seats were filled as Members rushed in to join the spectacle, and utter pandemonium ruled as The Speaker vainly tried to make his cries for order be heard above the cacophony of charges and counter-charges. Wilkins was on his feet, demanding a Point of Order, but Wendell refused to give way and harshly told him to "Siddown and shuddup!"

By this time, howling and desk thumping emanated from all quarters of the chamber as poor old Maddingly pounded his gavel again and again. Frustrated beyond endurance, he screamed, "The House is adjourned!" into the tumult and scurried out by the side door.

There being nobody in the chair, the sitting could not continue, so chaos reigned while Members continued to hurl epithets from one side to the other across the aisle.

Not finding this display either edifying or particularly entertaining, largely because I was disappointed at Wendell's temper and vulgarity, I slipped out and retreated to the legislative library, where I grabbed a magazine and sat in a corner, hoping nobody would find me.

My wish was not to be fulfilled, because no sooner had I settled than two women came over and sat at the same table.

"Are you the same Marc LeBlanc who wrote the books? The private investigator?" asked a pleasant redhead whom I guessed to be about forty-five.

"I am, yes."

"I loved the books. I've read them all. Are they all true?"

"Yes, as far as I know. I'm sorry, but who are you?"

"I'm Ellie MacLeod and this is Martha McNaughton."

"You're...opposition Members?"

"Yes, I'm from Colchester and Ellie is from Queens," said Martha, a stout, pony-tailed woman in her thirties.

"Wasn't that a real ding dong?" Ellie asked. "A real dust up!"

"I've never seen anything like it," I said. "Has it happened before?"

"A couple of times in this session," said Martha. "This is my first term, like you, but Ellie was first elected four years ago, so she's seen this kind of thing many times."

"Yes," Ellie said, "it usually happens when things are quiet and humming along well. Then he comes in and all hell breaks loose."

"Who, Wendell? You would say that, wouldn't you?"

"Don't be a dope. Martha and I like Proctor. He's brilliant and very good looking. I wish he was on our side, but he's like a red rag to a bull."

"More like he can't pass a hornet's nest without giving it a poke," Martha said.

"He's a personal friend of mine, but I must admit that I was a bit shocked."

"You'll get used to it. Our guy, Wilkins, can get carried away by times. But in case you were wondering, there are much worse people in this place than either of them. Some of them are real bottom feeders."

"I only got here yesterday, so I haven't even met most of my side yet, but to date I have seen a few who might qualify for that description."

"I can guess who they are," said Ellie.

"Yeah, we've got some real bozos on our side, too."

"Your guys Wong and MacNamara seem to go out of their way to be unpleasant."

"They're the designated provocateurs," said Martha. "But they're like that in real life, too."

"Does my side also have provocateurs?"

"Oh yes,' said Ellie. "Leaman, MacPhee and Parish. When they get going, it's like a pack of rabid wolves on the loose."

"I don't know Leaman or MacPhee, but isn't Parish the black lady who sits in front of me?"

"Yeah. She's the worst. She has a voice like a thunderstorm in a garbage can, and a tongue like a rusty razor blade."

"The way you describe things, I'm glad that I'm just passing through."

"What do you mean?"

"Just that. I'm a one-term Member."

"You're not forty. Why would you be quitting?"

"I'm not in this by choice. But that's a long story."

"Sounds weird to me," said Martha. "I thought the whole point of being an MLA was to get re-elected."

"Maybe for you. Not for me. I'm an investigator and a writer. The sooner I go back to that, the better I'll like it."

"Okay, Weirdo, what are you doing for dinner?" Ellie asked. "It doesn't look as if old Ernie is going to reconvene, so the evening is ours."

"Sure. I'm free. But before we go, tell me about Maddingly. When I met him before, he was a minister."

"Yes, and before that he was premier for a brief spell. I guess Proctor wanted him out of the cabinet because he was too much of an old woman, and Ernie insisted on running again, so they gave him the Speaker's chair so he could save face."

"I kind of thought the speakership was a stepping stone to the cabinet, not a retirement home."

"It always was before Ernie, but when you come to think about it, it makes much more sense this way," said Ellie. "If you put some young whippersnapper in the job, he or she is going to try to please the boss by being partisan. And that's just what the Speaker shouldn't be."

"So, progress is being made in some areas," I said.

"Yeah, but not in many," Martha said. "Let's go eat!"

10

My night out with Ellie and Martha was extremely pleasant. They were great fun and did not at all seem like "the enemy". Nor were the political points they advanced from time to time uttered with the vehemence of those who feel they have been appointed by God to save the world. In fact, they were so reasonable in both their arguments and their assessment of those on my side of the aisle, that I was impelled to ask the question which had been on my mind for some hours.

"So, what are the essential differences between your side and mine?"

Clearly, they had not been expecting me to ask this, and they needed to think about it before answering.

"There are more than twice as many of you as there are of us," Martha said.

"And three times the number of women," said Ellie.

"You have the most handsome leader, by far."

"And probably more good speakers."

"Yes, we have Wilkins, Downey and Cohen, but as well as Proctor you have MacKinnon—he's terrific—Joan, Chester McCormack and Stephanie Gilmour."

"And Bill Clark."

"Yes, Clark can be very good."

"I think you may have misunderstood my question," I said. "I meant real differences."

They stared at me and then at each other. They both laughed.

"That's easy. You're in and we're out!" Ellie said.

"That's it? There's no philosophical or ideological difference?"

"There are policy differences, but when you think about it, a lot of the time we're only against something if you guys are for it."

"And *vice versa*," Martha said.

"What about the other lot?"

"Dana Edward's bunch?"

"Yes."

"Well, they're every bit as hypocritical as your party and ours, and just as mendacious, but when they tell lies they think they're doing God's holy work."

"Yes," Martha cackled, "when Dana gets going you'd swear she was nailed to the cross."

"And a lot of the time she sounds as if she's been tortured. 'Oh My Lord help me to battle the raging storm and fight the good fight against these monstrous barbarians.' She's good at that sort of thing."

"I get a kick out some the people behind her when she's like that," Martha said. "They're desperately trying to keep straight faces, but they have to hide their heads in their hands or pretend they're reading something."

"I have a feeling they would be difficult to get to know," I said. "I don't imagine two of them would go out to dinner with me."

"I doubt it, although I think if Winnie Saccary could be pried away from the rest, she might be almost human."

"Which one is she?"

"She sits in the back with Andrew MacEachern."

"I don't know him. I know hardly anybody."

"It won't take you long to know them all," Ellie said, "And then you'll wish you didn't!"

George Savory had told me there would be a caucus meeting that morning. I thought I recalled his saying it started at ten-thirty, so at that time I trooped along to the conference room to find, to my deep embarrassment, that the proceedings had started at ten. Arrayed around a large oval table were all of the other thirty-one government MLAs. The Speaker, by tradition, did not participate in any partisan activity, so was not present.

I found the only available space and squeezed in between a big burly man I later discovered was Fred Askey, from my own county, and a very smartly-dressed woman who reminded me of Rosalie.

"You've been a naughty boy," she whispered to me. "I'm Emma Mitchell from Chester."

I nodded, grateful for any crumb of friendship, made myself as inconspicuous as I was able, and peered around the room. At the head of the table was Freeman Murphy, a bustling, self-important, middle-aged man who reminded me of an actor who perennially played the mayors of American towns. To his right was Wendell, his head higher than all others, his steely gaze constantly roving around the table as if searching for treachery. When his eyes met mine, the look he gave me suggested he might have found it.

On the other side of the Chairman was John Trevor, managing to appear even more sinister and brutish than when I had seen him yesterday. I picked out the Minister of Finance, Chester McCormack; Joan Howard; Angela Stairs; Angus MacKinnon, Minister of Economic Development; Labour Minister Gloria Jones; Tourism Minister Mark Gardiner, with whom I had a very unpleasant meeting two years previously; Pierre Dorion; George; Art; Zila ; Delia and, seated just behind the premier, Tom Aldridge. I failed to recognize anybody else in the room and thought it rather ridiculous that I could not.

"Now, folks," said Murphy, speaking in the back of his throat, "the premier would like to say a few words."

"More than a few, Freeman," said Wendell, rising and towering over the assembled company. "I've come to the conclusion that we've been coasting, not really *doing* anything really worth doing. I've decided that we need to make a splash. Now the election is behind us, I propose to stop farting around and kow-towing to all and sundry because we might lose a vote here or there. We've got four years to win back those we lose now—"

At this I noticed that people were shifting in their seats, suddenly uneasy.

"—and the best time to do unpopular stuff is at the beginning of a mandate. Now, you know that I was opposed to electric vehicles because they rely on exploitation of black people in Africa, but also because I think it is a damn fool idea—"

Some light murmuring accompanied these words. Several people leaned forward.

"—and so is ruining our landscape with God awful windmills—"

A few nods this time.

"—so this government is coming out four-square against this nonsense. Period. No more of either from now on."

A collective intake of breath could be heard.

"And before this mandate is over, we're going to have a real redistribution of seats based on population, not on race or ethnicity."

Some eyes widened and some jaws dropped.

"Right now we have fifty five seats for a population of just over a million. That's ridiculous. Even more ridiculous is drawing seat boundaries in the belief that people will, and should, only be represented by those who look like them or speak their language—"

A few Members slapped the table, whether in agreement or in protest I could not determine.

"In fact, it's racist!" Wendell spat out the word. "The notion that Preston can only be represented by a black person, or that Clare, Richmond and Argyle can only be represented by Acadians, is anathema to me."

I noticed that Pierre Dorion from Argyle and Gloria Jones, who represented Preston, looked particularly agitated.

"We constantly hear a lot of blather about 'institutional racism.' Well, let's face it, we have institutionalized it in our legislature. Our House is a monument to racism."

The room was now silent.

"And I say, as a black man, as the first black premier, that it's time we got rid of the pernicious idea that only certain people can be racist and certain other people can't be."

Some heads were nodding, but others were shaking from side to side, obviously distressed. Delia Parish looked as if she were about to suffer cardiac arrest.

"If you discriminate on the basis of race, it is racism. Whether against or in favour. Any decision based on race is racist, and my government is going to stop doing it. Now!"

Muttering had now become a loud murmur of competing sentiments.

"And while we're at it, this government is going to take back our language!"

A hearty "hear, hear," came from George Savory.

"Changing the meaning of words, titles and terms so as to make them more palatable in certain quarters is going to stop. If you'll excuse the expression, we're going to call a spade a spade," Wendell said with a huge grin.

A nervous laughter erupted, but only from some. Those who did not laugh were frowning deeply.

"One of our charities is called 'The Association for Community Living.' If you landed in a space ship from Mars would you have the slightest idea what it did or who it served? Of course, you wouldn't. How many times have we change the name of the department of—I hardly know what to call it—it started as the Department of Welfare, which is what the common people still call it, then went to Social Services, then to Community Services. Why? Because someone decided they were offended. Our words have to say what they mean and mean what they say."

I heard Emma Mitchell muttering to herself, "He doesn't get it. He doesn't understand."

"To cabinet I say, go back to your departments and root out this nonsense in your literature and guidelines. Dozens of words have been banned—almost made illegal—because some moaning Minnie somewhere found them offensive. We're going to change that. My government is declaring war on Woke!"

I judged that about two-thirds of those present applauded heartily. Roughly half a dozen looked aggrieved or afraid, I could not tell which, and the rest sat in silence, probably trying to calculate the effect of the premier's remarks and if they would personally derive benefit from these changes.

With that, Wendell stalked out, Tom Aldridge following at a close distance.

"Alright," said Murphy, trying to sound as if he knew all along what the premier would say. "You've all got your marching orders. As there is no further business, I declare the meeting adjourned."

But most had already left, talking to each other in hushed tones as they went. I saw that Delia Parish and Gloria Jones had stayed behind, huddled in a corner. The only words I could discern clearly were Delia's "Stabbed in the back!"

George came up to me, his face wreathed in smiles. "Finest kind! I been awaiting almost thirty years to hear that, Mr. Man. This baloney was just getting under way in my day, and it's gone too darned far."

Art Sullivan joined us. Until he spoke I could not tell whether he was pleased by what he heard or disapproved of it.

"What did you think, Art?" George asked. "Some good, wasn't it?"

"We in Cape Breton never went in for this woke stuff as much as the rest of the province. So I don't think it's going to make much difference to me. But elsewhere, I'm not so sure. At any rate, I'm sure of one thing."

"What's that?" I asked.

"The boss said he wanted to make splash. He's sure as hell going to get one!"

11

Following the caucus meeting, I naïvely thought we might be given some time to absorb what many Members were calling the premier's "bombshell". However, the splash Wendell said he intended to make was only just beginning. The House met at two o'clock that afternoon, and as soon as The Speaker called for a "moment of quiet reflection", Wendell jumped to his feet on a point of privilege.

"Mr. Speaker, I rise to protest this nonsense. For over 260 years this Legislature listened to a prayer from the chair prior to its proceedings. It was a Christian prayer because this was, and is, a Christian province. Today 60% of Nova Scotians , including our black and native citizens, identify as Christians, the closest other religion being Islam, with a mere 1.5%. In those 260 plus years, if any Members' sensitivities were offended by the prayer, they could have stayed beyond the bar of the House until it was over. Yet this was changed by a lily-livered government kowtowing to the minority. I wish to inform the House that this government will, by means of a substantive motion, be seeking to reintroduce the daily prayer."

The House was stunned by this announcement and none more than The Speaker, Ernest Maddingly. He opened his mouth to speak, but before he could get a word out, Wendell continued.

"I invite the House to now join me in prayer. 'Our Father which art in Heaven, hallowed be thy name. Thy Kingdom come, Thy will be done, on earth as it is in Heaven. Give us—'"

The rest of his words were drowned out in a pandemonium of some joining Wendell in saying the prayer, some howling in protest, desk thumping and the pounding of The Speaker's gavel. But if any thought the show was over, they were to be quickly disabused.

As soon as order was partially restored, the Clerk, Dudley Morton, straining to make himself heard, proceeded to read the Orders of the

Day. Presenting and reading petitions, presenting reports of committees, tabling reports, regulations, and other papers all were read without response until he announced, "Statements by ministers."

Wendell was quickly on his feet again. Amid cheers and catcalls he outlined to the House all the initiatives and reforms he had adumbrated to us in caucus that morning. This took him about fifteen minutes, but you could tell that he was just warming up.

I was curiously excited, in an almost-disinterested way, but I could see that others were taut and on the edges of their seats.

"Sounds like he's going to drop the other shoe," Zila said to me. "I hope it's not going to be a fucking big boot!"

"Now then, Mr. Speaker," said Wendell, his voice clear as a bell and becoming louder, "this province is $42 billion in debt. That's roughly $40,000 for every man, woman and child in Nova Scotia. Every year we are paying around $750 million in interest. That's money which can't be used to provide doctors, hospital beds, schools or roads."

The Opposition were listening to him in silence, obviously puzzled as to where he was leading. A few clucking sounds could be heard from the government benches. Angela Stairs was staring at the premier as if hypnotized. Chester McCormack had his head in his hands. Joan Howard was nodding vigorously.

"In addition to that, and despite the best efforts of our excellent Minister of Finance, we are running a $670 million deficit on our current account."

"You put it there!" Denis McNamara shouted.

"Yeah, you ran it up!" echoed Sammy Wong.

The Opposition Members were smiling and hooting. Our ranks were quiet. Some hung their heads. Others looked as if what they were hearing was complete news to them.

"We are shovelling—and I used that word advisedly—shovelling $750 million a year to universities which, when they are not teaching irrelevant or questionable subjects like Modern Jazz and Women's Studies, are indoctrinating our kids with Marxist ideology, anti-Semitism and insane notions that all white people are born evil. And we are $42 billion in debt."

A number on our side were nodding. Howls arose from across the aisle. Wendell waved them down contemptuously.

"Siddown! You'll get your chance to squawk later. All departments,

Mr. Speaker, are riddled with inefficiencies and items of expenditure which are illogical, incomprehensible, unexplainable and unjustifiable."

"Your lot did it!' John Wilkins yelled.

"Yes, and your lot, too. It's been going on for decades. Every government of every party has perpetuated this disgrace. The problem with any government programs or grants, Mr. Speaker, is that they start by being temporary but quickly become permanent until nobody can remember why they were put there in the first place. And all the while these items are costing the taxpayers more and more of their hard-earned dollars. And we are $42 billion in debt. Those who have been in this House for more than five minutes know I am right."

The sudden silence suggested that they all had knowledge of expenditures fitting Wendell's description.

"Let's take one department. Not because it is special, but because it is typical. This year we are projecting $125 million for the Department of Culture and Tourism. Of that amount, Mr. Speaker, nearly $70 million is going to Culture and another $10 million to Acadian, African and Gaelic Affairs."

"So what?" shouted Eric Downey, a portly black man sitting next to John Wilkins.

"So, I wonder how much of that is actually going to help people and how much is going to create and perpetuate petty bureaucracies? Can anyone across the way tell me? No, I thought not. And we are $42 billion in debt.

"Incidentally, while I have great respect for the few Gaelic speakers sitting alongside and behind me, I don't understand why they can't support their own language themselves. If it was that important, they would see to it that it survived and was nurtured."

Joan Howard gave Angus MacKinnon, who was known to be a Gaelic speaker, a little dig in the ribs.

"Taxpayers also support individual paid bureaucracies in outfits for Choral, Craft, Dance, Visual artists, Writers and"—he paused for dramatic effect—"Strategic Arts Management, whatever that is. The question has to be asked: why do each of these activities need a taxpayer-funded bureaucracy? If people want to sing, let them sing. If they want to paint, let them paint. If they want to write, let them write. If they want to dance, let them dance. Why can't those who pursue these inclinations support them with their own resources? "

"Philistine!" Dana Edwards shouted.

"Book burner!" Joyce Babin yelled.

"You don't understand," cried Dayle Doucet.

"I understand $42 billion in debt!" Wendell shot back. "Furthermore, Mr. Speaker, if you look closely at the supplements to the Public Accounts, you will see that every year government gives over $120 million in not hundreds, but thousands of handouts to clubs, associations, societies, legions, centres and every conceivable type of organization which at one time were voluntary and supported by their members and communities."

Zila had her head on her desk. A man a few seats from me whom I could not identify was biting his nails. Wendell was now in high gear.

"Do you know, Mr. Speaker, the government now funds a number of so-called advocacy groups which spend their time and resources lobbying the government for more money and to get their pet projects approved—which in turn would mean spending more of the taxpayers' money?

"Well, enough is enough! No more! I am asking the Minister of Finance to trim the provincial budget by at least $300 million this year, $500 million by next year and $750 million by the year after that.

"The day of reckoning has arrived. The gravy train stops here! And I commend this statement to the House."

The noise level was no lower than it had been the day before, when Wendell had been scrapping with the Opposition, but now it was of a different nature. There was as much bewilderment as there was anger on the Opposition benches, and not a small amount of fear and uncertainty on ours. I saw John Trevor shaking his head. So were Delia Parish and Zandili Joseph, a brightly-dressed black woman whom I remember had been Speaker before Maddingly.

George Savory. strained to catch my eye and gave me the thumbs-up signal. Joan Howard and Angus MacKinnon were busy congratulating Wendell, but Chester McCormack, I noticed, seemed very thoughtful.

When I leaned back and looked along the row to where Art Sullivan was sitting, he had a smile on his face and was looking at the ceiling. Then I saw that he had earphones on and was happily listening to music.

The Speaker called the next order of business and the House settled back into its usual tedium. When Wendell left the chamber, I followed him out.

"Wendell!"

"Oh, hello, Marc. How're you settling in?"

"Okay I guess. That was quite a speech."

"Yeah, well, it's time we put the fox among the chickens."

"How do you think it will fly?"

"Same as always. The complainers won't like it. The suck-holers will love it until they get stick from their constituents, then they'll howl like wolves. Look, I gotta go, but first I want to say something."

He gently took my lapel and drew me into the cloakroom. Then looking over his shoulder, he motioned me to the window.

"Look, Marc, when we're in public it's better if you call me 'Premier'."

"But you once told me not to call you 'Premier', but instead to use 'Wendell'."

"I know. That was when you were on the outside—"

"When you needed me. Now you don't?"

"Don't be like that." His eyes bored into mine. "It's just that I can't look like I'm playing favourites. I'm only asking you to play along when others are around. It may not be for always, just for now."

"Okay...Premier."

"Okay. So, this is your second day?"

"Yes."

"How do you like it?"

"Not much. I'm not a politician. I don't think I'd ever get used to all the theatre."

"No, I guess not. Still, if you're in it, you have to play your part upon the stage. What did you think of my announcements?"

"I never had any strongly-fixed political views, so I'm not sure I agree or disagree, but it sounds right and I must say you put it across very well."

"Thanks. I'll get back to you when you've had time to digest it. Do you have any sense of how it's going down with our people?"

"It's hard to say, but I'd guess you have made enemies of about a quarter of the caucus, friends of another quarter and the rest are on the fence."

"That sounds about right. The question is, will the enemies remain enemies for life or can they be bought or cajoled."

"I don't know them well enough to be able to say one way or the other. What's your own guess?"

"I'd say Zandili and Gloria are susceptible to flattery, but only a cabinet post will get Delia back on board. Not sure about Dorion. He's a queer fish."

"You've made a friend for life of old George Savory. You might want to drop a nice word in his direction."

" Old George, eh? Thanks for the tip."

"And a kind word to Art Sullivan wouldn't go amiss. I think he's there for whoever gets to him first."

"You're learning fast, Marc. Pretty soon you'll be a real pro."

"I don't think so. But you love all this wheeling and dealing, and sparring and catcalling, don't you?"

"Sure do." His grin revealed gleaming white teeth. "It's the only game in town."

"How's Cynthia?"

"Good. I don't see as much of her as I should. She keeps busy with charity work and such."

"Please give her our love. Rosalie's and mine."

"Sure will."

"And how's Grace?" Grace was the premier's voluble, busybody sister.

Wendell just rolled his eyes. "Have you seen Tom since you arrived?"

"No, I wasn't sure I should."

"Come on over. He'll be glad to see you."

"I will. I'll drop by tomorrow."

"Do that. And buckle up, Marc. It's going to be a bumpy ride!"

"Premier, that much I already knew."

12

I poked my head around the chamber door to see what was happening, but the debate sounded uninteresting and was droning on. As I was withdrawing my head, I saw that John Trevor had noticed me and was coming my way. He caught up with me at the Library door.

"LeBlanc, where are you going?"

"Hello John. I'm just popping into the library, if that's alright?"

"I guess so, but I need to know your movements at all times. Either tell me or Fred Askey where you're going. We need to know in case you're needed for a vote."

"Why Fred Askey?"

"He's the Annapolis Valley whip. Each region has its own whip, and they report to me."

"I see. I didn't know that."

"You should know it. Learn these things. They're important."

"I'll do my best. I promise."

"Where were you earlier? I saw you disappear, and you were gone for some time."

"I was having a chat in the cloakroom."

"You're not here to have chats. Who were you with?"

He was beginning to seriously annoy me, so I thought I would bait him. "An old friend."

"Don't play games with me. Who was it?"

"If you must know, it was the Premier. We were catching up on old times."

He glared at me with sheer hatred, then turned on his heel and stalked back into the House.

As I went into the Library I saw something which immediately struck me as unusual. In the corner was one of the assistant librarians, a young woman, looking as if she was being hemmed in by Denis

McNamara and Sammy Wong.

Thinking they were harassing her, I started towards them, intending to rescue her, when I got a glimpse of her face. Far from being harassed she was smiling and clearly sharing some kind of confidence with the two men.

Instinctively, I backed up and went to the Members' lounge, which I had not yet visited.

The lounge was quite small, accommodating six small tables surrounded by armchairs. At one end was an alcove containing a small kitchen equipped with a coffee urn and a small stove. There were seven Members sitting around drinking coffee or eating soup. One of them was Angus MacKinnon, the Minister of Economic Development.

"Marc LeBlanc!" he called, smiling as he got up. "How nice to see you again. In a different capacity, albeit."

"Hello, Mr. MacKinnon. I remember our last meeting. You were very kind to me and were generous with your time."

"Not at all. You did us all a great service. Had it not been for you, our Premier might have been assassinated. And, please do call me Angus."

MacKinnon's remarks attracted the attention of the others in the lounge.

"What's this, Angus?" asked a dapper, middle-aged man with a healthy, tanned face.

"David, this is Marc LeBlanc, our newest Member. Marc, meet David Cohen."

We shook hands. Cohen then ushered me around the room, introducing me, in turn, to the other occupants.

"Eugene Comeau," He said, as a jolly-looking man of about 60 jumped up to welcome me.

"I'm from Yarmouth. Like David here, I'm with the opposing army," he said with a grin. "But that's life. Wouldn't do for everybody to think alike."

"I agree with you, Mr. Comeau," I said.

"Everybody calls me Gene." He sat down and went back to his bowl of soup.

Next we came to a table where two men were playing cards. They looked up with annoyance at being interrupted.

"Marc, here we have Cliff Wolf and Bill Jenkins."

I heard Jenkins just managing a grunt of recognition, but Wolf said nothing. I could only describe his visage as 'glowering'. I was aware that appearances may be deceptive but, on looks only, I judged these two to be thoroughly nasty pieces of work.

Cohen gave me a wink as we moved on to the last occupied table, where two women were poring over masses of papers spread before them.

"Marc LeBlanc, I'd like to meet our Minister of the Environment, Jill Rutledge; and Carol Walters, the Member for Cape Breton East."

I bent over and shook hands with Rutledge who gave me an angelic smile, and whose hand was as soft as silk.

"Hello, Marc. You won't remember me, but I recall seeing you in the cabinet room a few years ago. The premier introduced you to us."

"Yes, that's right."

I reached over to take Carol Walters' hand but it was not proffered. Instead my gaze was returned by one of absolute malevolence. Not having any idea why she should harbour such dislike for me, I was disconcerted, quickly pulled back and stepped away.

"You two know each other?" Cohen whispered.

"No. I can't imagine why she seemed so hostile."

"Go figure! I guess Hashem will take care of it in his own time."

We returned to MacKinnon's table, where I sat chatting with him until a messenger appeared in the doorway.

"Premier's up again!" he called excitedly.

We all rushed back into the Chamber, almost falling over each other at the big brass bar, and bowing in unison to the Speaker. As we scurried to our seats, Wendell was on his feet.

Looking around, I could see that I wasn't the only one who wondered why he had risen, because the legislation before the House was an uncontroversial measure dealing with financial accountability of municipalities.

"Mr. Speaker, I may be a little off topic but I'm sure you will indulge me if I speak about accountability in a more general way."

"If the honourable gentleman does not get too general, I will allow it." Maddingly was at his most majestic.

"Thank you, sir. First, let's take a look at an organization which has a great deal to do with our municipalities: The Utility and Review Board. This group of unelected, highly-paid individuals has the power to regulate electricity rates, to fix the prices of gasoline and diesel, and to control planning, property assessment appeals and public passenger vehicles, and all without democratic accountability.

"Furthermore, this body can change the boundaries of municipal units and amalgamate them without even consulting the people, if they wish not to. And the only recourse the citizen has is to go to court...if he or she happens to have the money to pay heavy legal expenses.

"This body was given all this power by a previous lily-livered government in an attempt to avoid difficult or sensitive decisions. Well, this government is going to change that! Legislation will be introduced to give the government the right to change the board's rulings if they think fit. If the people don't like the final decision they can kick the government out."

"They will kick you out!" shouted David Cohen across the aisle.

"We'll see about that!" Wendell retorted. "You didn't do so well last time!

"Another matter relevant to accountability, Mr. Speaker, is the Auditor General—ah, this will get them going. The Auditor General was originally, and properly, charged with seeing that the province's finances were all in order. Nothing wrong with that but, again, a previous lily-livered government gave him—an accountant—the power to review and criticize all government programs."

"Your programs need to be reviewed!" barked Celia McArthur, a woman in the second row of the Opposition.

"Yes," Wendell said, leaning over his desk and pointing in her direction. "That's your job! What a greedy bunch. Not satisfied with two opposition parties, they want a third in the form of the Auditor General. How and when did *he* become an expert on fisheries, agriculture, environment, mines, culture, tourism and all the rest? What makes *him* qualified to judge public policy? Public accounts, yes. Public policy no! That's going to change pronto!"

The House erupted. About ten Opposition Members were on their feet, shouting, "Point of Order!' or, "Point of Privilege, Mr. Speaker!" Some unidentified member was singing *The Worker's Flag is Deepest Red.* Another was yelling "*Sieg Heil*!"

Wendell stood there, letting the insults and catcalls roll off him, as he stared down the Opposition.

Maddingly sat back in his throne, seeming to enjoy the performance. Having been an MLA for forty years, he had seen it all, and some of it was far worse than this. In his time he had witnessed physical assaults, the entire Opposition walking out, Members throwing water bottles across the floor, and the all-too-frequent use of extremely *unparliamentary* language.

"Lastly, Mr. Speaker," said Wendell, "this government is going to actively discourage the excessive use of hyperbole—that means wild exaggeration, for those across the way who did not go to school—and we will deliberately give more scrutiny to those who resort to the practice in order to get their way. A case in point is domestic violence, which is hysterically being alleged to constitute an epidemic."

"It is! It is!" Joyce Babin screeched from the third party.

"Really? Let's see what the dictionary says.. I just happen to have one with me, Mr. Speaker. I advise the honourable lady to likewise consult her own—if she has one. Here we go: *An epidemic is the rapid spread of disease to a large number of hosts in a given population within a short period of time.* Now, the situation may be serious, very serious; it may call for increased attention by police and government, but it is *not* an epidemic.

"This kind of rhetoric will not get us to consider a problem any quicker or any more seriously. So, let us be done with it!"

He sat down amid howls and jeers. As best as I could judge, there were a few in the Official Opposition who appeared to agree more with Wendell than with their own front bench leaders. I had less unobstructed vision to examine our side than theirs, but, apart from Carol Walters, Emma Mitchell and a tiny woman called Jennie Chan whom I had not yet met, it seemed to me as if Wendell had solid support. Of course, George Savory. was hugely delighted and, as before, Art Sullivan appeared to be in a world of his own.

I was wondering if Wendell had remembered my words of advice regarding these two men when, as if reading my mind, he got up and, threading his way through the desks, stopped first at George's and put an arm around the older man's shoulder. Then he went to the back row and sat on the edge of Art's desk. I saw Art whip off his headphones and, grinning, lean forward to receive the boss's blessing.

I was both pleased and surprised that Wendell had lost no time in buttering up Art and George. If a crunch was coming anytime in the near future, they would be in our camp. I thought that George would stick by Wendell through thick and thin, but that Art might need an occasional refresher of charm.

I shuffled along the wall and down a space between the desks until I got to Fred Askey's place. I crouched down beside him.

"What do you want?" he asked.

"I want to go out for a bit and John told me I should let you know."

"Yes. Quite right. Where are you going?"

"Out."

"Don't be an asshole. I need to know where you are so I can get in touch if I need you."

"Oh, sorry. I'll be at the Premier's Office."

"What?"

"More specifically, Tom Aldridge's office."

"What are you doing there?"

"Seeing some friends."

"What old friends? What are you talking about?"

"Tom and Susan. Wendell told me I should go over and see them."

He took a few seconds to digest this information and showed every sign of it having given him heartburn. He grunted and turned back to watch the debate.

"Don't be long. Your job is to be in here," he muttered out of the corner of his mouth.

I went into the lobby, down the ancient staircase, out through the western door, across the street, in by the back door of One Government Place and by elevator to the seventh floor.

Susan Greenlaugh was the guardian of the gate of the inner sanctum, where only Wendell and Tom's offices were located, and was the filter for incoming requests, reams of information, and outgoing correspondence and directives. Initially she had given me a hard time, but eventually we became great friends.

She seemed as delighted to see me as I was to see her. It had been almost two years since I last saw her, at which time I was in and out of the office over a period of several months. She seemed unchanged, as upright and formidable as ever, immaculately attired and business-like.

While we were joking around, Tom emerged from his office at the end of a short passage. "Is that Marc LeBlanc's voice I hear?" he called.

"I'd know those dulcet tones anywhere."

"Hello, Tom. Wendell told me to come and visit you."

"Well, come on in."

He led me into his large room, which was connected to the premier's office by a padded, double door. The place was a lot more untidy than it used to be, and Tom himself looked considerably worse for wear. The incessant pressure of being the point of contact between Wendell and the outside world had taken its toll.

Tom's job was to be the "fixer" who did all the dirty, manipulative work, and to take the blame for things which went wrong. He had to make Wendell look good, and in that service he was prepared to go to any lengths and endure any humiliation.

Tom was now, I guessed, approaching fifty, still relatively good-looking, but since I last saw him he had gained a paunch and quite a lot of grey hair around his ears.

"How's Heidi?"

Heidi was Tom's very beautiful wife, who was a lovely person, but many years his junior. She was the daughter of Premier Brenton Granger, who had preceded Wendell, but had tragically died in a drowning accident. She and Tom had married five years ago after a tempestuous, on-and-off relationship[3]. She was the manager of a bank on Hollis Street in Halifax, and they lived in a modest house in the city's west end.

"Heidi's great. My rock in the storm!"

"That's great. I'd love to see her again."

"Why don't you come to supper tonight? It'll be potluck, but we probably can scrounge something. I'll call her right now."

After Tom obtained her ready agreement, he grabbed his jacket and propelled me to the door.

"Go home, Susan. The Boss won't be back today. I'm off to entertain a rising political star."

"Before you go, Susan," I said, "would please call over to the House and leave a message for Fred Askey?"

"Sure, Marc."

"Tell him I am dining with the power behind the throne."

---

3   As described in *The Premier's Daughter*

13

I had been at Tom Aldridge's house before, when Rosalie and I had been invited there for dinner about two years previously. Rosalie told me later that she could not remember any home which exuded more love and warmth. Tom's toughness as a political in-fighter and Heidi's muscular firmness as a bank manager were instantly cast off as soon as they arrived home.

Although they had been married for over five years and there was a twenty year age difference between them, they behaved like two young lovers barely out of their teens. At first, it was slightly disconcerting to watch them touch each other and exchange kisses at the slightest opportunity, but one soon accepted it and even came to admire it.

Tom's devotion to Heidi was not difficult to understand, as she was highly intelligent, had a marvellous sense of humour and was stunningly beautiful. What kept Heidi deeply in love with him was more difficult to comprehend. He was no longer what most people would call handsome, as the years had taken their toll, and he was starting to put on weight around his middle. And she knew what was required of him as Wendell's Chief of Staff, the often brutal things he had to do, how he had to wheel and deal for his friend and boss and the rough, often crude, language he employed in his work. Yet she saw something continually endearing, kind and generous of which the outside world was not vouchsafed.

Apart from Rosalie and myself, I could not think of a happier, more congenial, more contented couple, and the restorative ambience they created for each other rubbed off on visitors to their house. In their house one felt warm, comfortable and, somehow, safe and protected.

Tom and I arrived as Heidi was pulling into the driveway. We hugged in front of the house, not made any easier by Heidi's being loaded with groceries, then tumbled indoors.

As we entered, Tom's phone rang.

"Sorry, sweetheart; sorry, Marc, I have to put out some unexpected fires. I shouldn't be too long."

He disappeared into his study as I helped Heidi carry bags into the kitchen. She laid them on the table and took off her coat. She looked amazing, her sunny smile melting away the cares of the day, and I thought that, next to Rosalie, she was probably the loveliest woman I knew.

"So, Marc. You're a politician now?"

"Sort of. Only temporary."

"You're not liking it? I must admit I thought it pretty unlikely when Tom first told me you were getting into the game."

"No, I don't like it. I'll be getting out at the end of this term, maybe sooner."

"Don't let Tom hear you say that."

"Why not? It's true."

"Your worth will diminish."

"But Tom and I are friends."

"Friends you may be, but he can't help seeing people as commodities to be useful to Wendell."

"That sounds harsh."

"You see, I know him. I know what politics has done to him."

"Yet you still love him?"

"Oh, yes. More than ever. And I need him more than ever. When all this business with Wendell ends, and it will end someday, he's going to need me more than at any time in the past."

She started unwrapping the food. "It's going to be a cold supper. Is that alright with you, Marc?"

"Yes, I love cold food."

"I swung by Pete's and grabbed some samosas, a pork pie, celery, radishes, lettuce, tomatoes and some rather dubious looking potato salad in a plastic container."

"Sound great to me. Give me something to do."

"Alright. There's a colander in the cupboard. You wash the vegetables."

"Okay, Heidi."

"Did you know that Tom was a politician himself when I first met him?"

"No. Really?"

"Yes, he was elected the term before Wendell. They became great pals, and when Wendell won the party leadership he asked Tom to be his Chief of Staff. So he stepped away and let Joan Howard have his seat."

"How on earth did she get involved? She was a big Hollywood movie star, wasn't she?"

"Yes. She was from Nova Scotia originally, but went to the States when she was quite young. Then a few years ago she starred in a movie which was being shot on the South Shore. While she was on set one day she met Harold Nickerson and they fell in love, so she gave up her acting career and moved here. Shortly after that she was elected in her area, but it was a shaky seat, so when Tom stepped down, she stepped up."

"Sounds to me like there's a lot more to the story than that."

"There is." Heidi laughed gaily. "If you're interested, we'll tell you all about it after dinner. Marc, would you open this wine, please? I got some red and some white. It probably won't be up to your standard."

"Nonsense." I looked at the bottles. The white was Chablis and the red Beaujolais Villages. "Nothing wrong with these, Heidi."

"Good. Marc..."

"Yes?"

"How do you find the old fellow?"

"Tom?"

"I only have one old fellow. Yes."

"He looks worn out, Heidi, to be honest. I'm guessing Wendell works him too hard."

"Yes, he does. Between ourselves, I'm almost hoping that Wendell loses the next election. I have a funny feeling that it might save Tom's life."

"Good God! Is he sick?"

"No, no, nothing like that. At least, not as far as I know. It's just this feeling I have in my gut that if Tom carries on doing this for longer than four years, he'll die."

"Who's going to die?" Tom asked as he appeared in the doorway.

"You will if you dare take any more calls tonight."

"Okay." Tom held up his phone. "Switched off."

"Good. Salad alright? No cooking tonight."

"Fine. Marc, come into the living room. Would you like a drop of scotch?"

"Sure. What is it?"

"Johnnie Walker Blue Label. I've been saving it for a special occasion. I guess the return of the prodigal qualifies."

"That'd be lovely. Speaking of Johnnie Walker, is Chedva still with us?" I remembered that Tom and Heidi's neighbour used to be a very old Jewish lady called Chedva Bensaid, who was devoted to single malt whisky.

"Oh, yes, Chedva's still hanging on."

"She must be in her upper nineties now."

"Ninety-eight. You may see her later. She doesn't always come down for dinner."

"Come down?"

"Yes, she lives with us now. You recall she lived next door?"

I nodded.

"Well it became too much for her so she gave the house to her daughter—Marc, you won't believe this—and as soon as she handed over the deeds, Sarah said to her, 'So, where are you going to live now, Momma?' So Chedva said, 'Well here of course.' And Sarah said, 'This is my house now. You'll have to find somewhere else."

"Jesus! That's incredible!" I could not recall anything so nasty and inhumane. "Is the bitch next door now, or did she sell the house?"

"Bitch is right. Within a month she sold it and I heard she moved to Ontario."

"Poor Chedva. I hope I see her later."

"She's still pretty lively on occasion, but mostly she's quite frail, and her sight has almost gone."

"Is she still able to take a dram of malt?"

"Is she ever! I'm hoping that when I open this bottle, she'll smell it upstairs and come prancing down."

Tom opened the whisky, but, sadly, Chedva did not appear. He poured out two generous measures and handed one to me. We then sprawled in two of the armchairs which were arranged in a semicircle around the television.

"So, you're the new boy on the block. Let me have it," he said, once he was seated.

"Let you have what?"

"Fresh eyes and all that. Your assessment of the government and where it may be heading."

"Ah. You know my knowledge of politics is very limited?"

"Granted. Even so..."

"And I've only been on the job—as it were—for a few days..."

"Spit it out, Marc."

"I agree that the time to do unpopular things is right after an election you have won."

"Yes. But?"

"Announcing so many controversial things at one time makes it difficult to digest and properly understand any of them."

"Fair point."

"I get the impression that each of these new initiatives has made the government enemies—"

"No doubt about that."

"The question is how many, and are they lost forever, or can you recover them by the time the next election rolls around?"

"Agreed."

"Also—and I haven't looked it up so I may have the numbers wrong—hasn't your party—?"

"*Our* party."

"Hasn't *our* party been in power for something like sixteen years?"

"Something like that."

"Any party in that long must expect to have outworn its welcome."

"Time for a change."

"Exactly."

"Marc, I appreciate your comments. They're more or less in line with my own thoughts. At the election we got 45% of the vote with the others receiving 34% and 21% respectively."

"I read that. Where do you think we are today?"

"This is in strictest confidence?"

"Of course."

"We put a private poll into the field two days ago."

"What did it say?"

"The government was down to 42%. And the poll was taken before Wendell went on this grand spree."

"So today, we're probably down to about 40% or lower?"

"That's my guess."

At that point, Heidi called us to the table and we trooped into the dining room. Despite its being cold and "thrown together" (as Tom put it), supper was delicious, all the more so for being enjoyed with such wonderful people.

We finished off the wine at the table then returned to the living room. There was still no sign of Chedva.

"It's getting late," Heidi explained, "and if she's coming, she's usually down long before this."

"Well, please give her my best wishes. Say, *Libe, aun gut vil.*"

"We certainly shall. She'll be happy to know you were here."

"Tom, Heidi was telling me earlier about your own days in politics."

"Back in the mists of time, I was an MLA and government Chief Whip."

"How did you come to make the switch from MLA to back room boy?"

"When Heidi's dad drowned, the movers and shakers in the party got together and chose Wendell as their nominee. He then went on to win against Angus MacKinnon."

"Darling, it wasn't quite as simple as that," Heidi said.

"No. They took a vote and asked the top few if they would—"

"Tom came first, but he declined."

"Why?"

"He was too heartbroken because I'd turned him down."

"That's about the size of it." Tom said glumly.

"Heidi, how could you have rejected him?" I teased.

"He was being boring," she said. "But eventually he wore me down and drew me into his tangled web."

"I'm glad I did. It was the best moment of my life when you said 'yes.'"

They joined in a long kiss.

"So, how did Wendell finally pull it off?" I asked, becoming somewhat embarrassed.

"We ran Joan as a stalking horse to get enough votes to draw the contest out. There were two other candidates, including Mark Gardiner, and Wendell needed to go to four ballots to gain enough steam."

"I was working for Joan," said Heidi. "And would again. I think she's wonderful."

"She is pretty amazing, I'll grant you that," Tom said. "Anyway, after the last ballot but one, Joan threw all her delegates to Wendell, and that put him over the top on the final ballot."

"I like Angus," I said. "Do you think he might ever try for the top job again?"

"He's loyal to Wendell now. And he'd be too old when that time comes."

"How about Chester?"

"Already too old."

"What about Joan? Would she ever go for it?"

"I'd like to see that!" Heidi said.

"Joan is Wendell's right arm. She'd never go against him. Maybe sometime in the future, if anything ever happened to Wendell—God forbid!"

"It's all too murky and involved for me," I said. "That's why I'm getting out."

Heidi shot me a quick frown, indicating that I should have taken her earlier advice.

Tom shifted position in his chair and leaned over towards me. "Listen Marc, I hear you've been saying that to all and sundry—"

"I wouldn't say that—"

"You've said it to everyone you've met since coming to Halifax. What's the big idea?"

"It's the truth."

"Is it? I hope not. I hope for all our sakes it's been a smokescreen."

"A smokescreen? No, not at all..."

"Well just shut up about it from now on. Nobody wants to hear how you're purer than everyone else."

"Tom!" Heidi interrupted. "Poor Marc doesn't deserve that."

"No," I said, having had time to think about it. "Tom's right. I guess being a prig is pissing people off. But I can assure you it hasn't been a smokescreen."

"We'll see about that," said Tom.

14

Over the next few weeks I was able to meet, if not get to know very well, most other Members of the House. Some Ministers were unavailable, or uninterested in a way Rosalie would describe as "snooty". I had tangled with Mark Gardiner two years ago and that episode had left a nasty taste in both our mouths, so neither of us was anxious for a rematch.

Kesegoo'e Sillyboy, Gloria Jones, Angel Stairs, and Lisa Hendricks all either looked past me or looked as if they had found something unpleasant on their shoes. I don't think I got more than a grunt from any of them as they swept off to their luxurious ministerial offices.

Ministers who not only stopped to talk to me, but were also kind, included Stephanie Gilmour, a rich and cultured woman in her midthirties; Angus MacKinnon; Jill Rutledge; Chester MacCormack, the Finance Minister, an imposing figure in his 60s; Hector MacNeil, a canny, wiry, little man from Cape Breton; Zandili Joseph, a large, cheerful, brightly-dressed black woman who was Minister of Lands and Forests; and Joan Howard, the deputy premier. She still looked like a movie star and had the aura of success which accompanied that. She was amazingly beautiful and, on first meeting her, most men were reduced to stuttering and burbling.

Of the backbenchers on our side of the aisle, there were three with whom I did not seek further acquaintance. They were John Trevor, Fred Askey, and Carol Walters, whose animus towards me was still a mystery. Almost as unfriendly as Walters had been were Sean Leaman, Cullum MacPhee, and Jeremy Reid, all of whom might be described as callow, but intensely ambitious youths; and Delia Parish, an angry black woman, whose face seemed perpetually contorted in protest.

Those I couldn't meet, for one reason or another, were Jennie Chan, a tiny, emaciated-looking Chinese woman representing Halifax's south end; Freeman Murphy, the caucus chairman; and Alaric D'Entremont, who hailed from Richmond County.

On the other side of the ledger, the friendly colleagues who shared the back benches with me were Zila, my seatmate; George Savory; Art Sullivan; Emma Mitchell; and Dan Nathanson, a former clothing store owner from Sydney.

Naturally, I did not have occasion to approach many of the opposition members, but Ellie MacLeod, Martha MacNaughton, Eugene Comeau, David Cohen and Phyllis Gordon all seemed to be thoroughly decent, friendly people. Whether or not it was because they were supposed to be "enemies", most of the rest of the opposition appeared to me to be uncongenial, and some seemed downright sinister. In this unsavoury group were Denis MacNamara, Sammy Wong, Cliff Wolf, Bill Jenkins and Liam Hudson.

During those weeks I also had a chance to explore this extraordinary building in which we met, and to learn something of its background. Among the most fascinating features was the story of how all the moldings on the cornices above the chamber came to be defaced. On these cornices and above the doors were plaster eagles. In 1838 a boundary dispute between Britain and the United States resulted in the U.S. taking part of northern New Brunswick. An MLA, Lawrence O'Connor Doyle, who represented Arichat in Richmond County, was so angered by this development he took a large stick and knocked the heads off most of the eagles. Apparently, his stick was not long enough to reach them all, so some remain to this day.

The Nova Scotia Assembly first met in 1758, but not in the present building. The Assembly moved around the city from pillar to post, meeting in houses, hotels and taverns, until in 1811 they decided to build a permanent home for the legislators. Some eight years and some $5 million (in today's money) later, the current structure was ready to be occupied by the Legislature, the upper house, the Legislative Council, and the law courts.

Sixty years later it was something of a squeeze accommodating 32 Members, and today 55 of us were packed uncomfortably into this space like sardines in a can.

However, what it lacks in floor space the chamber gains in charm, with a very high ceiling and surrounding galleries which can accommodate around 100 spectators, although those visitors are subject to some draconian and, to me, unjustifiable rules. While I readily understood why observers should not be allowed to indicate approval or disapproval of anything that takes place during proceedings, including applause, cheering, whistling and any other audible expressions, I could not comprehend why they cannot take notes, record or photograph the proceedings.

Most mystifying to me was the rule that spectators could not wear hats "unless of religious or cultural significance", indicating to me a stupid degree of political correctness. If hats were thought to be hiding places for weapons or bombs in the general public, one would have thought that it would also be the case for Muslim women, nuns, and those wearing native headdresses.

Our party caucus was to meet again at the beginning of March. The legislative session was in its dying days, most of the government's legislation having been passed or requiring only the formality of Third Reading, which normally went through on the nod with a shout of "Aye." All Wendell's controversial proposals were in this category, except for his initiatives on electoral redistribution, which he announced would be delayed "for further consultation." I suspected he wanted to hold this over the heads of MLAs like Jones, D'Entremont, and Dorion like a sword of Damocles. If he proceeded with his ideas, their seats would disappear, and the threat might be enough to keep them in line.

The first sign of trouble came with the vote on renaming government departments, programs and titles to get rid of so-called "woke" appellations. After Dudley Morton, the Clerk, read the title of the bill and the Speaker asked, "Shall the Bill pass?" a chorus of "Nays" caused Ernest Maddingly to call for a standing vote.

First the "Ayes" were called for and I stood up quickly so I could see what others were doing. The first thing I noticed was that, on the opposition side, Ellie, Ed Gallant, and David Cohen were voting for the bill. The second thing I observed was that Gloria Jones, Leila Hendricks, and Delia Parish had slipped out of the chamber. The Opposition's defections cancelled our own so the Bill passed.

This occurrence had not gone unnoticed by Wendell, since he was not facing the Speaker, but standing with his back to the aisle. His face wore an expression of intense anger.

The second, much more serious, occurrence came to my notice on the next day, when I was going into Province House. As I was going up the steps a reporter, Bob Michaels, came up to me.

"Hey, Marc. What do you think of the scandal?"

"What scandal?"

"You haven't heard? It is all over town. Frances Mullens has accused the Premier of improper sexual advances."

"What? Who the hell is Frances Mullens?"

"You must know her. She works in the library."

"What library? What are you talking about?"

"The Legislative library. She's the cute, dark-haired one."

I had to think for a second to figure out who Bob meant, then I had a flash of a young woman's laughing face, in the corner with two men.

"What's he supposed to have done?" I asked, my mind reeling.

"I don't have all the details, but the story going around is that he got her on her own, took his old boy out, and said, 'Here it is. I know you want it.'"

"That's crazy! I never heard anything so preposterous in my life."

"So, you're saying she's lying?"

"Of course I am. Now let me pass."

I was about to push past him, but on impulse I turned around, crossed the street and went into One Government Place. When I got to the seventh floor I could see that Susan was going frantic, answering one phone call after another.

"We have nothing to say at this time," she was saying. "A full statement will be issued later."

When I made faces and pointed towards Tom's office, she nodded, so I went ahead.

I did not knock and went straight in to find Tom with Agnes Mackillop, who had succeeded Charlie Simmons as Chief of Halifax-area police.

"Come in, Marc. You know Agnes?"

"Yes, I do. Hello, Agnes."

"Hello, Marc."

"You've heard the news?" Tom asked. "That's why you're here, I guess."

"Yes, from a reporter at Province House."

"You understand we have to treat this seriously, just like any other similar allegation," Agnes said.

"Yes of course," said Tom.

"But will you?" I asked.

"What do you mean?"

"Will you treat this the same? Will you pursue all leads surrounding the case to test its veracity?"

"Er...yes. Of course," said Agnes. "What kind of leads did you have in mind?"

"You might ask Ms. Mullens what are her connections with Opposition MLAs Denis McNamara, Waverly Fall River; and Sam Wong, Halifax Atlantic."

"What have they got to do with this?" Tom asked.

"A few days ago I saw the three of them very closely closeted in a corner of the Legislative Library, clearly gleeful about something."

"Really?" Tom jumped up.

"Did they see you?"

"No. When I saw they were in private—almost intimate—conference I backed out quickly."

"That doesn't constitute proof of any kind," Agnes said.

"But it is suggestive," I insisted, "My guess is that if she were questioned she would not be able to come up with an intelligent reason for the three of them being in a tight scrimmage."

"Maybe," said Agnes. "We will follow it up."

"Tom, do we know anything about Ms. Mullens?"

"I don't. Give me a minute and I'll find out."

Agnes and I walked to the window and looked out at the passing traffic while Tom worked at his computer. A few minutes later, he looked up.

"She was engaged as Library Assistant just after the election. She was hired by the Legislative Librarian. We had nothing to do with the appointment—"

"You mean politics was not involved?" Agnes asked.

"Not by us, anyway. But she gave as one of her references—"

"Let me guess—Samuel Wong?"

"No, Denis McNamara MLA. He's her cousin."

"Aha!"

"That certainly makes a difference," Agnes said. "Tom, will you ask Susan to call the Speaker and see if I can use his office for an interview? If he agrees, have her ask Ms. Mullens to meet me there."

"I'm on it," Tom said.

"But before we do that, there is an important step I must take."

"What's that, Agnes?"

"I must see the accused and ask him if there is any truth to the allegation."

"Of course! What was I thinking?"

"So, let's go ask him."

"Follow me. Marc, you'd better come in, too."

Tom pushed open the padded double doors and we entered the Premier's office.

Wendell was pacing up and down, obviously disturbed by the accusation. "What's this? A delegation?" he almost snarled.

Agnes related to him the circumstances that I had described. Wendell's eyes filled with rage.

"Those dirty bastards!"

"Now, Premier, I'm sorry I have to do this, but I have to ask you how you respond to the charge made against you?"

"How the hell do you think I respond?!"

"Just answer my question and we can be out of here."

"I utterly, categorically deny the allegation!"

"Thank you. One thing I have to say, and then one more question."

"Go ahead."

"If the young woman persists with the accusation, it will have to be subject to a formal investigation, probably followed by a trial at some date in the future. In that case, you should engage legal counsel immediately."

"Right. What's the question?"

"This: If the young woman tells me that she was pressured into making the accusation, or something of that nature, do you want criminal proceedings launched against her or the men involved."

"You bet!"

"Wendell," Tom raised his voice. "Don't you see that would be madness? It would be all out warfare. The House would become a blood bath and the media would never let it go!"

"What do you suggest, genius?"

"Get her to make a retraction—a written one—withdrawing the complaint and saying it was all a misunderstanding. Something along the lines of a bet or a joke which got out of hand."

"And she—and they—would just walk away scot-free?"

"Yes"

"I agree with Tom," I said. "It would be a bitter pill, but you've no choice but to swallow it."

"If we can get it," Tom said.

"Agnes, what do you think?" Wendell asked.

"They're right. It's by no means perfect, but it's the best solution available."

"Alright. Go ahead. Keep me informed."

"Of course."

We went out into the hallway, where Susan told us she had made the arrangements to use the Speaker's office and that she had conveyed the other message to the Legislative Librarian.

"Marc, you'd better come with me. It will be better if I can confront her with an actual witness rather than just say that 'somebody' saw them together."

We walked across the street together, and I let Agnes in with my pass at the western door. We walked down the steps to the main hallway, turned left and went to the far corner.

The Speaker's secretary said that Maddingly had stepped out for lunch, but had said it was fine for us to occupy his office.

We sat down, Agnes at the desk and me on an ornate chair in the corner. Agnes picked up an ancient fountain pen and tapped it incessantly against the polished wood.

At length there was a knock on the door and Frances Mullens entered.

It seemed apparent to me from the outset that she presented a far from defiant demeanour, and was nervous and confused. Tentatively, she sat down on the very edge of the chair offered to her. She was, I judged, about twenty-three, of average height, very attractive but displaying a little of what used to be called "puppy fat". She looked as if she had been crying.

"Frances," Agnes began, "do you mind if I call you Frances?"

"Most people call me Fran."

"Okay, Fran it is. Do you know who I am?"

"No."

"I'm Chief of Police for Halifax Regional Municipality."

"Oh."

"You know why I'm here?"

"I guess so. Why is he here?" She asked, nodding towards me.

"This gentleman is here because he saw you and your cousin and Mr. Wong looking as if you might have been plotting something. Isn't that right, Mr. LeBlanc?"

"Yes, it is, Chief."

"Do you have anything to say about that, Fran?"

"He saw that? Oh, fuck!"

"Well?"

"Will I lose my job?"

"I don't think it needs to come to that, Fran. Tell me what happened."

Stumbling through her tears, Frances told us that it started as 'a bit of a laugh' over drinks one night, when she suggested to her cousin that she could seduce half the guys in the House if she wanted to. This had caused her cousin to ask if she thought she could seduce the Premier. She'd said, 'Why not?'

Then he'd said something to the effect that it might not be possible to get close enough to the Premier, but she could pretend she had. By that time, she said, she was quite drunk.

During the following day they joked about it in the library, and the next thing she heard was that Denis had put it about that she'd actually made the accusation.

"So, Fran, there was never anything in it?"

"Fuck, no!"

"Will you of your own free will withdraw the accusation which your cousin made on your behalf, saying that it was not made at your request or with your knowledge?"

"God, no! You can't name him!"

"Calm down, Fran," said Agnes. "How about we say 'made on your behalf by *others*'?"

"Yes, that'd be okay."

"All right. So your statement would read, 'I, Frances Mullens, of my own free will, withdraw all accusations against the Premier made on my behalf by others, without my consent or knowledge'."

"Yeah, if you want. I will keep my job, though?"

"If the Legislative Librarian wants you, yes. It is she whom you need to convince."

"Okay."

Agnes asked the Speaker's secretary to step in, and dictated the withdrawal to her. In minutes she returned with an original and several copies. Very slowly, she read the text to Frances, who nodded agreement.

"All right, my dear," said Agnes, after Frances had signed the documents, "now you run along and make your peace with your boss. And if you take my advice, you will not talk to the media about this, and will definitely not engage in this sort of silly and dangerous behaviour again."

"No way, fuck, no," said Frances gratefully, and slipped out of the room.

"I wish that could be the end of it," Agnes said to me once Fran was out of earshot.

"How do you mean?"

"Despite our having the withdrawal in writing and signed, a large number of people will believe the accusation was true."

"Sure, the Opposition will spread it, because they will want it to be true. But sensible people will understand what happened, and our caucus will understand that it was a political stunt."

"Don't be too sure, Marc. There'll be more than a few who will believe it, regardless of the evidence."

"Like who?"

"There are thirteen women in your caucus."

"Yes."

"I bet you at least eight of those will turn against him because of this. See if I'm not right."

15

Chief Agnes Mackillop was not exactly right in her prediction, but she was not far off. I made it a point to talk with as many of the female MLAs as I could following the release of Frances Mullen's denial, and was astounded by what I discovered.

Only one woman, and that one an Opposition Member, Ellie MacLeod, told me she thought it was "a lot of old crap" and that there had never been any doubt in her mind that Wendell was innocent. Martha McNaughton told me "she wasn't sure" and that "we might never know the truth." Others I spoke to on the opposition benches were ferociously and sanctimoniously declaring that they "knew" Wendell was utterly guilty. Dana Edwards was almost hysterical and waxed at length about the iniquity of all men everywhere throughout the course of history.

On my own side of the House, things could hardly have been much worse. While some, like Zila and Jennie Chan, whom I finally met, said that, of course, they would stand behind the Premier and give him their solid support, they nonetheless intimated that they thought he was probably guilty. Emma Mitchell and Delia Parish came right out with and said they thought Frances must have been "forced" to retract the accusations.

When I tried to discuss it with Zandili Joseph, she said she could not comment because she was in the cabinet, which was such a poor excuse it suggested that she, too, subscribed to Wendell's guilt.

Naturally, I did not attempt to speak with my nemesis, Carol Walters, but I overheard her in the lounge, saying to Gloria Jones that "boys would be boys," and that, perforce, they had to "plaster over the cracks". As the chief Law Officer, Angela Stairs could not properly comment, so I did not approach her.

The only women on our side I thought would completely believe in

Wendell's innocence were Joan Howard and Stephanie Gilmour, but I did not get a chance to speak to them.

Most of the male Members on my side to whom I spoke were indignant and expressed complete confidence in the premier's unimpeachable character. Some, like George Savory and Dan Nathanson, were seething with rage. George swore he would raise the matter in Question Period, but I told him I thought that might only exacerbate the situation. It is important to note that, to none of the people, male or female, did I mention that I knew McNamara was behind the accusations. Had I done so, some of them would certainly have "gone ballistic", to use a phrase my wife often employs.

At some stage, the word must have been quietly circulated to members of the Official Opposition that McNamara and Wong had instigated the farrago, and that if they were not careful the whole affair could boomerang and damage them. Their leader, John Wilkins, must have issued orders to his caucus to "keep a lid on it."

So it was that when the House convened and Question Period commenced, the first inquiry from Wilkins was a fairly low-key one about problems in one of the hospitals. The next question, which also went to Wilkins party, and put by David Cohen, was similarly uncontroversial, but everyone was bracing themselves for the third question, which would be from Dana Edwards.

Looking across at her I could see she was flushed, her eyes were glaring, and her nostrils flared. There seemed little doubt that she saw herself as being on a Holy Mission.

"Mr. Speaker," she bristled, her earth-coloured robes swaying around her, "my question is for the Premier. Under other circumstances, perhaps, I would refer to him as the 'honourable premier', but that cannot be the case now. I want to ask him if he has the slightest excuse for his reprehensible behaviour which has been related in an accusation by an innocent young woman—"

Members on our side were shouting, "Shuddup! Siddown!" Wendell was impassive, staring straight ahead.

The Official Opposition members were putting up a pretense of being uninterested in the bedlam around them, and were busily consulting papers on their desks. Ms. Edwards' supporters were howling like wolves out for blood. The Speaker stood up and called for order.

When he had restored it, Edwards continued, "Will he now apologize for his heinous conduct?"

Everyone, including me, was expecting Wendell to rise in his wrath and demolish her with verbal fireworks and dexterity, but instead it was Angela Stairs who caught the Speaker's eye.

"The Chair recognizes the Honourable the Minister of Justice."

"Thank you, Mr. Speaker."

Looking as disdainful as the Ice Queen, she addressed the Chair in her frostiest tones. "The young person to whom the Member across the way—under other circumstances, perhaps I would refer to her as the 'honourable lady' but cannot now do so—has referred, has issued a clear and unambiguous statement indicating that these trumped-up allegations were not made by her, but by others who did so without her consent or knowledge. Mr. Speaker, I will now table the document in question for all to see. That should be the end of the matter."

She sat down, composed, unruffled and dignified. But Edwards was not finished and jumped up again.

"I want to ask the premier by what means was this denial *extracted* from the young woman? Under what duress? What threats or promises were made to induce this retraction?"

"Mr. Speaker." Again it was Angela Stairs who rose. "Of course, the Member opposite may imply or charge what she likes in this House, subject of course to your own rulings, sir, but I warn her that if she speaks outside those doors as she has done in here, she will become the subject of a vigorous criminal slander action."

Edwards rose again and attempted to speak, but the entire thirty-two Members on our side howled her down so loudly, she was unable to make herself heard. Epithets such as "Guttersnipe!" and "Slanderer!" were continuously hurled, so, thrusting her arms in the air, she appealed to The Speaker.

"Order please," he said. "I would not advise the lady to attempt to continue in this vein. The question was asked and it was answered. She may not have liked the answer, but it was given nonetheless. Let us move on!"

Throughout the remainder of Question Period several members of Edwards' party tried to ask the same question, but phrased differently, but the Speaker ruled them out of order.

George Savory, against my advice to him earlier, managed to catch The Speaker's eye and directed a question to the Premier. "Will my honourable friend tell the House if this whole shemozzle was a put-up job, engineered by his political enemies who turned to work and, by jingo, take advantage of this poor young creature?"

"I thank the Honourable Member for his question, Mr, Speaker," Wendell said quietly and slowly as he fixed his gaze on McNamara. "I can only tell him that something of the kind has been communicated to me. I was asked if criminal proceedings should be pursued against the perpetrator, but in the interests of harmony and good relations in this House, I declined to take the matter further."

Everyone on our side, including Parish and Mitchell, were on their feet, cheering and thumping their desks. Zandili tried to initiate "For he's a jolly good fellow", but was drowned out by the whooping and cheering.

I looked across to the other side and noticed that Edwards and her six comrades were contorted with rage, but Wilkins' people were silent and staring at the ceiling as if they had no comprehension of what was occurring. Ellie, who was almost directly opposite me, flashed me a wink and a tiny smile.

I needed to go to the washroom and left the chamber to find Tom waiting outside the lobby doors.

"Marc, I need to talk to you."

"Okay, but wait until I have a leak. Will you be here?"

"No, I'll be in the Red Room."

When I went to the Red Room a few minutes later, Tom was leaning on the ledge in the furthest window.

"Tell me what happened?" he asked, rather brusquely.

"Weren't you in the gallery?"

"Yes, but I want you to tell me what you saw and what you know."

"Alright."

I then told him what I had observed during the Question Period and what I had discovered from talking to MLAs of different parties prior to that.

"Hmm. So, you're saying that you think Gilmour, McCormack, Howard, MacKinnon, Stairs, Clark, MacDonald, Murphy, Askey, MacNeil, Nathanson, Trevor, Leaman, Sullivan, MacPhee, Savory, and Reid are solid. You are not sure about Dorion, Sillyboy, D'Entremont and Rutledge. You are suspicious, or wary, of Franks, Walters, Jones, Hendricks, and Gardiner. You think that Joseph, Mitchell, Chan and

Walters could be trouble, and that Parish is definitely trouble?"

"Yes, that's about it. Some of them are just impressions I got, without actually hearing them say anything."

"Fair enough. Well, good work, Marc. Very useful."

"You're welcome."

"Are you more, shall we say, committed now?"

"How do you mean?"

"Are you one of us?"

"One of who?"

"One of the Proctor diehards."

"I guess you could say that. After all, he's the only reason I'm here."

"Great. We weren't sure about you, but now I can report to Wendell that you're all-in with us?"

"I guess. Sure."

"To the end?"

"Okay, to the end." I thought, why not? I had nothing to lose.

"Good. Wendell's likely to want to bring you into the inner circle and have you be more active."

"Really? What would that mean?"

"Come to his office this evening. Caucus meets when the House rises, so come along after that adjourns."

"That could be quite late."

"Yeah. Whatever time it is, we'll be there. And keep your eyes and ears wide open at the caucus. Try to read the expressions on their faces even if they don't say anything."

"I'll do my best."

"Right. See you tonight."

It was after nine o'clock when we filed into the caucus room and Freeman Murphy gavelled the meeting to order.

16

I was one of the last to get to the caucus meeting. Just in front of me in the lineup were George Savory and Art Sullivan.

"How's she goin', b'y?" Art asked me.

"Good, Art. What's new?"

"George and I have got something up our sleeves."

"Yes, sir, Mr. Man, we surely have," said George. "Art and me are going to flush 'em out."

"Flush who out? What are you talking about?"

"Those who are saying stuff about our premier and trying to sit on the fence. I'm going to turn to work and move a confidence motion."

"Confidence in what?"

"The premier, of course."

"Oh no, George, I'm not sure that's a good idea." If I sounded worried, it was because I could foresee many problems with his plan. "Far better to let lie for now. In a few weeks everyone will have forgotten all about it."

"No, sir. Doing nothing is why everything has gone to the dogs. In my day we saw the whites of their eyes and met them head on."

"It's got to be done," said Art, "either to make them come out in the open and say where they stand, or silence the bastards. We have to shake up the ones who are on the fence. Some of them are as stunned as Tom Cunt's bulldog."

"You make your point very colourfully, Art," I said with a laugh. "But I don't think Wendell will like it."

"Well, I'm going to do it, Mr. Man."

George was emphatic, so I let it go. To be honest I, too, wanted to see where the lines would be drawn.

By the time we got to the table, Murphy had started the meeting. The normally-assigned seating wass abandoned so we had to find seats wherever we could and, to my horror, I found myself between Carol Walters and Delia Parish.

We dealt with a few housekeeping matters which were leftover from the previous meeting, before Murphy buttoned his jacket and delivered his report.

"Tomorrow, maybe as late as the early hours," Murphy was saying, "the House will be adjourned and we won't be back here until the fall. The House Leader, our good friend Angus MacKinnon, tells me we will be wrapping up third reading on all the bills pertaining to the Premier's announced reforms; that's bills number 16, 167, 83, 102 and 111. Bill 102, dealing with electoral reform, will remain on the Order Paper, and might be revived in the fall session. I want to thank you all for your hard work and hope you don't waste the summer months with vacations and stuff like that..." A murmur of laughter ran around the room. "There's not going to be an election for at least another..." He turned to Wendell, looking for direction.

"At least a year," said Wendell, to gasps.

"Maybe three..." The gasps turned into sighs of relief.

"Possibly four." Now everyone was laughing.

"Well, there you have the definitive word," said Murphy, hoping, in vain, to get an even bigger laugh. "But don't be wasting your time having fun when you could be visiting picnics, attending ball games, and going to church suppers."

He looked at his watch, and turned a pleading face to the assembled company. "It's very late, so if there is no further business—"

"Mr. Chairman. There is further business," said George, heaving himself to his feet, "By jingo, there is."

"The Member for Shelburne," said Murphy wearily. "Go ahead, George, if you must."

It might have been my imagination, but I swear I could both feel and smell the hostility suddenly emanating from Walters and Parish as they shifted in their seats.

"You bet I must!" George said loudly. "Mr. Chairman I move, seconded by the Member for Cape Breton Centre-Whitney Pier, Mr. Sullivan, that this caucus expresses its fullest confidence in the Honourable the Premier, Wendell Proctor, and offers its fullest thanks to him for his exempl..." George seemed to have difficulty pronouncing 'exemplary", so ploughed on. "...leadership, for his excellent reforms, brilliant ideas—”

“Brown nosing bastard,” Walters muttered.

“Fucking old fool,” Parish mumbled.

“And we hope he continues to lead us for many years to come!”

George sat down amidst a spontaneous eruption of cheers and applause from well over half the caucus members.

I leaned across the table to see who was not applauding. I quickly picked out Mark Gardiner, Emma Mitchell, Gloria Jones, Jennie Chan, Leila Hendricks and, of course, my neighbours Delia Parish and Carol Walters. Those who were obviously just going through the motions of applauding included Zila Franks, Pierre Dorion and Zandili Joseph. Excluding myself and Wendell, all of the remaining twenty were exuberantly clapping and cheering.

“Order please!” Murphy shouted. “Are you ready to vote?”

Something unpleasantly warm and woolly brushed against my side as Delia Parish rose in her wrath.

“No, we are not ready to vote! Some of us want to speak to this motion. Some of us want to speak *against* this motion—” Muffled cries erupted around the table. “Wendell has let us down. Especially those of us in the black community. He has not consulted with us. He has betrayed us. We are expected to sit and vote for whatever he says… like slaves! Well, I want him to know that I ain’t nobody’s slave!”

She sat down to a little applause, but it was more than I expected. I was so fixed on Parish, who was fulminating so close to me, that I couldn’t see where it came from.

“Are you ready to vote now?” Murphy asked.

“No, Mr. Chairman.” Carol Walters rose beside me, an even warmer, more objectionable presence rubbing against my shoulder. “I just want to say that I agree with what Delia has said, and I want to add that a number of us are not satisfied with the answer we’ve been given about the assault—”

At the word ‘assault’, a roar went around the table. Chester McCormack shouted, “Whoa!” Stephanie Gilmour cried, “Watch it, Carol!”

I just heard Joan Howard, who was a few places away from me, say, “Disgusting.”

Hector McNeil’s voice rose to utter the epithet “Bitch!”

“—assault on a young employee,” Walters continued undeterred, “For these and many other reasons, I shall vote against the motion.”

"Order please!" Murphy shouted. "It's getting late. How much longer is this going on? Yes, Emma Mitchell, you want to speak?"

"Yes, I do," said Mitchell, her voice weak and tremulous. "I have searched my conscience and I have to vote against this motion because women must be believed."

"But this one hasn't said anything to be believed!" Bill Clark bellowed at her. "She denied having anything to do with it!"

"But...but... there's the question of whether she was...coerced to—" at this point Mitchell broke down in tears. "I must...I have to..." She flopped down in her chair, sobbing.

"Mr. Chairman." It was Jennie Chan now, looking like a tiny blade of grass in the midst of a wild garden. Although her voice was thin, it somehow cut through the hubbub. "Yes, yes, yes. Women must be believed!"

"Are you stupid?" Bill Clark yelled.

"We know there was something not right about this," said Chan, defiantly standing her ground. "And I won't be bullied into backing down."

"Go and ask the girl yourself. She'll tell you!" said Angela Stairs, uncharacteristically becoming heated, and waving the denial statement.

As soon as she said this, I knew I had to say something, so I waved my arm to get Murphy's attention.

I saw that he initially had no intention of recognizing me until Wendell whispered to him.

"The chair recognizes Marc LeBlanc, our newest Member, who has not spoken before either in caucus or in the House."

There were palpable waves of hatred coming from the women on either side of me as I rose. I heard some hissing from over on the far left, but saw George and Art thumping the table in my support. Against all expectations, I was not in the least nervous, and once I was on my feet, I took my time in surveying the room before speaking.

"Thank you, Mr. Chairman." I spoke deliberately slowly and as loudly as I could, short of shouting. "I just wanted to point out to my colleagues that I was present when the young woman agreed to, and signed, the document of denial—" Expressions of surprise came from all quarters, some in disbelief.

"I was asked to be a witness by the Chief of HRM Police, who was also present. I wish to assure you, Mr. Chairman, and *all* of my colleagues, that there was absolutely no form of coercion or intimidation; no hint of threat or bribery; not the slightest pressure or harassment of any kind whatever. She was asked by the Chief of Police—" Several growls of anger came at me. "If anyone here wishes to impugn the integrity of the Chief of Police, I would remind them that they are *not* in the House now and are therefore not protected against suit for slander."

Over a dozen people thumped the table and loudly cheered me on. "As I was saying, Mr. Chairman, the Chief of Police asked her calmly and quietly if she had made an allegation, and when she said she had not, asked her if she had asked or authorized anyone else to level an allegation on her behalf. When she said she had not, she was asked if she had knowledge that the allegation had been made. She said she had not. Those are the facts. I would invite those who have condemned the premier without a single shred of proof to now withdraw their remarks."

Art and George were going wild. I could see Joan Howard looking at me with an enormous smile. "I would not expect those people to verbally apologize"—I deliberately turned to my left and right to look Parish and Walters in the eye—"but I expect them to do so by voting for this motion. I shall certainly be doing so myself."

I could not abide the thought of sitting next to them any longer and, as I left the table to stand against the wall, I estimated that at least two-thirds of the room was vigorously cheering my remarks. I was beginning to think that I might enjoy politics much more than I had anticipated.

A surprise punch in the arm caused me to turn to see Tom edging up to me.

"Marvellous!" he whispered. "Well done! First class!"

"Order! Does anyone else want to speak?" Murphy asked, sweating profusely.

"Yes, I do."

Wendell rose. He seemed somehow to extend his six feet, three inches' height until he towered over the room. "Every Member here is entitled to have an opinion, to express it and to act according to that opinion. But they must understand that there are consequences to exercising those rights.

"I could not help noticing that, in the House recently, several members absented themselves during a vote. That will not be tolerated again without there being repercussions. Any member of cabinet who abstains on a Government bill will no longer be in the cabinet. Anyone who votes against a government bill without a very good reason will have to find another party."

The room was deathly quiet. The only sound was people's breathing and chairs creaking.

"With regard to the vote tonight, any cabinet member who votes against the motion may consider themselves dismissed immediately. Anyone who is not currently in the cabinet and votes against it can forget about ever getting in while I am premier. Anyone who abstains can expect to hear from me...one way or another."

As Wendell sat down there was a chorus of "Vote! Vote!"

Angus MacKinnon caught the chairman's eye.

"The chair recognizes Mr. MacKinnon," said Murphy, battling against the noise.

"I move the previous question," said Angus.

"Are you ready for the question?" Murphy asked, and, not waiting for an answer, continued, "All those in favour say 'aye'."

The 'ayes' were absolutely deafening.

"All those against say 'nay'."

The 'nays' were noisy, almost braying, but at best no more than a quarter of those present.

George and Art were on their feet shouting, "Standing vote!"

"A standing vote has been called." Murphy was enjoying his role having turned out to be more than mundane. "Those in favour will please stand."

I took a few steps forward so I could see the whole table.

An overwhelming mass of people stood up. Remaining seated were Gloria Jones, Delia Parish, Carol Walters, Emma Mitchell, Leila Hendricks and Jennie Chan. The number was greater than I anticipated, but the real test would be to see how many of those would actually stand up at the Chair's next call.

"Those opposed, please stand."

Only Parish, Walters, and Chan had the courage of their convictions and slowly rose. While I was decidedly on the other side, and while I personally disliked each of them, I could not help but admire them. Any ambitions they might have had in politics could now be forgotten.

Unless Wendell were to be overthrown in some other way at some other time, I was sure he would see to it that they were undermined in their constituencies and not re-nominated at the next election.

It suddenly occurred to me that the only hope they had of keeping their seats might be for them to cross the floor to the Opposition. If that were to take place the government would still have a reasonably comfortable majority of seven votes.

Of more concern than those who stood against the motion were those who did not stand at all, the abstainers. One of them was Emma Mitchell, who might be dismissed as a principled, but silly and misguided woman; but two of the abstainers were ministers of the Crown. This begged the question that if they neither supported nor opposed the motion, what exactly were their sentiments? Although I did not agree with what they had done, I sympathized with them over the awful, tongue-lashing and dressing down Wendell would heap on them.

Wendell stood up, waved to the room and made for the door. On his way, I noticed that he stopped by Hendricks and Jones, leaned down and whispered to them. It is difficult to interpret people's expressions under such circumstances, but to me the looks on their faces did not suggest that they were unduly nervous.

Excited thumping and cheering accompanied the Premier as he stalked out.

"Meeting is adjourned!" yelled Freeman Murphy above the cacophony.

"Let's go," Tom said.

17

When we were halfway to the elevator, Tom's phone rang. He stopped and had a short, muttered conversation, leaning into the wall.

"Marc," he said, pocketing the phone. "That was Wendell. Could you go back and ask George Savory and Art Sullivan to drop by my office in about half an hour?"

"Sure. What's up?"

"Just go tell them. You'll find out later what it's all about. And see if you can find Hector McNeil and ask him to come up, too."

Retracing my steps, I found Art and George still sitting in the Caucus room, and gave them the message.

"What's this about?" George asked.

"I don't know."

"I hope he's not going to give us shit," Art said. "I don't like being dressed down by a hireling."

"Tom's hardly a 'hireling', Art. Besides which, I suspect it's not him you'll be seeing."

"Oh-oh, Mr. Man. That sounds ominous." George rubbed the back of his head. "Still, we'll be there."

I rushed back to where I had left Tom, to find that he had gone on ahead.

As I was about to go out into the street, Gloria Jones and Leila Hendricks, rather rudely I thought, pushed past me. It became clear that, like me, they were heading to Tom's office.

I slowed down because I did not want to share an elevator with them, given the tension created by the meeting. When I got to the seventh floor, they were milling around Susan's desk.

I hung back, but Susan breezily called to me over Hendricks and Jones' heads.

"Oh, hello, Marc. You can go straight in."

The two ministers did not look at all pleased with this develop-ment, clearly believing they should have precedence over a lowly backbencher, and scowled at me as I edged past them.

I went into Tom's office, but it was empty. I hesitated, but since I was now one of "the inner circle", I felt it entitled me to go directly into Wendell's office.

"Oh, hi, Marc," He said with a huge grin. He was sprawled behind his desk with his feet up, and Tom was standing near the window. "Getting an education?"

"Yes."

"Ready for more?"

"You bet."

"Okay, watch and learn. Tom, ask those snakes to come in."

Tom left us alone. I felt a little uncomfortable.

"Glad to hear you've come in," said Wendell. "I have all kinds of work for you to do, if you're willing."

"If I can, Premier, I will."

"Fuck that 'premier' stuff now. You're one of the gang. It's 'Wendell' from now on."

"Thanks," I said, thinking it was indeed strange that this was the second time he had asked me to use his first name, having asked me not to use it in the interim. I was certainly flattered, if slightly con-fused, but I was starting to get used to the fact that politics, as George had told me, was all about 'wheels within wheels.'

"Take a seat," he said. "And, for fuck's sake, keep it!"

"What do you mean?"

"When others come in, don't be getting up and offering them your chair. You stay put!"

"Oh, alright."

At that moment we could hear muffled sounds from beyond the door.

"Here they come," he said, rubbing his hands together. His eyes were gleaming.

Tom came in, followed by Gloria Jones and Lelia Hendricks, the lat-ter nodding obsequiously.

"You wanted to see us?" Jones said. She looked round and, seeing me sitting while she was standing, uttered a disapproving snort.

"Gloria, Leila. I may have been misinformed, so correct me if I'm wrong, but I've been told that you both abstained on the confidence motion in caucus. Is that true?"

"Yes." Jones said. "Do you want to know why?"

"I don't give a shit why."

"*That's* why. Because you don't let—"

"Okay, shuddup! You're fired. Effective immediately. Leila, did you abstain?"

"Maybe."

"*Maybe*?"

"It was confusing. There was a lot going on."

"Is that the best you can do? That you were confused? That you didn't know what you were doing?"

"Wendell…Premier… you don't understand—"

"You're right I don't. You're fired, too. Now get out, the pair of you!"

The women looked at each other, not quite believing what had transpired.

"Go! And don't either of you go back to your previous departments. Any personal effects you left in your offices will be sent to you tomorrow or the next day."

"You'll be sorry for this, Wendell." Jones said with a snarl.

"Maybe I will, but not as sorry as I am for having put your sorry asses in my cabinet in the first place. All you ever did there was attention-seeking, whining and complaining."

When they had gone, Wendell got up and did a little dance around his desk. "God, I'm glad to be rid of that dead wood."

"You may have to kiss Preston goodbye," said Tom.

"Don't you believe it! I was out there the other day with Senator Carvery, and the people were telling me they're as sick of Gloria Jones as I am. Anyone else out there?"

"Yes," said Tom, "McNeil, Savory and Sullivan."

"Okay, wheel them in."

As each of the men entered, he gave me a quizzical look. Forgetting my instructions, I started to get up to give Hector my seat, but Wendell fiercely waved me back down.

"Welcome, gentlemen. It's my pleasure to inform you that Ms. Hendricks and Ms. Jones have departed the Executive Council of Nova Scotia."

"You don't waste much time," Hector said.

"No, sir."

"How can I help? I mean, why am I here? You going to fire me, too?"

"God, no, Hector. But I am going to promote you."

"That sounds good. Where am I going, Wendell?"

"Education. Are you okay with that?"

"You bet. I wonder how the elites will react to that post being filled by a man who only has his Grade Twelve!"

"Fuck the elites! Alright, Hector, get over to the department now and if there's anybody still there, tell them to gather up Leila's effects. If there isn't anyone there, do it yourself."

"Aye, aye." McNeil gave a salute and left.

"Premier," Art said quietly, "what are George and I doing here?"

"Art, you're going to be the new Minister of Labour. Think you can handle it?"

"Wow! Thanks Boss. Labour? Uh…yeah…I guess I could handle that."

"Okay. See Adrian MacIsaac first thing tomorrow, and get him to swear you in. Same for you, George."

"For me? What's going on? What's going to happen to me?"

"Don't look so nervous, George. You're going to be Minister of Agriculture and Fisheries."

"Boys, oh, boys! Finest kind! You got yourself a deal, Mr. Man!" George smiled from ear to ear. "I did that job back in my day, before things went to the dogs. I can do it again."

"Alright, now fuck off, the pair of you and don't get too drunk tonight." Wendell cheerily waved them out.

After Art and George had left, Angus McKinnon poked his head around the door.

"May we join the party?"

Behind him were Joan Howard, Stephanie Gilmour, Bill Clark and John Trevor.

"Come in, guys. Sit down, if you can find somewhere to sit. I want to bring you up to date. Hector has been moved to Education." There were murmurs of agreement. "I thought of sending you there Steph, but you're doing such a good job where you are."

"Thank you Wendell," said Gilmour, delicately arranging her elegant posterior on the corner of Wendell's desk.

"Tom, break out the Scotch and glasses. Make sure everyone gets a drink."

Tom went to a wall closet, took out the whisky and started to pour out generous measures. When the first bottle was empty, he fetched another. The glasses of Scotch were awkwardly passed around.

"Okay. This may surprise you, but you'll be joined in cabinet by George Savory at Ag. And Fish, and Art Sullivan at Labour."

"Holy cow!" Said Bill Clark. "What about Leila and Gloria?"

"Gone! I sacked them. They are now on the back bench."

"What about the three who voted against the motion of confidence?"

"Can't expel them for having an opinion, but they are now at the far end—where Marc used to be." He gestured in my direction. "What's up, Marc? Why are you frowning?"

"I'm wondering what will be the effect of both being female? It may not look good that you replaced them both with men, and with—"

"And with not very remarkable men. Is that what you were going to say?"

"Not exactly."

"That was a message to others that loyalty will be rewarded, but disloyalty will be punished. I've still got six women in the cabinet. That's not bad."

"I'm not sure the media will see it that way."

"But, Marc, I couldn't replace them with other females. That would have meant Zila and Carol."

A collective shudder went through the company.

"What I would like to see is those people replaced by their constituencies."

"Leave that with me, Premier," said John Trevor. "I don't think I'll have any chance with Parish—she's solid in her riding—but I can work on Chan and Mitchell. Don't be surprised if either or both resigns within the year."

"Really?"

"It might mean you'll have to offer some job in the public service."

"That's okay, but please check with me before you make any concrete offers."

"Wendell, could I make a somewhat gloomy observation?" Angus McKinnon asked.

"Go ahead, Angus."

"This is only the beginning. The challenge is over for now, but it will re-surface. These things are never over. They always come back in one form or another. I'm not exactly sure how many are unhappy or who they are—"

"Marc, give us the names."

"I will, Wendell, but before I do that, I think it's important to remember that there is now a bloc of five MLAs—on *our* side of the House—who will be looking for an opportunity to bring you down. In my judgment, that bloc could expand by as many as four others—"

"Wow!" Joan said. "If nine ganged up on you, it would be very serious. The media would make tremendous hay out of it."

"Nine! Who are they, Marc?"

"From my observations, Wendell, I would say that Carol Walters and Zili Franks could not be relied upon in a crunch."

"That only comes to seven," said Bill. "Who are the other two?"

"Both Reid and Leaman are very ambitious young men, Wendell. I'd guess that you can count on them only if there is something in it for them."

"He's right there, Wendell," said Joan.

"Hmm. You mean I'd have to expand the cabinet. It's already pretty large. I'll have to think about that.

"But it gets worse, I'm afraid," I said.

"What do you mean, Marc?" Angus asked.

"Well...er..."

"Go ahead!" Wendell said.

"I'm not sure this is the right time and place. And I'm not certain. I could be wrong..."

"Oh, for God's sake, spit it out!"

"If you insist."

"I *do* insist!"

"I think there are some members of the cabinet on whom you cannot rely unquestionably."

"Who?"

"As I say, I can't be certain, but if I were you, I would keep a close watch on Joseph, Rutledge and Sillyboy."

There were murmurs, some gasps and a long whistle from Bill Clark. Wendell frowned and stared ahead.

"If you think about it, Wendell, you know it makes sense," said Angus, "when you add it all up. We all know that Kesegoo'e will jump in any direction if it serves her own purposes. Zandili is perpetually aggrieved and is like a stick of dynamite rolling around looking for a fuse. Not so sure about Jill. Why do you include her, Marc?"

"She and Hendricks are as thick as thieves and, watching her during the motion today, it looked as if she wished she could vote with her."

"So…" Joan looked thoughtful. "That means if worst comes to worst we would have twelve against us in a showdown. To be honest, I don't think you could survive that."

"It still leaves twenty on our side," John Trevor said.

"We'll just have to see that it never comes to that point," said Wendell. "We prorogue tomorrow, then we'll have all summer to build bridges and mend fences. I have a plan to sound out the backbenchers and make sure we know where they stand. Marc will be going around the province to visit each of them—"

"I will?" I was so astounded I stood up, knocking over my glass of whisky.

"Oh, didn't I mention it?" Wendell said with a laugh. "Sorry about that. Does that mean you won't do it?"

"Well…"

"Okay, that's settled. Good grief, look at the time. Let's adjourn. The House sits in less than seven hours."

18

The House met at ten o'clock, and by twelve-thirty it was all over. Maddingly zipped through over a hundred bills, and had them all read for the third time and engrossed in record time. The Lieutenant Governor was summoned, and in customary fashioned intoned, "In His Majesty's name I assent to these bills."

He then trooped out and the House was adjourned, to be summoned again at the call of the Speaker.

When we first filed in, some of our own MLAs found that the name plates on their desks had been changed, and we had trouble finding where we supposed to sit. As we milled about, rather like cattle at a market, the Opposition members watched in complete amazement. They were surprised and puzzled by the fact that Hector now sat at the end of the first row, where Gloria Jones used to sit, that Art and George were now in the second row just over Wendell's left shoulder, and that nine backbenchers, including me, had been "promoted" to more senior seats.

But what shocked onlookers most was seeing the seats with the lowest precedence now occupied by Delia Parish (where I used to sit), Emma Mitchell, Jennie Chan, Leila Hendricks, and Gloria Jones. Instead of having the most junior place, I was now second from the Speaker's end in the back row.

Our own MLAs had some inkling of what had caused the changes because they had been present at the previous day's caucus meeting, but the opposition were completely at sea. Two ministers, previously close to the Premier, were now as far away from him as was possible. The hum of speculation was so loud The Speaker had to gavel for order on several occasions.

When they thought they had figured it out, the opposition benches came alive with shouts and jeers.

Revised seating chart for the government

1 – Ernest Maddingly **Speaker**
2 – Harold MacDonald
3 – Kesegoo'e Sillyboy
4 – Angela Stairs
5 – Angus MacKinnon
6 – Joan Howard
7 – Wendell Proctor **Premier**
8 – Chester MacCormack
9 – Stephanie Gilmour
10 – Mark Gardiner
11 – Bill Clark
12 – Pierre Dorion
13 – Hector McNeil
14 – Daniel Nathanson
15 – Alaric d'Entremont
16 – Sean Leaman
17 – Art Sullivan
18 – George Savory
19 – John Trevor
20 – Jill Rutledge
21 – Zandili Joseph
22 – Fred Askey
23 – Freeman Murphy
24 – Carol Walters
25 – Cullum MacPhee
26 – Jeremy Reid
27 – Marc LeBlanc
28 – Zila Franks
29 – Gloria Jones
30 – Leila Hendricks
31 – Jennie Chan
32 – Emma Mitchell
33 – Delia Parish

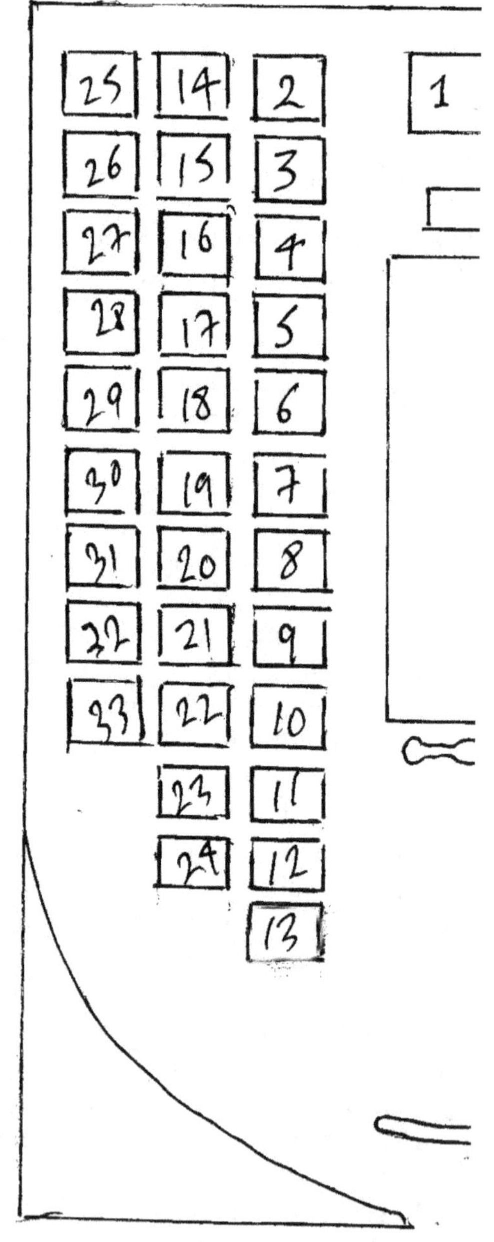

"The night of the long knives," bawled McNamara.

"Who's been naughty girls, then?" This from Cliff Wolf.

"The brown-nosers getting their reward," shouted Bill Jenkins.

"What's up, Delia, did you fail to kiss the boss's ass?" Sammy Wong hurled at Parish in the 'dunce's seat'.

"Oh, oh, trouble in paradise!" Eric Downey jeered.

Liam Hudson was singing *I Did it My Way,* and Michael Winters and Ed Gallant were shouting, "Chop! Chop! Chop! Who's next, Wendell?"

"Order! Order!" Maddingly barked. "I will have order!"

When order was restored, the silence was broken by Martha MacNaughton softly singing "Memories..."

The opposition dissolved into laughter, causing Maddingly to pound his gavel and threaten to eject anyone who spoke out of turn.

I was interested to see if any of the five rebels would try to vote against any of the bills. The third and last 'reading' of a bill is nothing of the kind. The bill is not read, only the title, and is pushed through the legislative process very quickly. If any of them wanted to create a scene, they would have to shout, "Nay" as soon as the Speaker said, "Shall the bill pass?" and then demand a standing vote. It has rarely, if ever, been done and would not be easy to accomplish, due to speed at which events move.

I was in a good position to see the rebels, as there was only Zila between them and me, but they said nothing and did not even absent themselves from the chamber to register their discontent. Hendricks was in tears and was silently sobbing. Mitchell and Chan looked as if tears were not far away. Jones and Parish glared defiantly.

When the House rose, Wendell asked me to go back to his office with him. He said he wanted to give me instructions as to my summer assignment.

I wanted to give him a piece of my mind about foisting the task on me without consulting me first. I had wanted to confront him last night, but others were in the room and I did not want to embarrass Wendell or myself.

It was when I was on my way over to Wendell's office that a thought struck me. I realized, to my horror, that when Ray Bland had told me about his financial difficulties, I had not offered him direct assistance. I could have lent him money or invested in his business, but neither had occurred to me at the time. I felt utterly ashamed at this bad lapse. Ray was one of my best friends and he certainly deserved better from me.

"Come on!" Wendell barked at me.

"I have to make a call," I said coolly. "I'll be there directly."

Wendell gave me a strange look, which suggested he was not used to underlings not jumping to his every order, shrugged and headed on to the elevator.

Ray picked up on the second ring. "Marc, is that you?"

"Ray, I feel terrible. I realized that I didn't offer you financial assistance when you first told me about your partner's embezzlement. Please forgive me."

"That's okay."

"You must have thought me a real jerk."

"Well, to be honest, I was a bit depressed about it."

"Let me make amends now. How much do you need?"

"I've managed to scrape along by cutting costs. I had to close one of my branches and reduce staff. At the moment I'm just holding our own, but if I get one really bad month, I'll go under."

"How much. Name it and it's yours."

"Could you run to a couple of hundred thousand?"'

"Of course. I'll call the bank as soon as we're though here."

"Thanks, Marc. What kind of interest will you want?"

"None. If you want, give me some shares in the business."

"Wow! Thanks."

"I wish I'd done it before. I guess my head was mixed up with all this political stuff."

"How's that going?"

"You would have been so much better at it than me. But I'm adjusting reasonably well. At first I hated it."

"How are you getting along with Wendell?"

"Good, I think. He says I'm now one of the inner circle."

"That's great!"

"I guess."

"What's wrong, Marc?"

"Wendell. I used to think he was such a great guy."

"You don't anymore?"

"I'm committed to him more than ever..."

"But?"

"But he can be a real prick sometimes."

"Yeah. He has a ruthless side to him, alright. I guess to be a successful premier, you have to be tough."

"I guess so, but he seems to enjoy being a prick."

"I haven't seen that side of him," Ray said. "But I have a suspicion that all heads of government get a God complex as soon as they take office. They think because the people elected them, they can do no wrong, and anyone who gets in their way is working for the Devil."

"That seems to be the way Wendell operates. You've known him for a long time—"

"But only socially. Never any of the backroom stuff."

"From what you've seen, how would you think he would react to someone—a colleague—standing up to him?"

"That sounds ominous. Are you planning something?"

"I'll tell you, Ray. I have a feeling that if I don't, he's going to treat me like a little dog. He's already doing it to some extent."

"Hmm. If you were a career politician I would say you should go easy. But since you've got nothing to lose, try it. See what happens."

"I think I will."

"I hope, with your help, I'll have straightened the business out by the time of the next election, so if you are not re-offering—"

"I won't be."

"I would be the candidate in Kings South."

"Sounds good. I've been keeping the great man waiting while we've been talking. I'm going to call the bank right away, so you go and see Malcolm MacGregor later today."

"I will."

"And, Ray, why don't you and Rachel come over for dinner the day after tomorrow?"

"Will you be back by then?"

"We just prorogued. I'm leaving as soon as I've had a word with his Highness."

As I was disengaging from Ray, Susan came out of the elevator, looking distressed.

"Marc! The Premier's waiting for you."

"Yes, thank you, Susan. Tell him I won't be long. I have to make some calls first."

"I think you should come now."

"I won't be long."

When she disappeared back into the elevator I called MacGregor and arranged for the money to be made available to Ray's business, and then I called Rosalie. Truth to tell, I was taking a childish delight in keeping the boss waiting.

"Sweetheart, I'm on my way home."

"Oh, good. It feels like the session went on forever."

"Two things: I given some money to Ray. I hope you don't mind."

"Why would I mind? I was surprised you didn't do it earlier. What was the second thing?"

"I invited Ray and Rachel over for dinner the day after tomorrow. That alright?"

"Of course. Shall I invite Joyce and Walter too?"

"Yes, please. I have to go see the Premier now."

"Ooh, what an important man you have become!"

"See you in a few hours."

When I got off the elevator, Susan was flustered and quickly ushered me to the end of the hall. I was used to entering Wendell's inner sanctum by way of Tom's office, but this time she pushed me through the large oak door beyond his.

"For fuck's sake, get in here," Tom whispered to me as I poked my head into the room.

"Back off, Tom," I heard myself saying. He looked startled and moved away. Wendell was at the window looking out over the street.

"Before we start," I said in a tone which made him quickly turn around, "I didn't appreciate your announcing I was undertaking a task before even telling me about it. How did you know Rosalie and I didn't have a trip to Europe planned? Or did you think we would just cancel any plans we had to fit in with yours?"

Out of the corner of my eye I saw Tom put his head in his hands, but in front of me Wendell's face was wreathed in smiles as he came towards me. He put his arm around me and guided me to a chair.

"I'm sorry, Marc. I should have asked you, I know."

"Well, for God's sake, let me know first the next time you have something you want me to do."

"Okay, it's a deal. I will, I promise. Tom, get Marc a drink."

"God, no, it's much too early for me."

"Alright. Will you do it?"

"Describe the assignment again."

"I just want you to circulate throughout the province, sounding out members of caucus, finding out where they stand, what their beefs are, what they see in their future, and so on."

"Do I have to visit them all?"

"Yes, please."

"And do I have to see Carol Walters?"

"Why not?"

"She hates me."

"Is that true, Tom?"

"I didn't know about this, Wendell."

"What did you do to her, Marc?"

"Nothing that I know of."

"She's obviously trouble but I don't know why. We might win her over if you were able to take a promise of rewards to come when you visit."

"Like what?"

"You could say you've discussed it at length with me—which is indeed the case—and hint that she could be the next in line for the cabinet."

"If I did, would it be true, or bullshit?"

"If it was a hint, it could be either," Tom said unhelpfully.

"I won't unless your word is good."

"Alright. You can say she could be in the next shuffle."

"Visiting the rebels will have to wait until later. To allow them time to cool off, if they ever do."

"Agreed."

"I'm not sure any approach to Jones or Parish could ever do any good. I 'd rather leave them out of the equation."

"Okay."

"I think with a lot of flattery and some promises, Hendricks and Mitchell might be brought back on board. I have no idea about Jennie Chan. She's a complete mystery to me."

"Look, why don't we leave it to your discretion?" said Wendell. "You see who you want and say what needs to be said. Within limits, you have my authorization to make promises, but only if you're sure they're absolutely necessary."

"Wendell, I'm not sure about this," Tom said.

"Marc won't play fast and loose. I trust him."

"Thanks," I said.

What was troubling me as I walked to the elevator was not whether I had the ability to carry out the task, but whether Wendell would back me up when I had completed it. If I made promises which he then didn't keep, it would make me look and feel like a lying, treacherous person.

The more I thought about it, the more convinced I was that Wendell would not give a fig for my feelings or reputation, but would use my findings in whatever way he saw fit.

19

As I headed out to the Bugatti, I took a quick look at my watch and saw it was not even two o'clock. I was anxious to get home and see Rosalie, but an intriguing thought entered my head. Why not exchange notes with someone who had known several premiers, and see how Wendell compared with others who held similarly high office?

With this in mind I slowly drove to the north end and parked the car on Brunswick Street. It was here that my old acquaintance Akerman and his wife had an apartment.

Fortunately, he was at home and invited me into a room whose walls were covered with paintings he had done over the years. This man, now in his eighties, had helped me with my investigations on numerous occasions. In his time he had been an archaeologist, a newspaper editor, a deputy minister in government and a radio announcer, but also an MLA for a decade.

"Marc, this is a surprise." he said as we settled in our chairs.

"Why should it be a surprise?"

"Because you are now an important politician." He laughed.

"Oh, you've heard about that?"

"Yes. Imagine my amazement when I was going through the election returns and saw in the winner's column: *Kings South, Marc LeBlanc*. At first I thought it must be some other Marc LeBlanc, but some discreet inquiries confirmed it was you."

"Yes, for my sins."

"I heard it was a landslide," he said, laughing.

"Yes. Eight votes, later reduced to three by the courts. Did you ever have a close race yourself?"

"Not me. If I recall correctly, my majorities were 1,500; 2,500 and 2,000. But there was one election, I recall, in which my wife's father was a candidate. On election night he led right up until the last two polls, which went for the other man."

"A real nail-biter."

"Indeed, yes. But, Marc, I thought you were a sensible guy. Whatever possessed you to get into the crazy game of politics?"

"I was roped into it. It all happened quickly. One minute I was an interested bystander at a meeting, and a phone call later I was the candidate."

"I don't understand."

"They were desperate because the man chosen, a friend of mine, had to pull out. So the premier called me and asked me to do it."

"And you couldn't say 'no' under those circumstances. You and he have history, don't you?"

"Yes, we got to be friends on a case I was working on for him[4]. You remember you helped me with it."

"So I did. That was when he was getting death threats?"

"That's the one."

"So, what brings you here today? What can drag you away from important affairs of state?"

"You've known a number of premiers well, haven't you?"

"I would say I've known three very well, and several more fairly well."

"Who were they?"

"The three I knew really well were premiers Regan, Buchanan and Hatfield. I had more than a passing acquaintance with Blakeney of Saskatchewan, Lee of Prince Edward Island and Bennett of British Columbia."

"Can we talk in absolute confidence?"

"What about?"

"I want to pick your brain—your memory, really—about premiers and why they act the way they do."

"So, why the secrecy?"

"I may say things about the current premier which I would not want repeated."

"Ah. Now I understand. Yes, you have my assurance that nothing we say here today will go any further."

"Thanks. That brings me to my first question. If you tell a premier

---

4   Recounted in my book *The Plot to Kill the Premier*

something in confidence, will he or she keep it?"

"Absolutely not. Nothing anyone says to a head of government will be kept secret unless it is something embarrassing to the premier in question. I give you an example. Once I was asked to investigate a situation for a premier. In the report—marked 'secret and confidential'—it was vital to give a negative assessment of a person appointed by a premier of another province. The next thing I knew I was being loudly chewed out in public by this other premier for attacking his pal."

"What happened?"

"Our premier casually handed the report to his counterpart without giving it a second thought. That action had a number of serious consequences."

"Are you saying you can't ever tell them anything and trust them to keep it to themselves?"

"Only until it can be used to their advantage. Then out it will come. Just like that!"

"Why do you think that is?"

"Premiers don't behave according to our rules. They are guided only by what is expedient."

"That seems a little harsh."

"They believe that, by virtue of their position—being chosen by the people—whatever they want is right, whatever they believe is true, whoever they like is good, whoever they dislike is bad, and whatever they know is all there is to know."

"Is that why they seem to be reluctant to take advice?"

"Yes. In their brains, if the advice being offered was any good, the person giving it would be the premier instead of themselves."

"That has a strange logic to it."

"On the few occasions on which they recognize that the advice is good, they pooh-pooh it at the time, tuck it away in their head, and bring it out at a later time as their own idea."

"What about promises?"

"Ah-hah. They will make as many promises as there are stars in the sky, if necessary to keep people in line. Here's how it goes.

"Suppose an MLA wants to be a cabinet minister and goes to the premier to present his request. The premier will look sad and pained and tell the MLA that, while he or she is an outstanding person of great ability, geography or ethnicity is against him or her, and that he can't have too many people like the supplicant in the cabinet because it would look bad.

"Or he will say, 'Yes, I'm glad you brought it up because I am planning to make you minister of ABC, but not yet. The timing is not right. As soon as it is, you'll be in the cabinet.'

"Or he will drop hints, and say things like, 'Bill, that was a marvellous speech you made today. We could use people like you in the cabinet,' and then move on quickly so he can't be pinned down.

"Another tactic premiers employ is to say, 'I've got a real problem, Bill, I want to share with you. I'm very anxious to get you into the cabinet, but I'm having an awful lot of trouble from some of the guys who are already in.' The supplicant will then express surprise and ask why he is disliked. The premier will lower his voice and say, 'You know as well as I do, you'd show them all up. They couldn't stand the competition.'

"One ploy premiers use is when the MLA asks to go into the cabinet, they say, 'Bill, to be frank, you'd be wasted in the cabinet. I've got something more important in mind for you. I can't say right now what it is or when that will be, but you know that these things take time.'

"Another one they use is if there's a rumour that the Minister of Fisheries may resign due to age or ill health. The premier will conspiratorially approach a troublesome backbencher and say, 'Bill, what do you know about fisheries?' Whereupon the man says, 'Actually, quite a lot, Premier. My father is captain of a fishing boat.' The premier's eyes will open wide and he will say, 'That's good to know, Bill. I'm very glad you told me that.'"

"I think you must be exaggerating," I said.

"Am I? Marc, what is gratitude when all is said and done?"

"Appreciation for having received something."

"Wrong. Gratitude is a lively expectation of favours to come."

"God, that's cynical!"

"Cynical it may be, but think about it. People who want something are much more likely to be loyal than those who have already got it."

"The corollary of that, though, is that those who are certain they won't get anything will be the most disloyal."

"I think that may be true. But in my experience, a great deal of disloyalty—by which I mean turning against a premier at a crucial moment—springs more often than not from some small, personal slight."

"You think?"

"Why do you think premiers are always glad-handing, back slapping, and having a joke with their troops?"

"They're friendly people?"

"Hah! No, they want to make sure that nobody thinks they are 'snooty' or 'stuck up'. A premier who laughs with one MLA, but not with another may be creating a resentment which can fester for a lifetime.

"You wouldn't believe the tiny, trivial things which can cause lasting grudges. When I was a politician, my good friend and next door neighbour told me he didn't vote for me because I didn't ask him. That I had taken him for granted because we were friends rankled so much he voted for my opponent in two elections."

"Did you get him in the third election?"

"He said I did, but I can't be sure. He was seriously upset by my oversight."

"It's hard to imagine people getting upset by so little."

"It's the little things most people really care about. One premier told me that, before he came to office, a party supporter who lived two hundred miles away from him said he could not back him for the leadership. When asked why not, he replied, 'Because you never invited me to your house.' No amount of reasoning would change his mind.

"The same premier told me that, after he was out of politics, a member of his party told him he had never supported him because he had, many decades earlier, thought he had 'sneered at him'. Neither man had any recollection of how and where this was supposed to have taken place, only that the complainant was sure it had occurred forty years ago."

"Any other cheerful things to say about premiers?"

"Some of them treat their staff and inner confidants very badly. That's when arrogance can almost become unpleasant. Brian Peckford was the worst I ever saw in that respect."

"Who was the best?"

"Bill Bennett. He was a wonderful man, God rest his soul."

"I guess it's the old story of familiarity breeding contempt."

"Buchanan was never like that. He was a charming fellow, but he did get staff to buy him shirts, ties, toiletries and never reimbursed them."

There was a lull in the conversation. Akerman went into his kitchen to get a drink of water.

"Why have you asked all these questions," he inquired on returning. "I'm guessing you have—if not exactly fears—concerns about Mr. Proctor. Why? You're not looking to get into the cabinet—"

"God, no!"

"And, despite your friendship, I would not think you're part of the inner circle—"

"Actually, I am."

"So, what's the problem?"

"If what you've been telling me is true, then Wendell has been laying away all kinds of trouble for himself."

"Arrogance?"

"And then some."

"Needlessly offending people?"

"For sure."

"Letting people think they're on the outside looking in."

"I would say so, yes."

"There's something else?"

"Yes."

I told him about the assignment Wendell had given me, what the terms of reference were, as best as I could grasp them myself, and that it had to be completed before the fall.

"That's quite a task he's trusted you with, but do not let it go to your head, whatever you do."

"What do you mean?"

"You may think it gives you some kind of power. It doesn't. Any kind of status you may feel is attached to this is strictly temporary—if it even exists. For a brief time you have a spot in the sun, or maybe you have a target on your back."

"That's cheered me up no end. Thanks a million."

"And, lastly, let me give you some advice from the heart."

"Please do."

"Be absolutely honest with the people you visit. You're too new at the game to be able to double-deal, so no bullshit."

"Okay."

"And no matter what Proctor told you, do not, repeat do not, under any circumstances make any promises. If do, you can be sure he will later deny that he authorized it. And one last thing—"

"What's that?"

"Have a good time. Enjoy yourself. If you're lucky, you might make a lot of new friends. You might need them someday."

"What's that supposed to mean?"

"It's politics. Do not say, 'Fountain, I will never drink of your waters.'"

20

It was good to be home, to see Rosalie and to look forward to a whole summer with her. However, I realized this could only happen if she agreed to accompany me around the province when I made my visits to other MLAs, and since I had not yet informed her of Wendell's assignment, I was totally unsure how she would respond.

As I nosed the Bugatti up the driveway, I wondered if she would strenuously object, and if she did, would I have the intestinal fortitude to tell Wendell I had changed my mind and that the plan was cancelled?

I tucked the car in the garage, which had been newly rebuilt after an explosion, grabbed my bag and hopped out. The garage was a massive-structure with steel doors and an ingenious closing mechanism. All this was necessary to satisfy my insurance company, and because I did not want to lose another Bugatti.[5]

I nipped around the side of the house to take a quick look at the garden, and was horrified by the state of it. It was a tangled mess of dead vegetation from last year and new weeds which had all appeared since I last looked a few weeks ago. This would require a great deal of work, and I seriously doubted that I would have time to do it. I would have to hire a gardener, at least on a part-time basis.

I looked out at my huge field, the woods beyond, and, far to my right, the vines of John Dempster's vineyard, and, not for the first time, I regretted having promised to undertake Wendell's mission. After all, what would it, could it, accomplish? Even supposing I was able to get these people to open up to me, which was by no means certain, and even if I could determine their attitude to the party leadership, their minds could change by the time of the next legislative

---

5 For the events surrounding this, see my book *My Brother's Keeper.*

session. If that was likely, would Wendell expect me to contact them all over again? If he did, I would certainly refuse.

Not the least of the many questions looming ominously in my mind was the extent to which I would have to suffer insults and abuse for some of those I went to see. I was aware that some of them already called me "Wendell's little dog", "Teacher's pet", and "Brown-noser", and those slurs were said in what you might call semi-public. How much worse would it be in private?

When it came to unpleasantness, Carol Walters, our MLA for Cape Breton East, continually cropped up in my thoughts. Why on earth did this woman, whom I had first met only weeks ago, seem to dislike me so much? I would have to do some digging on her background because, though I had racked my brain, I could think of no rational reason for her animus.

After I had dropped my suitcase in the hall, kissed Rosalie and given her the sapphire brooch I had bought for her in Halifax, I casually asked her if she had any commitments at the university during the summer months. When she told me that she would only be required for two weeks for reviewing masters' and doctoral theses, I dived in.

"How do you fancy spending the summer going around the province?"

"Oh, we've never done that. How many stops would it involve?"

"As many or as few as we like. I would guess at least a dozen. We'd interrupt our tour and come back for your thesis marking."

"It's not exactly marking. You make them sound like high school exams."

"Sorry. Are you up for a Grand Tour?"

"Yes, I think it could be fun," she said excitedly, "There are many places neither of us have ever seen."

"That's certainly true. So, I'll get moving on booking hotels, shall I?"

"Or I could do it?"

"No, I'll do it."

Rosalie and I have only been married for six years, but if there is one thing I have learned—or should have learned—about her is that she has an extraordinary sixth sense of being able to detect when I am sugar-coating a proposition. I do not know how she does it, but when she gets an inkling, she homes in like a deer fly after its quarry.

"I usually do the booking for trips," she said, looking at me with a frown. "Why do you want to do it this time?"

"No particular reason…"

"Marc!"

"Well, if you must know, Wendell has asked me to drop in and see some of the other MLAs this summer, you know, to sound them out on how they feel about his leadership."

"Wendell! I might have known! How many?"

"How many what?"

"How many MLAs?"

"Oh, just some of the government members. Obviously I won't be going to see Opposition Members."

"Answer my question! How many?"

"No more than fifteen."

"And what would I be doing while you're interviewing these characters?"

"You could come with me if you want. Or go walking about, investigating this beautiful province."

"Okay. Tell me where they live and I'll do the bookings."

"You want a list."

"Of course I do."

"Now?"

"Why not?"

"Alright. Let me see. Lunenburg, Chester, Halifax, Windsor, Sheet Harbour, Pictou, and Arichat."

"That's only seven."

"Is it? We can add to it if you wish."

"No I think this will be enough. I'll see what I can find on the net."

"Okay. I'll rustle up something for dinner."

"Speaking of which, you haven't forgotten that we're having the Brysons and the Blands over tomorrow night?"

"No, I haven't forgotten. I don't know what we'll give them to eat. I'm tied up all morning in the constituency office, handling problems."

"Until what time?"

"I would guess about one."

"That won't leave much time to prepare."

"No, it won't. I guess we could go with the old standbys, smoked salmon and shepherd's pie."

"Do we have kosher cream and butter?"

"Yes. Not a lot, but enough. I'll get some cabbage on my way home. If I clean it thoroughly it should be alright. Could you make your famous lemon tart?"

"I only have four or five lemons in the fridge so I can't make the real thing—"

"Doesn't that require something like a dozen lemons?"

"Yes, and ten eggs! And it takes a long time to prepare. Leave it with me. I have some rhubarb and a few apples. I could make a crumble."

"Wonderful."

"What will we have tonight?"

"It'll have to be cold. Whatever I can put together."

"Okay. But you'd better sort out tomorrow's wines now so you won't be rushed."

"Right."

I flicked on the cellar light, resolving as I had so often in the past to replace the bulb with a stronger one, and descended into the cool dampness. Around me the myriad bottles twinkled, some of them only faintly due to the dust they had gathered over the years.

After the Bugatti, this cellar was my pride and joy. I had spent enormous sums of money and many years accumulating my collection of fine wines, some of them going back to the 1940s. I was particularly proud that I had managed to get my hands on a number of 1961s and 1966s from the first and second growths in Bordeaux. Some of the latter were a little past their peak, but most of the former were in perfect condition. The 1961 Bordeaux vintage was one of the best of all time, producing small, ripe, sweet, thick-skinned berries making the wines rich and tannic, and requiring many years to mature.

Since the food would not be anything spectacular, I thought our guests deserved some rather special wines. The smoked salmon would need a big, strong white to stand up to the saltiness so I chose a *Château La Mission Haut Brion Blanc* 1961. The main course would be somewhat rustic, so to elevate it I thought a *Château Latour* 1961 would be more than suitable. To accompany Rosalie's crumble we would have a *Château Suduiraut* 1959.

Having stood the Latour up to allow the sediment to settle, I took the Suduiraut and La Mission upstairs and placed them on a slate counter in the pantry. When the time came I would give them only a short stay in the fridge before serving.

I searched around and found a big chunk of Cheshire cheese, some nice looking ham, tomatoes, celery, radishes and a not very enticing lettuce. I washed and dried the salad items, then tossed them in olive oil, lemon juice and chopped dill.

Having set the food on the table and pulled a bottle of Chablis from the fridge, I called Rosalie.

"You know," she said, making herself comfortable. "I'm rather looking forward to this trip. I think getting to meet all your colleagues might be fun."

While I was happy that my wife was now fully on board with the touring plan, I harboured some doubts about her being able to blurt out strong opinions to people who might be more amenable to the velvet-glove treatment. Still, the *quid pro quo* was necessary, and I knew I had to learn to live with it.

21

After a superb breakfast of homemade sausages, fried bread, eggs, mushrooms, tomatoes and Jamaican Blue Mountain coffee, I headed into town to encounter my constituents. I had done this several times since my election, always on Saturdays because the House sat during the week.

Initially, I had managed to rent a small office on the upper floor of one of the older buildings on Main Street, but within days I was told that the premises were not wheelchair accessible, a condition, unknown to me at the time, required by legislation. Forfeiting the already paid rent, I had to find somewhere else which was both legal and convenient. It took me, and Rosalie and Gerald in my absence, almost a month to find somewhere even remotely suitable.

Eventually, we discovered a space—it does not merit a better description—in an old warehouse on Front Street, which had at one time been the dispatching area of some kind of haulage company. It took Mary Driscoll and Maud Taylor several days' hard work to make it presentable, this despite Maud's recent leg operation. They told me the place was filthy, "like a pig sty", in Mary's words. Their difficulty had been compounded by the necessity of creating a waiting area in addition to the office itself.

I was extremely grateful to the ladies for their efforts, but the result was barely acceptable. There was a rickety old card table on which the telephone sat precariously, with my hard-backed chair behind it. The visiting constituent had a much more comfortable armchair which, although it had definitely seen better days, was relatively clean.

It would have been easier had we been able to put "the waiting room" near the "office", but since there was no partition, this would mean that constituents could hear the others' private business. So we had to put it closer to the yard, which entailed another gargantuan cleaning effort and required those waiting to be partially exposed to the elements due to ill-fitting windows with missing panes.

On his return from visiting his sister in Winnipeg, Reg Harkness had found an assortment of chairs to furnish this area. None of them matched as to condition, colour or style, but were not likely to give way unless a very large, heavy constituent were to sit on them.

I had engaged, sight unseen, Joe's niece, Cheryl, as my constituency secretary and installed her at another, smaller, card table in the "waiting room". She was a small young woman, and if she had not worn ridiculously long stiletto heels she would have been diminutive.

While she was very agreeable and greeted the public with cheerful politeness, her secretarial abilities were far from exemplary and she frequently got people's names wrong and made mistakes in my correspondence. Even if her errors increased, I knew that firing her would never be an option because there would be cataclysmic repercussions in the local party organization. Old Joe was a local institution and was not a force to be trifled with.

As I entered, I saw about half a dozen people bunched up in the waiting area as Cheryl came clack-clacking towards me.

"Good morning, Dr. LeBlanc."

"Good morning, Cheryl. How many patients do we have today?"

Pretending we were doctor and nurse was a game we played after I told her that in Britain the Members of Parliament called their constituency offices "surgeries". She thought that hilarious and milked the joke—weak though it might be—for all it was worth.

"I have five patients for you today. All of them are ambulatory."

"If they weren't they wouldn't have been able to get here, would they?"

"I guess not." She giggled. "They'd be in ambulances!"

"Who's first?"

"Er...I wrote it down somewhere." She frowned, and searched her notepad. "I think it's Mr. Dexter. Yes it is, Mr. Dexter."

"Alright, thank you nurse. Wheel him in."

"He looks like he could use a wheelchair. He must be close to a hundred."

"Keep your voice down please, Cheryl!"

"Okay, Doc." She giggled again.

Mr. Dexter was indeed extremely aged, and seemed very confused as to what era he was living in. He started by addressing me as Mr. Haliburton, and when I told him that the gentleman he had named had not been the MLA for Kings South for more than sixty years, he looked surprised.

He was a man of little education and few manners. After much meandering, he came to the reason for his visit. "I want to get the widows' pension."

"But, Mr. Dexter, need I point out that you are not a widow?"

"I believe the woman next door is getting it, so why can't I get it?" He was extremely surly.

"The legislation relates to widows of men who were killed at work, but that is not the point. You are not a widow."

"I bet some trans person could get it," he said, suddenly brightening. His expression reminded me of cartoon characters whose acquiring ideas was illustrated by a light bulb above their heads.

Confounded, I just stared at him, not having an inkling whether he was right or wrong. Even were such a thing possible in the past, for all I knew it could have been superseded by Wendell's "anti-woke" campaign. The best I could do under the circumstances was to tell him that, even if what he said was true, in order to establish a claim he would have to produce evidence of some kind of treatment, possibly involving surgery.

At this he jumped up with a snarl and left at a speed which belied his years.

The next constituent was, if anything, even more hostile than Mr. Dexter had been. His complaint was that his neighbour's dogs were continually knocking over his garbage cans, making a noise which woke him up in the middle of the night. When I said he might try securing the cans in position with bricks or concrete blocks, he became incandescent, demanding to know why it should be his responsibility when the dogs were to blame.

As his rage increased, so did my own impatience, and finally I said he should see his town councillor since dogs knocking over garbage cans was not a matter within provincial jurisdiction.

He left, roaring that we were no longer living in a free country, but one run by "communionists."

Mrs. Archibald, the next constituent, was a genuinely aggrieved woman who had been injured at work, but due to a technicality had been rejected for Workers' Compensation. I advised her how to go about the appeal process, but also that she would stand no chance of success without compelling medical evidence, so the first step should be to obtain her doctor's opinion in writing.

There was a steady flow of people, mostly seeking information about government programs and grants, continuing well into the afternoon. This experience considerably strengthened my view that the online substitution for services previously rendered by live human voices had severely diminished the public's access to government. This was especially true for the old, the poor, and the uneducated, many of whom either botched their efforts to make contact or simply gave up.

I resolved to mention this to Wendell, as I thought it might appeal to him. I could easily imagine him pledging to bring back humanity to the government's interaction with the people.

I had let Cheryl go home at one o'clock, but I didn't get out of the office until after two-thirty.

Just as I was leaving, old Alfred, whom I had met at the fateful pre-election meeting at Reg Harkness' house, "dropped by to chat" about how I was liking my new role. If I had allowed him, he would have talked all day, so it was with some effort that I extricated myself with excuses that I had to go shopping for Rosalie.

As soon as I got home, I set to work on the evening's meal. The smoked salmon was no problem, and all I needed to do to smarten it up was to surround it with strips of peeled and sliced cucumber, thinly sliced apple, wedges of lemon and capers.

To make the shepherd's pie, I put about eight large potatoes on to boil, and sautéed chopped onions in a large pan. When the onions were soft, I added lots of button mushrooms and then lean ground beef and lamb in equal quantities.

When that was partially cooked I added peas, chopped carrots, salt, pepper, parsley, thyme, garlic, nutmeg, basil, half a cup each of good red wine and beef stock, and a generous amount of Chinese oyster sauce. When that was cooked a little longer I poured it into a large baking dish, mashed the potatoes with cream and butter and spread them evenly over the meat mixture.

Having grated *Parmigiano reggiano* on top of the pie, I set it aside to be put in a hot oven about twenty minutes before serving with the sliced, buttered cabbage dressed with a few caraway seeds.

Ray and Rachel were first to arrive. Rachel immediately gave me a wonderfully-warm hug and kissed me on the cheek, while Ray put his arm around me and squeezed.

"You saved our lives," he said.

"Yes, thank you, darling Marc," said Rachel in that lovely silver voice. "Your investment pulled us back from the brink of bankruptcy."

"I should have done it earlier, but I was too wrapped up with this political nonsense," I replied. "Are you okay now? Is the business back on its feet?"

"Yes, we're back on an even keel," Ray said. "It's a huge relief, I can tell you."

Just then Rosalie came downstairs and the kissing and hugging was repeated.

We were just moving into the lounge when the Brysons called through the open door. "Anyone at home?"

We ushered Joyce and Walter into the large room with floor-to-ceiling windows, and settled everyone on the expensively-soft chairs and couch. As soon as I had served *Billecart Salmon rosé* Champagne, inevitably the conversation was all about my new occupation as a representative of the people.

"What's it like, Marc?" Ray asked. "Do you think I would have enjoyed it if I'd been able to run?"

"I'm not entirely sure. I think you might have gotten along with it better than I am because you've been politically active for some years."

"But not as long as Walter," said Rachel.

"No," I said, "Walter would be as happy as a pig in muck."

"That's because he gets to shoot his mouth off almost every day," said Joyce with a laugh. "He'd have no trouble getting up on his hind legs and spouting off in Halifax."

"I gather you didn't like it, at least at first. Is that right, Marc?" Rachel asked.

"You're right. For the first few weeks I positively loathed it. Listening to stuff which had no meaning to me, and observing rank hypocrisy all around me. They just threw me on the back bench, and had some snotty professor type—"

"I'm a professor," interjected Rosalie. "Be careful what you say."

"You're one of the good ones, my love. Probably the only good one. But, as I was saying, this character gave me my marching orders, as it were, and—"

"What were they?" Walter asked.

"Basically to do as I was told, and not to ask questions. And definitely not so say anything."

"So you haven't given your maiden speech yet?"

"Not in the House. Apparently, when they think I'm ready, they'll tell me what to say."

"You'll become known as Silent Marc," Walter said with a grin.

"I've spoken once in caucus and got a few boos—"

"Oh, that's too bad."

"—and a huge round of applause."

"Well done. What did you speak about?" Ray asked.

"Can't say, sorry. Caucus is confidential."

They all hooted with laughter, as though I had deliberately cracked an enormous joke. I thought it best not to explain that I had been serious.

"What changed your mind?" Rachel asked. "You said you loathed it at first."

"Mainly because I got to know a few of others—"

"Are they nice?"

"Some are, some definitely are not."

"On the opposition side," Rosalie said firmly.

"No, sweetheart, some of them are really nice people. I made good friends with about three of them." I could see Walter nodding. He had been a member of the opposition party for years. "And, frankly, some on our side are absolute swine."

"What else?" Rachel inquired.

"You mean what else helped to change my mind?"

"Yes."

"Well...er...I'd really rather not say."

"Oh, come on!"

"This is going to sound stupidly conceited, but I started to enjoy it more when I became a member of...the...er, inner circle."

"The *what*?" they exclaimed in unison.

"The group around Wendell. One day Tom Aldridge came up to me and said I was in the inner circle."

"I think he was having a bit of fun," Joyce said.

"Maybe not," Walter said. "Marc, who's in the inner circle apart from yourself? When you meet, who's there?"

"Tom Aldridge, Joan Howard, Angus MacKinnon, Stephanie Gilmour, Bill Clark and John Trevor. That's it."

"Hmm. I'd say Marc is definitely a member of the inner circle." Walter was emphatic. "Those are the names of Proctor's closest advisers."

"Gosh!" This from Joyce.

"I'm so glad for you," said Rachel, placing her hand on my arm.

"Before Marc gets too swollen-headed we'd better go and eat," said Rosalie, rather coldly and a little too flippantly for my liking.

She jumped up and went into the dining room. The rest of us followed and sat wherever we found seats.

While I was serving the smoked salmon and pouring out the wine, I wondered at Rosalie's surprising attitude. I could not imagine that she was in any way jealous, but it did occur to me that she might have liked to have been asked to be the candidate herself, as she was in many respects more suited for the job than I. Maybe it was because we had first met Wendell together, had stayed at his house and had gone to London as a team in search of the person who was threatening his life. Did she feel that I was...for want of a better word...hogging Wendell to myself and keeping her out of the relationship?

The first course was enjoyable without being special, and the *Château La Mission Haut Brion blanc* looked years younger than its age, showing fresh citrus, lemon peel and honeysuckle, and was full-bodied and concentrated, so it stood up to the smoked fish quite well.

The shepherd's pie was robust and comforting, but here again the wine far overshadowed it. It was amazing to think this wine was sixty-four years old, as it was very deep in colour, showing little or no signs of its age. On the nose it was exquisite, with pure and refined tinges of blackcurrants, coconut, and mint. On the palate it was spectacularly intense and almost so powerful it was difficult to take more than a small sip at a time. It was not only one of the best *Château La-tours* I had ever tasted, but one of the all-time best wines, too. Others seemed to be as impressed as I, and there was a chorus of "oohs" and "aahs" around the table.

Rosalie's dessert was excellent and it went very well with the

Château Suduiraut, which was the colour of autumn leaves and full of apricots, honey, butterscotch and marzipan. Quintessentially sweet, it also had great balance provided by an edgy acidity.

For Ray, Rosalie and Joyce this was the wine of the evening, but Walter, Rachel and I far preferred the *Château Latour*, which was still providing a remarkable bouquet from the remnants left in our glasses.

In view of Rosalie's obvious aversion to the subject, I wanted to avoid the conversation returning to politics. So, when we had returned to the lounge, I pursued the matter of Ray's business. "Did you ever manage to bring Willis Parker to book?"

"Who's Willis Parker?" Rosalie intervened, rather aggressively.

"He was my business partner," said Ray, "until the bastard cheated me out of a few hundred thousand dollars."

"Did you catch up with him?"

"You'd better ask Walter. He is representing me in this."

"I'd rather not say much." Walter said. "It might conceivably be prejudicial, but at the moment it does not look promising. Parker covered his tracks quite well and, frankly, Ray's hand on the tiller was not as firm as it should have been."

"I know, I know. I trusted him. He was a friend."

"That's to your credit, darling," Rachel said, running her hand over his back. "I'd rather have you like that than as a hard-nosed, no-nonsense, grinding tyrant."

"It would be best not to discuss it any more," Walter said firmly, which shut us all up abruptly.

"I hear you're going on a provincial tour," Rachel said to Rosalie.

"Maybe. It's not settled yet," Rosalie answered, in a tone which tightened my stomach.

"But I thought you were making the arrangements," I said, knowing before the words were out of my mouth that it was foolish to utter them.

"I said, it's not settled," she snapped.

"Walter, I think it's time we went," Joyce said, standing up.

"Yes, it is rather late," said Rachel.

I called them taxis, and while we were waiting for them to arrive, we stood around in the hall chatting. Eventually they left and I watched the tail lights of the cars disappear into the night.

I dreaded going back in, but had no choice. In any event, I was resolved not to be the one to raise the matter again. I figured that whatever it was that was bothering Rosalie, she would tell me in her own time.

When I went back to the lounge it was empty, and going through to the kitchen, I found she was not there either. I sauntered back and poured myself a glass of Dalmore sherry cask.

There was no point in going to bed, because I knew I would not sleep. My Uncle Romuald had once told me that in relationships one should never go to bed leaving a dispute unsettled. I had found it to be good advice, and I firmly believed it to be true. Unfortunately, my wife did not share that belief.

22

I was hardly out of bed the next morning when the phone buzzed. Rather than risk waking Rosalie, I rushed downstairs and took the call in the kitchen.

"Marc?"

"Yes. Who's this?"

"Wendell. Did I get you up?"

"Kind of."

"Jesus, I've been up for hours. You should get your ass in gear."

"What can I do for you?"

"Couple of things. The first, I'm sure you already thought of, is that even during the summer, except for weekends, members of cabinet won't be in their constituencies, they'll be in Halifax."

"Good point. No, I hadn't thought of it."

"Okay. The second is that eleven members of our caucus are in the Halifax area, so you may as well stay with Cynthia and me while you're seeing those."

"Thanks very much. That'd be nice. Rosalie might be with me. Is that alright?"

"Sure. Cynthia would love that. Where are you going to start?"

"I thought I'd do the ones who are within a short driving distance of here first. That would be Askey and Franks."

"Okay, but see John Trevor first and get his advice. I don't want his nose to be out of joint."

"Yes, I was going to do just that."

I then took the opportunity to tell Wendell about my opinion that substituting online methods for services previously rendered by live human voices had severely reduced the public's access to government. I said this was especially true for the old, the poor, and the un-educated, many of whom either botched their efforts to make contact or simply gave up.

"You might be able to make some hay with it, promising to bring back humanity to the government's interaction with the people," I concluded.

"Good idea. I like it. When you see, Tom mention it to him in case I forget."

"Okay, I will."

"Who's that, Marc?" Rosalie had just come downstairs and into the kitchen.

"Is that Rosalie?" Wendell asked. "Put her on!"

"It's for you," I said, handing her the phone.

As they were talking, I went out onto the deck, walked around and peered at the jungle of a garden. It truly was an awful sight. Before going to see Trevor, I decided I would call Joe and see if he had any other relatives looking for part-time work.

When Rosalie hung up the phone she was all smiles. I took this to mean that the domestic crisis was over, but I was not entirely correct, as I soon discovered.

"Wendell asked us to go and stay with him and Cynthia."

"Wonderful!" I decided not to say that he had asked me already.

"So, when are we going?"

"I thought in a few days. I have to see a few of our people within driving distance first."

"Hmnph. You really are such a prima donna, Marc."

"How do you mean?"

"All that stuff about confidential meetings!"

"Well, the caucus is confidential."

"What did you discuss—nuclear secrets?"

"Wendell's leadership was on the line, if you must know."

"I'm sure you exaggerate."

She went over to the counter and poured herself a coffee. "And boasting about being in 'the inner circle' wasn't what I expected from you."

"They asked and I told them." I decided that was as defiant as I dared be, and hastily added, "Look, this political business is all new and confusing to me, so I'm bound to get a lot of it wrong."

"Yes, I understand that. Maybe in time you'll get the hang of it."

"Yes, maybe I will."

I left her to make her own breakfast and called Joe to see if he could find me a part-time gardener.

"I've got just the man," he said, not surprising me in the least.

"Another member of your family?"

"Yes, Marc. My nephew, Bamby."

"Bamby?"

"Yeah, short for Bambatha. My sister Florence got carried away. She thinks we have Zulu blood."

"And do you?"

"Who the hell knows? Anyhow, Marc, Bamby is a good fellow, if the lines of demarcation are clearly drawn."

"I'm not sure what that means."

"It means you need to spell out clearly what you want done. If you said to him, 'Go plant stuff,' you never know what might happen."

"A garden full of cannabis?"

"Haha! Something like that. Shall I send him over?"

"Sure. I'll pay him twenty bucks an hour."

"Sounds good. He'll be there within the hour."

When he arrived later on his bicycle, Bamby was not at all what I expected. He was very short and clean-cut. No dreadlocks or brightly coloured clothes, and clearly a man of considerably more intelligence than his uncle had suggested.

As I took him around to the garden, he told me he had just completed his Masters' degree in physics and was about to embark upon his Ph.D. Before I could tell him what I wanted, he quickly adumbrated a comprehensive plan of action.

"Yes, I see," he said. "All this needs to be cleared. Then the ground should be prepared for planting. That's digging, raking and fertilizing. Herbs along the edges and near the house. Tomatoes, peppers over there, where you get the most sun. Other veg in raised rows here. Maybe a row or two of pretty flowers for Mrs. LeBlanc."

"Yes," I said. What he had outlined was exactly what I wanted.

"Okay. I'll get cracking. Do you want to stick to the hourly payment or come up with a figure for the whole job?"

"Like piece work?"

"If you want. If you go the hourly route you won't be able to know if I have put in the time."

"I trust you."

"Why? You don't know me."

"I trust Joe, and you're his nephew. That's good enough for me."

"Do you think I can get all this done in a week?"

"You'd be working hard, but I would guess you might be able to."

"Let's say a thousand dollars. That way I'll have to get it done even if it takes me longer."

"Okay. It's a deal."

I showed him where I kept the tools and wheelbarrow and went back inside. About an hour later, I looked out of the window and saw that he was attacking the job like a man possessed, and had already accomplished as much as I would in an entire morning. It was clear that, unlike Cheryl, Bamby would need no overseeing.

So, it was in a positive frame of mind that I drove over to Berwick, where John Trevor lived in a huge, three-storey white house on Union Street. I parked alongside his SUV and knocked on the front door. Getting no response, I went around to the back, picking my way through hundreds of daisies.

John was at the bottom of the garden, dressed in old clothes and sporting a cap which looked as if it were at least thirty years old.

"Ah," he said as if he had known I was coming, "there you are."

"Hello, John."

"Look, Marc, before we start, let me say that we got off on the wrong foot. I'm sorry if I wasn't at my most collegial, but I had you down as some wealthy dilettante playing at politics. Now I know you're serious, we can start again."

"That suits me."

"Let's go in."

"Okay," I said, heading towards the house.

"No, not in there. Let's go into my shed."

The shed was almost invisible behind a huge compost heap and a tangle of vines and ivy. He led the way into a tiny, darkened space containing two boxes. John pulled out a bottle from under a battered workbench, sat on one of the boxes and invited me to take the other one.

"There! We can be cozy here," he said, holding out the bottle. "Drink?"

"What is it?"

"Shine."

"No thanks."

"It's good stuff. Made by a fellow just a few kilometres from here, up in Rockland."

"I'm sure it is good, but it's much too early in the day for me to be drinking."

"To be honest, I spent much more time in here than I do in the house…since Helen passed away."

"Oh, I am sorry. When did your wife die?"

"Helen wasn't my wife, she was my Labrador bitch."

"Oh."

"My wife was Marjorie. She took off with some guy from Morristown."

"I'm sorry to hear that."

"While I was in Halifax attending the Legislature—I was first elected in 2005—they were fooling around here in the house. That's why I don't much like spending time there."

"Ah."

"Still I think it's been getting me a sympathy vote ever since."

Suddenly, he uttered the most awful, braying laugh, harsh and somehow cruel. I just sat there, not knowing what to say.

"Right. The Boss has put me in the picture as to what your mission is. I think he's smart to use a newcomer to do it. I approve."

"Thank you," I said, although I did not think I needed his approval.

"You'd better start with me."

"What?"

"You have to find out who is loyal and what it will take to stay loyal to the Boss. So start with me. But you can be blunt with me. The others will require a certain amount of finesse."

"Oh, alright." I felt stupid asking the question. "John are you loyal to the premier?"

"Yes."

"Will you stay loyal to the premier?"

"Yes, but…"

"But what?"

"I will *stay* loyal, but I would like some recognition of my loyalty."

"What kind of recognition?"

"I want a department. It doesn't matter which one, but I'd like Municipal Affairs."

"When?"

"Certainly before the next election."

"A year? Two years?"

"Definitely within two. Preferably within a year."

"How about Speaker?"

"You are learning, aren't you? If push came to shove, I'd take it, but I'd much rather be minister of a department."

"Duly noted. Any advice before I see the others?"

"Watch out for D'Entremont."

"He's the one in front of me in the second row?"

"That's him. MLA for Richmond. The most treacherous bastard you could find. He'd sell his own mother for ten bucks."

"Thanks. Anything else?"

"Are you seeing ministers as well?"

"Yes, some of them."

"Gardiner is a prick."

"I already know that. I've had dealings with him before."

"Harold MacDonald. He's the biggest liar on God's green earth. Don't believe a word he says."

"Right."

"Chester McCormack is a good guy. A superb minister. I'm guessing he would be loyal, but he plays his cards close to the chest."

"What about Angela Stairs?"

"The Empress of Antarctica! Very capable, but who knows where she stands on something like this. I wouldn't have had a clue until she spoke up in caucus about the library assistant. If I were you, I wouldn't waste my time on her. You'll be none the wiser at the end of it."

"What about the young Turks?"

"Ah, you mean Reid, McPhee and Leaman?"

"Yes."

"They all have that lean and hungry look, don't they? My guess is that they usually hunt as a pack and that they'll be loyal to the Boss—and to each other—only as long as there's something in it for them."

"Thank you, John. I must get going. But before I do, can you tell me why Carol Walters is so hostile towards me?"

"Is she? I didn't know."

"She hates the air I breathe and the ground I walk on."

"Bad as that? No idea what's up her nose. You two have history?"

"Not that I know."

John walked with me to the Bugatti where he whistled.

"Wow! That is some machine, Marc. Absolutely marvelous. I won't ask you what it cost."

"It was a gift."

"You've got some very generous friends."

He walked around the car and delicately ran his hand over the hood. "Where you going next?"

"To see Askey."

"Hmm. Fred's a prickly bastard, but he's one of us. At least for the time being. I'd be interested to get your take on him."

"You shall have it."

As I headed eastwards back to Kentville, where Fred Askey lived, I reflected that Fred was one of John's handpicked whips, yet even he was unsure of his loyalty. I was learning that in that sphere almost everything was temporary, and that almost nothing could be taken for granted. A friend today could be an enemy tomorrow without any apparent reason.

Fidelity to a chief could depend solely on whether he could be expected to provide some gift, no matter how small. I was glad politics was not my life and that I was not a leader, constantly looking over my shoulder. I was starting to understand why those for whom politics was a central force in their lives clung so tenaciously to it and went to extraordinary lengths to resist any attempt to dislodge them. My political education was proceeding apace.

23

Fred Askey was a big, heavy-set man in his early 50s, with a permanent five o'clock shadow. He was a very loud breather, sometimes almost wheezing, and needing to take a gasp of air before beginning even the shortest sentence. This was accompanied by an inordinate amount of face rubbing with huge, ham-like hands.

I had seen him frequently in the House of Assembly, but had not noticed until quite recently that he walked with a pronounced limp, something I later discovered had been caused by a gunshot accident, although some hinted at a more sinister origin,

When I went to his house, his wife, a tiny, grey, mousy woman dressed in a knee-length cardigan, told me he was at his constituency office on Church Avenue. This proved to be upstairs in a large brick building near Main Street.

At once, I wondered about disabled access and if Fred had somehow obtained exemption from the rules, but when I went through the narrow, yellow street door, I saw that there was an ancient elevator in the far corner.

I took this to the third floor, the minute cage shaking and vibrating violently as it struggled with the ascent, exited into a set of rooms, painted in similarly loud yellow, and found myself facing an enormous, middle-aged woman dwarfing a desk built for far lesser mortals.

"What can I do for you, dear?" she boomed.

"I'd like to see Fred. I'm one of his colleagues in the legislature."

"Are you, now? Do you have a name?"

"Marc LeBlanc."

"Aha. You're the one, aren't you?"

"Am I?" I asked, having no idea what she meant.

"I'll see if Mr. Askey is available."

"Please do."

She swivelled her chair 180 degrees and kicked a door behind her desk. It swung open to reveal Fred listening to some sports event on a small transistor radio.

He looked up and switched off the radio. "LeBlanc! It's you. You'd better come in."

"Hello, Fred. I guess John told you I'd be coming."

"Yeah. He called about ten minutes ago. Said you and him had a long, cozy chat."

"Yes, we did. I was hoping you and I could have one, too."

"Oh yeah? What do you want to know?"

"I won't beat around the bush, Fred. I'm here because the premier sent me."

"He could have called me himself." Fred rubbed his hand over the back of his neck. "If he had any questions, he could have picked up the phone and called me. I don't know why he thought it necessary to use a middleman."

"Yes, I'm sorry about that, Fred. But he's extremely busy."

"Hah! That old excuse. Busy!"

"It happens to be true."

"Busy for me. But I'll bet not busy for others!"

"I can't comment on that."

"Well, what *can* you comment on?" He was now furiously running his hands over his face.

"I was asked to convey a request from the premier. He wants to know who he can rely on if things get rough in the future."

"If he had asked me, I would have told him that things always get rough in the future if you wait long enough."

"I guess that's true."

"So there you are. Are we done?"

"Not yet."

"What now?"

"He wants to know if he can rely on you. You haven't actually an-swered that one way or another."

"You're so smart. You figure it out."

"Fred, the premier is not only going to want to know what I learned, but how easy or how difficult it was for me to obtain the in-formation."

"What's that supposed to mean?"

"I think you know what it means."

"You little shit! Who the fuck do you think you are? You've only been in this business five minutes and already you're lording it over the rest of us."

"I'm not lording it over anyone. The premier asked me to do something and I'm trying to do it."

"Well, you can fuck off and do it somewhere else!"

"Thank you, Fred, for your time," I said quietly as I stood up. According to my instructions, I would report my findings and the nature of my reception to the premier and John Trevor.

When I came out of Fred's office, the constituency assistant was standing at the window, blocking most of the light coming into the room, so at first I had difficulty seeing the outer door. I muttered my thanks to her and navigated my way into the shaking elevator.

I had expected a rough, but comradely, reception from Askey, and was surprised he was so hostile. I imagined that if this was what I received from him it would be a great deal worse from others. The question which bothered me was whether Askey's hostility was towards me or towards Wendell.

When I got back to the Bugatti I called John. "I've just seen Fred."

"How'd it go, Marc?"

"Couldn't have been worse. He was foul-tempered and called me names."

"What did he call you?"

"A little shit."

"Hmm. Could be worse, but it's not good. I guess we have to put him in the 'maybe' column?"

"I'm doubtful about that, even. I put the question to him head on: Could the premier count on him if things got rough."

"What did he say?"

"He wouldn't give me an answer."

"Really? The bastard."

"Does he get paid as a whip?"

"Yes. It's not much. A few hundred a year."

"Not much leverage there."

"Not much. I'll have a word with him. If he gives me a hard time, I'll give his job to someone else. Who're you seeing next?"

"Zila Franks."

"Shouldn't have any trouble there."

~

I wandered around eastern Hants County, but could not find Zila's constituency office. It had been some months since she had been elected so she should have had time to find and open a place where her constituents could come to see her. For some reason, I had her home address, but not one for her office, so I gave up the search for the latter and drove to the outskirts of Shubenacadie, where I found her dwelling.

Zila lived in the bottom half of a medium-sized house on the main road. The place badly needed a coat of paint and the yard could certainly have used a thorough clean-up. The door to Zila's apartment was at the rear of the house, so I picked my way there through lumps of old concrete and rotten fence pickets. There was no bell or knocker so I thumped on the door.

For a second or two, when Zila opened the door, I thought it was someone else. I had not taken a lot of notice of her at Province House during the session, but she had registered in my mind as a bulky woman of about forty-five with dirty blonde hair. I suppose I must have been aware that, when in the Legislature, she wore her best clothes and a fair amount of makeup, but not that these created, in effect, an entirely different person. The only thing the woman standing in the doorway had in common with the one I knew in Halifax was her size, for she now appeared to be well into her fifties, her face lined and blotchy, and her hair grey and dishevelled.

"Marc! Good God, what are you doing here?" As she asked the question she maneuvered herself into a position where more of her was outside than in, a move I took to indicate that she did not want me to enter the house.

"Hello, Zila. I looked for your constituency office, but couldn't find it."

"It's temporarily in Stewiacke. It's over the border in another riding, but that's all I could find for the time being."

"Ah, that explains it. I'm sorry to intrude, but may I come in? I need to talk to you."

"What about?" she asked, not budging from her sentinel stance.

"The premier asked me to see you."

"Oh God." She stared at me like an animal at bay, then started to weep.

"Zila, it's not bad news or anything like that."

"I hope not, Marc, I've got plenty of that already."

"Let's go inside."

"Oh, jeepers." She looked over her shoulder as if she were being hunted. "The place is a mess."

"That's okay. I'm used to messes."

She paused for a moment then, with a huge sigh, flung the door open.

She was right. It was a mess, but rather than the expected piles of laundry on chairs and unwashed dishes, it looked like burglars had ransacked the place. I did not ask what had happened, but removed a vase, two books and some kind of musical instrument from a chair and sat down.

"I guess this is not a good time, but—"

"No, it isn't."

"I won't take long, I promise."

"Okay. Go ahead."

"The premier wanted to know if he can rely on you if things get rough for him."

"How? When?"

"Whenever. However. It's an abstract question, not related to anything specific."

"Oh. Not that library assistant."

"No."

"Because I may have muttered something about that."

"Yes you did. I remember. But you were satisfied when she signed the denial?"

"Yes. Pretty much."

"Pretty much?"

"There are always doubts hanging after something like that."

"Not serious doubts?"

"No, not serious."

"Well, that aside, how would you answer the question?"

"What was it again? I'm all at sixes and sevens today."

"If he can rely on you if things get rough for him?"

"Yes, I guess so…" She trailed off, her eyes reviewing the disorder around us.

"I need something a little more definite than that."

"It would depend, wouldn't it?"

"Depend on what?"

"On what happens between now and then, I guess."

"I am not sure I know what to tell the premier, Zila. Does that mean you'll back him unless something dramatic happens?"

"Yes, something like that."

"But not a drop in polls? A decrease in his public popularity wouldn't drive you to, say, backing a non-confidence motion?"

"No, I guess not."

"You're not making it easy for me. The premier needs to know where you stand."

"Oh, for God's sake, stop hounding me, Marc!" she shouted and immediately burst into tears. She sobbed quite violently for at least five minutes, during which I thought it best to hold my peace.

"I guess I haven't caught you on a good day," I said when she had stopped crying.

"The very worst day. Just look at this fucking place, will you?"

"What happened? Did you have burglars?"

"Yeah, you could say that. My own damn son ransacked the place and robbed me blind."

"Your son?"

"Yes, he's nineteen. The little bastard is what they call a problem child. You know, booze, drugs, all that stuff. He's been impossible to handle ever since his father went."

"Went? Where did he go?"

"Who the fuck knows? Just disappeared one day and I have never heard from him again."

"Oh, I am so sorry. What did the boy take?"

"All my jewellery, although that's not worth a whole lot, and the cash I had drawn out for the rent and what I owed to the store for the last two weeks' orders."

"How much would that have been?"

"About two thousand dollars."

"Do you know where he went?"

"Same place he always goes after he comes home and takes everything he can get. Somewhere in Toronto. I don't exactly know where."

"Do you...er...have other...resources?"

"Resources? *Resources*? What the hell is that?"

"Money. Do you have any money put by?"

"No, not a damn bean." She sniffled and wiped her nose on the edge of her sleeve. "And the landlord said that if I was in arrears one more time, she'd kick me out."

"Zila. I can let you have two thousand. No problem at all."

"You're joking?"

"No, of course I'm not joking."

"Oh God, Marc, you are a real star."

"Will two grand be enough?"

"I think it will tide me over until next payday. Thanks so much, Marc."

"I don't have that much in cash. Is a cheque any good?"

"Oh sure. I can get to the Scotia Bank before it closes. Thanks again, Marc."

With some difficulty I cleared a space on the table, wrote a cheque for twenty-five hundred, and handed it to her.

"I made it out for a bit more, just in case you need it."

For a second I thought she might throw herself at me and try to kiss me, but she just grabbed my hand and shook it vigorously.

"I'd better get going before they close," she said as she snatched her purse and rushed out, leaving me alone in an unlocked house.

As I wandered back to the Bugatti, I reflected that politics was not the domain of riches, excitement and luxury which many imagine it to be. After all, I thought, there was no reason why the elected MLAs should not fairly accurately represent the people who chose them, being a cross-section of society in all its gaiety and suffering, its triumphs and woes, its anger and its hopelessness. I had certainly seen a little of two of those conditions today.

24

The next day was the one on which Rosalie had decreed we should go to Halifax. I had it in my mind to do the western end of the province first, but she said she was anxious to see Cynthia and Wendell again, so I acquiesced because, in the long run, it made no difference to my mission.

There were ten of our MLAs in the Halifax area (eleven, if one counted Wendell), and while I should rather have seen them in their homes, I realized it would not always be practical and that the four ministers would have to be seen in their offices. I further realized that I should take this opportunity to see those who were ministers but from outside Halifax County. Since there were nine of them, I was looking at a week's stay in the capital.

This would enable Rosalie to spend time with Cynthia, go shopping and see our great friend Ruth Kennedy, wife of an RCMP superintendent with whom I had been associated on a number of cases in my capacity as a private investigator. That would suit me, because I thought taking my wife with me to meet the MLAs would not be a good idea in all cases. There were some visits, such as to Jill Rutledge and Jennie Chan, where Rosalie might be an asset, but many interviews would be sensitive and, not being in possession of all the background, she might say the wrong thing and exacerbate an already-tense situation.

Having told myself that about Rosalie, it dawned on me that I myself had been guilty of the same kind of solecism. From the outset I had been asking directly what their intentions were in respect of Wendell's leadership, when I should have been asking for their *advice*. The kind of advice they gave me, and the manner in which they gave it, would likely reveal as much, if not more, about their designs and aspirations. The same objection would doubtless be raised that Wendell could have called the MLAs in person rather than employ a go-between, but an approach seeking counsel for the premier would almost certainly be better received than a demand to know the status of their support.

"It will be so good to see Cynthia again," she said as we were crossing the Avon causeway. "She is such a lovely person."

"I agree. She's very special. But it was not always wine and roses with her and Wendell. Tom Aldridge told me that they had a hard time when they first went out together."

"Why was that? I vaguely recall Cynthia telling us something about it."

"You remember. Wendell's family were dead set against the relationship, especially his mother Blossom and sister Grace."

"Oh yes. I can believe it about Grace. She is one loud, bossy woman. What was her problem with Cynthia?"

"She thought Wendell should marry a black girl."

"Ah yes. How did they get around that obstacle?"

"When Wendell was running for the party leadership, Grace's husband, Matthew, told her that he'd get more votes if he had a white wife!"

"Good God!"

"From that moment on, it became Grace's idea and she suddenly became Cynthia's best friend."

"Matthew is a nice guy."

"He's more than that. He's a really smart gentleman. He doesn't have much to say, but his head and heart are always in the right place. I'd trust him with my life."

"I called Cynthia yesterday to let her know when we were coming. She said we could stay as long as we liked."

"That's Cynthia. She's kindness itself."

"She asked how long we'd be staying, but I didn't know what to say."

"You can stay as long as you want, sweetheart. I figure I'll be there a week, then I'm heading east. Eventually to Cape Breton."

"If it's alright with Cynthia, I might stay another week. Or until you come back from Cape Breton. Do you know when that would be?"

"Three days, four maximum. I have only four people to see. One in Pictou and three on the island."

We lapsed into silence and I closed my eyes. I cast my mind back on my experiences to date. My one on one meetings were limited so far to three, but they had caused me to think much about what politics does to people: how "normal" people one day could become fanatics the next, and how those with few ambitions could acquire a burning motivation for advancement.

I was a prime example. Only a few months ago I was totally apolitical, had no interest in politics and could not have told you the policies of any of the parties if you had put a gun to my head. Now, through an initial freak accident, I was a staunch partisan, in the inner circle of government, and carrying out a delicate task for the leader of my party.

When I asked myself how this had happened, the answer also explained what induced the attitudes of the others I had seen. I supposed that all human beings wanted some sense of belonging, if possible some perception of being special and some degree of recognition. I recognized that I was where I was because I had been flattered, first by being asked by Wendell to be a candidate, then by Tom telling me I was one of the "in" group, and finally by being asked to undertake an important role in the leader's future.

Reduced to that, I reflected that it did not paint me in a very creditable light. But, to a large extent it seemed to be the *raison d'être* of politics. It was clear to me that Fred Askey, Zila Franks and even John Trevor would respond to any kind of positive attention from Wendell. It might be only a kind word (as I saw him administering to George Savory and Art Sullivan in the House); but a personal phone call would be better, and an appointment to some kind of office, such as Whip, better still. The ultimate preferment for all who were outside that august body would be elevation to the cabinet.

At whatever level an MLA might find him- or herself, they lived for some indication that they might rise to the next. Their days were spent hoping, maybe even praying, for a suggestion from above that the leader smiled on them and might one day reward their loyalty. Thus it was that some undistinguished backbenchers might spend years waiting for gradual promotion from insignificance to prominence, hanging on the leader's every word and gesture.

Politics had its rewards, but it was not a place for those with thin skins or easily-hurt pride. It made people do things they would not otherwise think of. It forced them to speak and vote for measures to

which they were personally opposed, to vote and speak against measures they supported. It encouraged them to boast, to exaggerate, to
sneer and condemn in circumstances which did not call for it. Worst
of all, it often compelled them to fawn, to flatter, to crawl and sometimes to beg.

I was forced to concede that I was not a better person now than I
was before I had been corralled into running in the election. Maybe
that was what Rosalie had spotted, or sensed, and it made her uneasy,
if not resentful.

~

Wendell and Cynthia Proctor lived in a large old house on upper Got-
tingen Street, in the heart of the premier's constituency. They had no
children, so there was plenty of room for themselves and for guests. I
gathered that sometimes some of Wendell's relatives from Truro
came to stay, and occasionally, Cynthia's parents visited from Ontario.

However, this did not mean that the house was very often empty
because, Cynthia told us, Wendell's parents dropped in frequently,
and so did his sister, Grace, and her husband, Matthew, together with
various uncles and aunts, most of whom lived in the city's north end.

Cynthia had once told me that when the Proctor family did des-
cend, the women loudly occupied the kitchen, while the men sat
around the living room, speaking in undertones. Grace, who was a
large, sometimes bullying, big-bosomed woman, made her presence
felt in no uncertain terms. She made it clear that she took credit for
Wendell's becoming premier and for his marrying Cynthia, on whom
she doted, having conveniently forgotten that initially she had been
violently opposed to the match. In contrast, Cynthia said Grace's husband was "a darling", a man of very few words and an extraordinarily
good and generous nature. Despite Wendell's exalted status, apparently, they all treated his house as if it were a community centre, coming and going pretty much as they pleased.

However, Cynthia told us, the premier had put his foot down now
that we were coming to stay. He had instructed the family to keep
their visits to a minimum, and on no account to come unannounced.
He had told his mother, Blossom, and Grace that since he would need
to have many confidential discussions with me, it would not be

proper to have them dropping by at all hours of the day and night. In the interests of the province, they had grudgingly agreed.

Cynthia had arranged it so that we had a bedroom and bathroom on the top floor of the house so we might have some privacy, but, unless we preferred otherwise, that we should eat with her and her husband. This involved a certain adjustment for us, at least for me, as we had become used to a somewhat rarefied diet and to particularly good wine with our meals. Simple food was to be the order of the day, but we agreed we would be none the worse for that.

Cynthia greeted us at the door with the warmth we remembered and took us up to our room.

"Wendell's in Truro for some meeting or other," she said as we followed her upstairs. "I never have any idea when he'll be back. We'll give him until six, and if he isn't back by then, we'll go ahead and have dinner without him."

"Can I help you prepare the dinner, Cynthia?" Rosalie asked.

"Both of you can help. I need to peel the vegetables."

"Marc's the man for that. He's a great peeler."

"Unlike Wendell, who is the great repealer these days." I said, but they did not get the joke.

"You can lay the table for me, Rosalie." Said Cynthia. "We'll drink wine while we do the work. With any luck we'll all be slightly drunk by the time we eat."

She said this in a surprising, almost sad, tone. I looked closely at her as she stood in the middle of what would be our bedroom. She was still beautiful, cheerful and impeccably dressed, but I noticed a few more wrinkles around her eyes and mouth. Being premier was a stressful job, but in many ways, being the premier's wife would be even worse because she had to suffer the consequences of decisions and actions in which she had no say.

And I knew from my own experience that Wendell was not an easy man. Certainly, he could be generous and hospitable and great fun to be with, but everything had to be done his way. He did not suffer fools gladly, and sometimes was impatient with and intolerant of those whose intellect was not as considerable as his own. In addition, like all heads of governments, he had a convenient memory and an infinite capacity to dispense with those who no longer served a useful purpose to him. Just as Rosalie was detecting unpleasant characteristics emerging in me, I supposed that Cynthia was seeing an over-abundance of them in Wendell.

We had a lovely, boozy time preparing, then eating dinner. We had steaks with potatoes, carrots and onions and a plain, but pleasant, Chilean Pinot Noir.

We exchanged stories, laughed a lot, and when we went up to bed after ten o' clock, Wendell had still not come home.

25

The next day I managed to see six of the ministers. Several of them questioned, logically and justifiably, why they should give their views to me when the premier could ask them himself. But most were tolerant and did me the courtesy of hearing me out.

Mark Gardiner, Minister of Tourism and Culture, was every bit as prickly and hostile with me as he had been two years ago when I had interviewed him, and it was quite clear that, while he picked his words with some care, his loyalty to the premier would only last as long as it was of practical use to him. Further than that, I detected a seething ambition, which suggested he was just waiting for Wendell to fall so he might make another bid to get into the premier's office.

"I hope you have what you want," Gardiner said as he opened the door, indicating that as far as he was concerned our interview was over.

"I think so. Thank you, Minister."

"It can't be a very pleasant occupation running errands for someone else."

"I don't think of it in those terms."

"Well, you wouldn't, would you?"

"I think the premier thought he might get a more accurate reading of where people stand than if he approached them himself."

"Really?"

"I think most people would be more sycophantic in person. More inclined to flatter."

"I wouldn't," he said defiantly.

"Obviously, I was excluding present company, Minister."

He gave me a scowl, and literally pushed me out of the office.

The Mines and Energy Minister, Harold MacDonald, greeted me like a long-lost friend, and nearly shook my hand off. A one-time miner himself, he was short and stocky, with a shiny bald head and what seemed like a permanent smile. He said that Wendell was without doubt the greatest premier within living memory, and that few other provinces were as fortunate as ours. He told me, over and over, how devoted and loyal to Wendell he was, and at first I thought he must be the premier's biggest supporter.

But then I recalled that John Trevor had warned me that MacDonald was "the biggest liar on God's green earth" and I was forced to wonder how sincere he was. I may have been wrong, but I judged that MacDonald would cling to the ship until it was clear it was going to sink, and only then would jump clear. Unlike Gardiner, this man did not long for greater things, but was happy being a big fish in a small pool and did not want anything to disturb that.

My interview with Justice Minister Angela Stairs was curious. I had expected her to be cold, aloof and generally unresponsive. The last time I had met with her one on one, she had clearly resented my being there and as good as said I was wasting her time, a charge with which I could not, in all conscience, have argued.

I found her to be very cold, and I imagined she would be ruthlessly efficient, but because she seemed more like a machine than a woman, I thought her an unlikely suspect to harbour strong feelings about any human being. I recall Wendell telling me that Stairs was his most able minister, and had called her a "frigid bitch."

Therefore, I was greatly surprised when I found that, on this occasion, she seemed glad to see me.

She started by saying how impressed she had been by my speech to caucus about the library assistant. Apparently, she had been somewhat taken aback by my not having been emotional, but having presented the facts in a precise manner.

"Are you a lawyer, Marc?"

"No. A private investigator."

"Really? I've been a member of the bar for almost twenty years and I don't think I've ever met a private investigator."

"There aren't many of us."

"I suppose not. Well, we'd better get down to business. I have a meeting across the street."

"Okay. It's just that the boss wants your advice on what he should and should not do to maintain the support of caucus and party."

"I see. Why did he send you?"

"He thinks the answers I get will be more candid than if he asked in person."

"How strange," she sniffed and sat back in her chair. "Well, I suppose the first thing to say is that I will support Wendell except under the most extreme circumstances."

"Which would be...?"

"I could not tolerate criminality. Or corruption."

"Administrative or moral?"

"That's a most intelligent question. Both, I guess. If proved."

"That's fair enough."

"But if he wants to be sure of his future, he must be less arrogant, less bullying, and must consult before dropping bombshells on the caucus."

"I would call that good advice. Thank you so much, Minister."

"Angela."

"Yes, Angela."

The Minister of Finance, Chester McCormack, had been a stalwart and rock of the party for many years. He was considered to be a man of impeccable judgment and considerable ability. He brought to his job dedication and hard work, but did not generally get involved in intra-party intrigue. I judged him to be in mid-sixties. He was tallish but rather stooped, and his face was still relatively free of lines and was pink and shiny. His most striking features were two bright-blue, laughing eyes and enormous bushy eyebrows.

Wendell told me that when the inner group were looking for a candidate for premier following Brenton Granger's death, he had come third in an open ballot. Tom Aldridge, who was then an MLA, had topped the list and McCormack had come second. When both of them had declined to accept the honour, Wendell stepped into the breach. He was widely liked and greatly respected not only by the party, but also by the media and Opposition.

Getting anything substantive out of McCormack was like pulling teeth. He would discourse at great length about public policy, but would not talk about party affairs.

"You know, Marc, gossip is rarely of any value to anybody. What is on everybody's tongues today may be totally forgotten by tomorrow."

"I understand. But if you were to give the premier one piece of advice, what would it be?"

"I would not be so impertinent as to give advice to my premier un-less it concerned matters within the purview of my portfolio."

"Let me put it this way, Minister—"

"Chester."

"Chester. If you were premier, what advice would you want to re-ceive?"

"I should want advice to the effect that I should continue whatever I was doing." He laughed heartily.

"I mean what advice would you *need*?"

"Ah, that's different from *want*. The advice I would need would be to always pay attention to the little guy. One little guy may be nothing, two almost nothing, but three little guys could be a rebellion."

"Point taken. Thank you."

As I walked towards the elevator, I thought that McCormack's age freed him from the slavery of ambition. It also probably meant he would not run in the next election. So, there being no personal motive to dislodge the present leadership, the likelihood was that he would provide strong, but mostly silent, support even in a serious crisis. Or so I hoped, as the doors opened and I stepped inside.

Stephanie Gilmour, the Health Minister, was a good-looking, soph-isticated woman in her late thirties. You could tell from looking at the way she was groomed and dressed that she came from money. I do not mean my kind of money, which was of relatively recent acquisi-tion, but what was often called "old money." Not that I was an expert in such matters, but I judged the clothes and jewellery she was wear-ing as being worth about $20,000. She was from Halifax aristocracy, very well spoken and with perfect manners.

As I looked at her, I recalled the rumour I had heard that she had been seriously in love with Tom Aldridge and that they had gone out together until he had fallen for Heidi. Apparently she was still single, and the word was that she still pined for Tom.

She made it clear from the outset that she was a confirmed Wendell supporter and would stay that way. Only his committing some heinous crime would get her to change her mind. Despite the fervour of her commitment to Wendell, however, she, too, thought he was too arrogant and high-handed and that, if not checked, this atti-tude might lead to serious trouble down the line.

Next to Tom, Deputy Premier Joan Howard was the closest to the premier and made no bones about her devotion to him. She was a most remarkable woman, with an even more extraordinary life story. An almost unbelievably-beautiful woman, Joan had spent her early years in Nova Scotia, had left for California when she was a teenager and had become an international movie star by the time she was twenty.

Some eight years ago, she had been shooting a movie on the South Shore and had met Harold Nickerson, whose long liner fishing boat had been hired by the production company for some sea scenes. They fell madly in love. Joan gave up acting, moved back to the province, and subsequently was elected to the legislature. Being highly instrumental in Wendell's selection as party leader, Joan had remained his number-one booster.

Clearly, Wendell had told her about my mission and she launched into paeans of praise as soon as I was seated. This suited me because, like most men, I found it difficult to talk to Joan because she exuded such beauty and femininity that it made me feel bashful and embarrassed. So, I just sat and listened...and admired.

I made notes on the day's findings and concluded that, added to results of the previous day's visits, so far we had two outright hostile, two unreliable, three likely solid and two utterly solid. The more I thought about that, the more worried I became.

26

I woke early the next morning and, creeping quietly so as not to wake Rosalie, I went downstairs to find Wendell in the kitchen eating a bowl of cereal. It was a ritual with him to have cornflakes very early in the day, then later to have his secretary bring him a fried egg sandwich from a café on the corner, which he ate at his desk. I knew from having stayed at his home before that he was a man who needed little sleep and was a very early riser.

He looked up and grinned. "Hey, Marc. How'd you get on yesterday? Manage to see many?"

"'Morning, Wendell. Saw six ministers. It didn't go too badly."

"Let me have all the details."

"If you don't mind, I'd rather wait until I have a bigger picture. With certain exceptions, providing the information in dribs and drabs could lead to a false analysis of the overall situation."

"Okay, If you say so. But you'll let me know if there are any huge surprises or warning signals?"

"I will."

I dragged up a chair and poured myself a coffee. "I haven't uncovered anything too wildly extraordinary to date, but there are a few points I thought I should mention."

"Anything which needs immediate attention?"

"Yes, one thing immediately. And one intermediate."

"What's the immediate?"

"You're not going to like it."

"I guessed that from the way you're pussyfooting about. What is it?"

"Friend and foe alike say you're too arrogant."

"Arrogant, me?" He laughed. "You mean, not listening, giving people the brush-off, not consulting, being big headed, et cetera?"

"Yes, exactly those things."

"Okay. I'll see what I can do to reduce their occurrence. What's the intermediate item?"

"Within the next six months you should elevate John to the cabinet. And before that, you should let him know you're going to do it."

"John Trevor? Is he shaky?"

"No, not exactly shaky, but he needs some recognition for his efforts and loyalty."

"Hmm. I was thinking of bringing in Freeman Murphy or Dan Nathanson in the next shuffle, but it'll be John if you think it necessary."

"Yes, I do, from a political perspective, and I think it would also be the right thing to do."

"If I did that, who would replace John as Chief Whip? Fred Askey?"

"Good God, no!"

"Ah." He looked surprised at my response. "I won't ask for details. At least not now. If not him, then who?"

"It's too early for me to offer advice. In a week or two I may be able to do that."

"Fair enough." He took his bowl and spoon to the sink and methodically washed them out.

As he was putting these on the draining tray, his phone buzzed.

"Yeah? Oh, hey, Susan. What does he want? Shit! Okay, give me his number."

He scribbled a number on some paper towel and turned to me. "Marc, take a look outside the door and see if *The Herald* has arrived yet."

The newspaper was on the ground, tangled up in a bush, but I extricated it and brought it back into the house. I moved my coffee cup to the counter, put the paper on the table and smoothed it out.

The primary headline was about war in the Middle East, but the secondary headline jumped out at me.

> GOVERNMENT MLA SAYS PREMIER TOLD HIM
> OKAY TO TAKE MONEY.
> NO COMMENT FROM PROCTOR

"Oh, fuck!"

"What is it?" Wendell demanded, trying to peer over my shoulder. "Read me what it says."

"Okay. *Richmond MLA Alaric D'Entremont, who has been accused by a constituent of demanding $500 from him following a successful pension appeal, says Premier Proctor told him it was okay to take the money—*"

"Like fuck I did!"

"*D'Entremont said he had personally researched and conducted the appeal on behalf of Albany Boudreau of Petit de Grat and had obtained a settlement of over $10,000. He said he asked Mr. Boudreau for 5% of the settlement to cover his time and expenses—*"

"Asshole!"

"*When he became aware that Mr. Boudreau might take the matter to the news media, D'Entremont said he asked the premier if it would be all right to take the money and the premier said that it would.*"

"Lying little toad!"

"*Premier Proctor could not be reached for comment.*"

"Bastards! I'm always available for comment!"

"Holy crap! What really happened, Wendell?"

"That was Susan just now. She gave me a message to call the paper. I'm going to do that right away."

"Wait 'til you've cooled down."

"Don't worry, Marc, I'll be plenty cool...Is this Bill MacTeague? Wendell Proctor here....If you'll stop talking and start listening, I'll tell you what really happened. Right. D'Entremont told me what happened. I told him to give the money back because he's already getting paid as an MLA...wait, I'm not finished yet...Then I said that if he had been a lawyer, it probably would have been *legal* for him to take it as a fee for service, but not *moral*...Wait will you?...But I said that since he was *not* a lawyer he had no excuse and should return the money right away....What? No, I'm definitely *not* saying that lawyers who are MLAs should take money from people. Get that straight."

Wendell took out a handkerchief and wiped the perspiration which had appeared on his brow. "Now, listen to me, Bill. I know you won't read a story back to me before it's printed, but just tell me the main points I have just made....What? If you don't, you never get another story out of me or my office....How about if I just list the main points?...Okay, I'll go over them again slowly. One, he told me what happened. Two, I told him to return the money. Three, I said that if a lawyer did it, it might be legal, but not moral. Four, MLAs should provide their services free of charge. Did you get that?...Okay."

"You certainly displayed a lot of cool there," I said with a grin, once he had hung up. "Did he ask you if you intended to discipline D'Entremont?"

"No, he didn't. I wonder why. I'll call Freeman and ask him to bring this up in caucus. If the Opposition demands that it be taken to the House Rules and Privileges Committee, it will have to be heard. It will depend on the skill of the committee chairman how it will be dealt with there."

"Who is the Chairman of the Rules and Privileges Committee?"

"I am." He was smiling from ear to ear.

"And I imagine we have a majority on the committee?"

"We have five, the Official Opposition have three and the other crowd has one. It could be quite a show. Dana Edwards is the on the committee and she will be a crusading voice for goodness and light. John Wilkins will be all right. He's a sensible guy and he's a lawyer, so he knows the limits of the committee's powers. But he has Cliff Wolf and Bill Jenkins as their other members, and they are slavering, rabid, partisan fanatics."

"So, in short: one will be calling a crucifixion, two for tearing Alaric to pieces, and the others will be voices of moderation and tolerance."

"More or less."

We sat drinking our coffee in silence for a few minutes, then Wendell looked across at me.

"Know what I'm thinking?"

"I never know what you're thinking." I said.

He sniggered. "You should cut short your visits here, and head straight to Cape Breton to see D'Entremont."

"What would I do, or say, to him?"

"First, tell him he is on the very thinnest of ice. Second, tell him he says one more word to the media, he's finished. Third, tell him to stay inside and talk to nobody until he is sent for. Fourth, tell him what to expect if it goes to committee—"

"But I don't know what goes on in that committee."

"You can guess. It'll be a brawl. Wilkins' people will demand a monetary fine. Edwards will demand expulsion. A compromise might be suspension from the services of the House for two weeks."

"Okay." I was busy getting these points into my phone. "What about caucus?"

"Tell him he could be expelled from caucus if he tells any more lies or is not fully contrite. He could be expelled from the party, but that'd be up to the Provincial Council, not us."

"What leeway would I have?"

"Anything you think will work."

"John Trevor told me that Alaric was treacherous, and would sell his own mother for ten bucks."

"Yes, he is totally without any morals. Completely unscrupulous. Frankly, we'd be better off without him, but if he went, our majority in the house would drop to nine. And if any of the women who were up in arms about the library assistant decided to leave, we could be down to six or even five."

"I doubt that would ever happen."

"You never know. It's always better to have a bigger cushion than a small one."

"So, with Alaric, should I go in as the heavy?"

"As heavy as you like."

"How about I paint as grim a picture of his future as I can, then say that his only chance of survival is if I can persuade you to intervene on his behalf?"

"I like it!"

"But that you'll take a lot of persuading, because he has put you in such a difficult position."

"Even better!"

"That covers the threats. I don't suppose there are any promises I could hint at?"

"Jesus, no!" He screwed his face up and peered at me through narrowed eyes. "At least, none that we would keep."

"You mean I should promise something I knew you would never honour?"

"I'll leave it to you. If you're not comfortable with that, I'll understand. But if you could leave the impression that there might be some rewards for a man who kept his nose clean over an extended period of time, well..."

"I'd have to think about that."

"Sure."

Wendell stood up and started to put papers into his briefcase. "I guess you'll have to tell Rosalie."

"Of course I will. I'll go up and tell her now."

"You have the Bugatti with you?"

"Yes."

"How's it running? Is it as good as the one you had before? I'll never forget that spin out to the airport we did."

"Even better." I remembered the event to which he referred. It was very early on a misty morning when, on his instructions, I broke the speed limit by considerable margins. "It runs like a dream."

"Good. If you leave within the hour, you could be in Arichat well before noon."

27

I had to wake Rosalie, and it took me a little time to tell her that I was leaving immediately for points east.

"What do you mean, you're going now? Where?"

"To Arichat. It's an emergency."

"Emergency? Don't be so stupid." She was still half asleep.

"It's for Wendell. He asked me to go."

She glared at me, then pulled the blankets over her head. A motioning arm stuck out on one side, but it was not so much a wave goodbye as a gesture to vamoose.

I lost no time in following her instructions, hastily packed a bag in case I might have to stay the night, and went out to the Bugatti. In the early-morning sunlight, its blue lines on the gleaming white body looked stunning and, as many times in the past, I gave thanks that I owned such a beautiful machine.

Once on the road, I put in a call to Tom Aldridge to see if he could tell me more about Alaric D'Entremont. Tom confirmed what Wendell and John Trevor had told me: that Alaric was a man of virtually no principles.

"But Marc," said Tom, "the man has an attractive personality which hides a ruthless con man. You must watch out for that. He could charm the birds out of the trees."

"It sounds as if you have personal experience of this."

"Indeed I do. When he was first elected almost five years ago he talked me into 'investing' in a surefire scheme. When I found out I'd lost all my money and confronted him, he just grinned like a Cheshire cat."

"Did he say anything?"

"Yes. He said: 'You win some, you lose some,' and walked away.

"I hope I don't get sucked in."

"Marc, you have to come at him like a ton of bricks. Don't take any crap."

"I don't know if I can do that."

"If you let him take the early initiative you'll be lost. Of course, you'll have to find him first."

"Why should that be a problem?"

"It wouldn't surprise me if he is hiding out somewhere. He drives a bright-yellow Nissan Juke, so keep a lookout for that."

It took me less than three hours to get to Arichat. I saw no RCMP vehicles along the way, so the Bugatti had a chance to perform, nowhere near its limit of 434 kph, but in admirable fashion.

One of the two great advantages of owning a car like this was that it occasionally allowed for stretches at speeds around 170 kph, and allowed passing other vehicles very quickly because the acceleration was so remarkable.

It had been a long time since I had been on île Madame, and it was good to revisit these sleepy little fishing communities which had been originally founded by ten Acadian families in 1758. When thousands of their countrymen had been deported from Louisbourg after the British had conquered the fortress, these adventurous families had slipped through the net and fled to île Royale, as it was then called. Today, some 4,500 souls inhabited the island, 40% of them claiming French as their first language.

On my way across Lennox Passage, I wondered if I could pull off this assignment. While I was by no means a shrimp or weakling, I was not stockily built and did not think I looked very threatening. In my previous occupation as a floor trader and merchant banker, I had needed to keep my nerve and often to be quite aggressive. I hoped that the first few minutes with D'Entremont might give me a clue as to how to handle him thereafter.

The whole task would be easier if we were face to face in private, but trickier if other people intruded. I certainly hoped that the media had got their pound of flesh, were too lazy to travel to what, for them, would be a backwater, and would concentrate on Wendell for any follow-up.

My hope for privacy was dashed as soon as I drove along the main street of Arichat and immediately saw a yellow Juke parked outside a restaurant called The Island Nest. I reluctantly concluded that the chances of there being more than one car of this description on the island were very low, so I pulled the Bugatti in alongside it.

Outside the door was a handmade sign advising me that the day's special was roast pork with carrots and mashed potatoes for $12.99.

The restaurant was a quite large, clean room containing about fifteen tables. On one side there was a bar and in the far corner a small stage, where I presumed a band played at night. There were about a dozen people lunching, all of them dressed in overalls, plaid shirts and ball caps.

Except one.

Sprawled at a table by the window at the far end of the room was Alaric D'Entremont. He was attired in a white linen suit and wore sunglasses, which I took to be an affectation, considering we were indoors and the light was not that bright.

Without waiting for an invitation, I sat down.

"Marc LeBlanc isn't it?" he asked with a big smile.

"You know it is," I snarled.

At that moment the waitress came to the table and asked if we wanted to order.

"Nothing for me," I said.

"Alaric, how about you?"

"I'll have the special, darling," he said, "but it says $12.99."

"Yes, that's right."

"How much without the potatoes?"

"Same price, Alaric."

"You should knock off a dollar or two for no spuds."

"I can't. I'd get fired. Do you want it or not?"

"Sure. Then I'll have the apple pie with the double header of ice cream."

"Okay," she said, scribbling in her notebook.

"And make sure it is a double header. Or there'll be trouble."

"And you can kiss my arse," the waitress said defiantly, tossed her head and walked back to the kitchen.

"Now, my good sir," he said, turning to me, "what brings you to île Madame?"

"Listen you piece of shit," I snapped, amazing myself at the feigned hostility I was able to summon. "Take those fucking sunglasses off or I'll knock them into next week!"

He was obviously taken aback, quickly removed the glasses, and stared at me wide-eyed.

"The minute you've finished your lunch, I'll see you outside. You got a phone?"

"Sure, I do."

"Give it to me. Now!"

Still somewhat in shock he slid it across the table. I put it into my pocket and stood up.

"Thirty minutes. If you're not out by then, I'm coming in to get you. Understand, you miserable, no good bastard?"

He nodded.

As I was walking out I passed the waitress, who was wearing a little badge marked 'Denise' attached to her apron. She glanced at me, nodded her head in Alaric's direction and rolled her eyes.

When I got outside I was feeling a little weak as a result of a mixture of fear and triumph. I had no idea what I would have done if he had answered back or, God forbid, hit me. But I knew the die was cast and that I had to continue to be the hard man to the very end.

I supposed I should have stayed in the restaurant, but I could not bear to watch him eat and I could feel my hand starting to shake.

Through the window I could see Alaric gobbling down his food, and even though his dessert did not appear to be adorned by a double portion of ice cream, he did not seem to mount any objection. As he paid his bill, I thought I could see that his hand was also shaking, something I took as an encouraging sign.

He came out and, keeping at a distance from me, asked what he should do now.

"Where'd you live?"

"Off the Grandique Road."

"Alright. You drive. I'll follow you. And in case you've got any stupid idea of getting away from me, don't forget I've got your phone and my car can do 400 kph."

"Yeah, I bet it can," he said, giving the Bugatti a respectful glance.

"Let's go, asshole!"

I followed the Juke down High Road and off to the left onto Grandique Road. A few miles up, there was a lake on the right hand side, and on the other side was a lane with a swing gate near the roadside.

As soon as we were through I stopped and pressed the horn. He stopped, got out and came to my window.

"What?"

"Shut the fucking gate! Do you have a lock?"

"No."

"Well, shut it anyway, and if you've got a bit of rope, tie it down."

"Alright," he said and went back to his car, where he struggled in the trunk, eventually finding a length of plastic rope the same colour as his car.

After fumbling with this, he managed some kind of knot, turned round and gave me a thumbs up sign.

I did not respond, but pressed my accelerator, producing a rich, throaty roar which he rightly interpreted as a sign of my impatience. He scurried back to his car and drove on.

About a quarter of a mile along the lane was an opening in the spruce which revealed a yard and a small, bright-pink bungalow. Here we parked and he led me into the house.

"The wife's visiting her mother," he said with a sheepish grin, "but then she spends a lot of time visiting her mother."

"Alright." I said, "Now sit down and shut up."

He meekly went to an old armchair and sat on the edge of its seat. I sat back and arranged myself until I was comfortable.

"The premier is sick and tired of your lying, fucking antics." I laid it on as heavily as I could. "Here's what you're looking at. Appearance before the House Committee on Rules and Privileges, where you would be fined several thousand dollars. If the boss is in a bad mood that day, it could be as much as five thousand dollars. Expulsion from the legislature, effectively immediately."

"Jesus!"

"What did you expect, you sack of shit? Telling lies about the premier to the fucking news media!"

"I thought he would be able to finesse it. I was put on the spot."

"And you thought you'd just walk away unscathed? Are you as stupid as you are worthless?"

"No. I guess I wasn't thinking." He actually smiled, which I found utterly repelling. "You must know how that is, Marc, when your nerves get the better of you and you say crazy things."

Momentarily at a loss, I stood up. He took this as a threatening gesture and cowered back in his chair.

Now back in control, I started to pace up and down.

"Is there any way out?" He asked weakly.

"Not the way things stand now."

I started to look thoughtful, and paused as if considering a course of action. "No, no," I said, shaking my head, "that won't work."

"What won't? What is it?"

"Maybe the boss could get you out of getting screwed with your pants on by the committee, but after that you'd be kicked out of the party and the caucus...unless...."

"Unless what?"

"Hmmn. Well, it would take some doing, but it might—just might—be possible."

"What might be possible?"

"Number one. Under no circumstances will you speak to a member of the media about this ever again, and not about anything else, either, for at least six months."

"I can do that."

"Number two. You will not discuss anything to do with this matter —including this conversation we're having now—with any fucking person alive. That includes wives, kids, relatives, friends or colleagues."

"I can do that."

"Then, you'd have to come back with me and grovel—well and truly, fucking grovel at the premier's feet."

"I can do that."

"*Then* you'd have to put out a statement admitting that you lied about his saying it would be alright to take the money...incidentally, did you send it back?"

"Er...not yet...no."

"You total, fucking, stupid, useless, brainless asshole!"

"I forgot."

"Forgot! You idiot. Where does this Boudreau guy live?"

"A few miles from here. In Petit de Grat."

"How did he pay you?"

"I asked for cash"—again he gave the revolting smile—"you know, income tax an all..."

"We'll take that back to him right after we're done here."

"Will that do it?"

"Maybe. Wendell Proctor can be a rough son of a bitch, but he can also be ridiculously forgiving. If you stay quiet and keep your nose clean, and after a lengthy period of good behavior..." Here I paused, realizing that if I carried on I would be deliberately lying. Hell, I thought, why not? D'Entremont deserved everything he got. "Then, after a discreet period, the boss *might* see his way to putting something your way."

"Cabinet?"

"You must be fucking kidding. Cabinet, after what you've done?"

"No, I guess not."

"Maybe a whip." I hated myself for saying this, but I was in for the whole hog. "I heard they might be looking for a Chief Whip soon."

"Wow, Chief Whip!"

"Any misbehavior or violation of confidences and the deal would be off."

"I understand."

"Alright, now get some sheets of paper and I'll dictate your statement. You dare change one word and everything is cancelled."

It took us over half an hour to compose, rewrite and sign the statement. I carefully folded it and put it in my pocket.

"Now, let's get that money back to Mr. Boudreau and your sorry ass to Halifax."

"Shall I follow you or will you follow me?" he asked.

"You're travelling with me. You think I'm going to give you a chance to wriggle off the hook?"

"How will I get back here?"

"What do I care? Get a bus."

"Okay, I guess. Can I have my phone back?"

"When we get to Halifax. After you've seen the boss, I'll give you your phone back."

I called Tom and apprised him of what had been accomplished. He congratulated me and said he would arrange for Wendell to see the miscreant as soon as we arrived.

As the Bugatti soared across the Canso Causeway, I reflected that my first impersonation of a Mafia button man had gone quite successfully. That acknowledged, I would not relish the prospect of having to do it again.

28

When I came downstairs the next morning, Wendell had finished his cereal and coffee, and was stuffing reports into his briefcase.

He looked up and grinned. "Hey. Good work yesterday. Well done!"

"Thanks. How did you get on after I dropped Alaric off at your office?"

"You should have stayed. We had a lot of fun with the little runt. He cringed at my feet in abject humiliation, begging for forgiveness. I bashed him around the room a bit until the poor bastard was in tears."

"He deserved it."

"But you know what his loudest, most earnest plea was?"

"No, what?"

"That I shouldn't let you go near him again!"

"You're joking?"

"No, you must have put the fear of God into him."

"I did my best. I'm glad it worked."

"You won't be surprised to learn that this has leaked out into the party ranks."

"Leaked accidentally or was deliberately leaked?"

"Haha! You're catching on. I imagine Tom might have had something to do with it."

"I'll bet he did."

"Anyway, you know what they're calling you in the party now?"

"I don't know why they should call me anything."

"Come now. You're too modest. Anyway, guess what your nickname is now."

"No idea."

"*The Enforcer.*" He burst out into hilarious laughter.

"No!"

"Yes! Isn't it great? I'll have to make use of this somehow."

"Please don't."

"We'll see. What have you got planned for today?"

"I'm hoping to see Angus MacKinnon, Bill Clark, Jill Rutledge, Pierre Dorion, Hector McNeil and Zandili Joseph."

"Good, but stop whatever you're doing before 2 pm."

"Why?"

"I'm calling a meeting of the Rules and Privileges Committee and I want you to be there."

"This is about D'Entremont?"

"Oh, yes."

"Have the opposition parties asked for the meeting?"

"Yes. Both of them. They want drastic action, but I have a plan to split them up so that Edwards will be on her own."

"How will you do that?"

"You'll see, but the first step has already been taken."

"And that is...?"

"I told Wilkins the meeting is at 2, and I told Edwards it starts at 2:30." He grinned. "A common administrative error."

"I don't see what—"

"Be there and all will be revealed."

"Okay, I will. Where's it being held?"

"In the Red Room at Province House."

My first stop was with Angus MacKinnon, the Minister of Economic Development. He was a powerhouse within the party and was called the "uncrowned king" of Eastern Nova Scotia. He was the man Wendell had defeated for the leadership almost six years ago.

Since then, Wendell told me, he had been entirely cooperative with and supportive of the premier. As he was now in his early sixties, another attempt at the leadership was out of the question, and he did his job competently and loyally. I liked him a lot and remembered his kindness towards me on a number of occasions.

"I'm glad Wendell has got someone doing what you're doing," he said as he sat across from me in an armchair in front of, not behind, his desk. "It's important we know where we stand. And whatever your findings are, they should be updated at relatively frequent intervals."

"I agree entirely. Things are volatile and could change substantially at any given time."

"Exactly. We don't really have to worry about the occasional abstentions in the House—such as we saw a few weeks ago—although, of course, if those abstaining were to sit mute, rather than sneaking out before the vote, it could be much more embarrassing."

"As you see it, Angus, what are the main dangers we have to watch out for?"

"The very worst scenario would be if enough of our people voted with the opposition on a major bill or motion, and defeated the government in the House. But that is so unlikely as not to be worth considering."

"What's the next worst?"

"Losing a motion of confidence at the party convention."

"How does that work?"

"The party constitution requires that a vote be held after we have lost an election, so that wouldn't be applicable for at least another four years, and not at all if we win again."

"Is it possible to have such a vote even if the party has won?"

"You mean, like now?"

"Yes."

"There are special provisions. If two-thirds of the Legislative Caucus wants a non-confidence vote, one has to be held at a specially-called convention."

"But I'm guessing that if two-thirds of the caucus wanted it, the leader would be so badly damaged that even if he won the convention vote he couldn't really recover."

"Precisely. Unless he swept the convention vote—say 90% or more —and, in effect, the party told the caucus to get in line. Shape up or ship out."

"And I suppose that any vote at convention could be dangerous. If, say, 30% voted against the leader the opposition could go to the public and say, '30% of this person's own party don't want him. Do *you*?'"

"Well, exactly. In my opinion, if the caucus asked for a confidence vote, any leader would be wiser to quit than try to tough it out."

"Thank you, Angus. You've given me a lot of food for thought."

Visits to Bill Clark and Hector McNeil were almost a formality. Both men swore loyalty to Wendell in no uncertain terms, but it was not what they said which convinced me of their sincerity, but the way they said it.

Two of those remaining were more difficult to gauge, but Zandili Joseph was not.

"Sure, I know he first made me Speaker and then put me in the cabinet, and I'm grateful. But I'm my own person. Nobody owns me. I'm nobody's puppet."

"What does that mean in practical terms, Zandili?"

"What do you mean, 'practical terms'?"

"If push comes to shove, where would you be?"

"I guess it would depend on the situation."

"You'll forgive me for saying so, but that isn't much help to me."

"How can I say what I'm going to do six months from now, if I don't know what's going to be happening at the time?"

"Well, supposing another unsubstantiated allegation was made against the boss, would you back him until the smoke settled or would you rush to judgment?"

"Why would I do that?"

"Do what?"

"Why would I rush to judgment?"

"Because, when I asked you what you thought about the affair with the library assistant, you gave the feeble story that you couldn't have an opinion because you were in the cabinet."

"So?"

"Let's not beat around the bush. If you didn't have reservations about the boss's innocence, you wouldn't have fed me that crap."

"You watch who you're talking to!"

"You'd better watch who *you're* talking to," I blurted out and immediately regretted it, but it seems to have had the right effect.

She glared at me with undisguised malice. At first, she made a play of pulling her African dress about her shoulders, then started spluttering. "Well...I didn't know you then....I mean—"

"I know what you mean."

"Just because I'm black, doesn't mean I have to support Wendell because he's black."

"That tells me what I need to know. Thanks for your time, Zandili."

"Wait!" she called after me from her office door, but I had no intention of listening to more prevarication.

Dorion was a cold fish. Being a fellow Acadian, he was not able to pretend that language and culture differences allowed misinterpretation in what he said, so instead he was distant. He pledged his support for Wendell, but in a way which left him lots of leeway to wriggle out if it. A lot would depend on whether the legislation regarding redistribution of seats re-emerged, he said, and that the premier could hardly expect him to vote his own seat out of existence. Apart from that, of course, he was loyal and would be loyal, but who could say what the future held? Mentally, I put him down as a fence-sitter...at best.

Jill Rutledge was a woman of a nervous disposition under normal circumstances, but her demeanour today strongly suggested that she had heard of my reputation as "The Enforcer" and was affected by it. She could scarcely construct a sentence, and whenever I tried to pin her down, she started to yammer but trailed off without actually saying anything. I knew that she was close with the dismissed Leila Hendricks and that she thought there was something irregular about the library assistant's statement, so she could babble as much as she liked, but I still wouldn't trust her.

As I came out of Rutledge's office I realized it was almost two o'clock, so I hurried over to the Red Room. I got there just in time, because Cliff Wolf and Bill Jenkins were just going in.

Wendell, Joan, Angus, Chester, Angela Stairs, and John Wilkins were already seated in huge red chairs around the massive oak table. Wolf and Jenkins sat flanking Wilkins, while I sat at the side of the room behind Wendell.

"Dana doesn't seem to be here, so we'll start without her," Wendell said, sounding pained at her non-appearance."The Chair will accept a motion that no action be taken in the unfortunate matter of Alaric D'Entremont."

"I so move," Angus said solemnly.

"Mr. Chairman, this motion is impossible," Wilkins protested. "The man must be punished. Justice has to be done."

"Give every man justice and who shall 'scape whipping?" Joan asked sweetly.

"Oh come on!" Cliff Wolf cried.

"You can't just let him go without even a slap on the wrist," said Wilkins.

"You're a lawyer, John," Wendell said in a friendly manner. "If D'Entremont had also been one, it would have been alright for him to accept a fee for service, wouldn't it?"

"But he's not a lawyer."

"So, are you saying there is one rule for lawyers and another for the rest of us?" asked Chester.

"Er...no...you know what I mean. What he did was wrong."

"Yes," said Angela, "But so also what Denis McNamara did was wrong. Wasn't it?"

Wilkins looked as if he had been hit by a punch to the solar plexus. His colleagues looked to him for guidance, but he said nothing. At length, in a weak voice, Wolf asked what Stairs had meant by her question.

"You don't know about that?" She spoke icily, "But John does, don't you, John?"

"Yeah." It was barely a whisper.

"So, here's the deal," said Wendell. "If you go ahead with D'Entremont, we'll revive the library assistant matter and haul not only McNamara but also Sam Wong in here, charge them with criminal activity, then use our majority to get them both thrown out of the House. If you agree to let D'Entremont off the hook, we'll let McNamara and Wong live to fight another day. Deal?"

Wolf and Jenkins looked stunned. Wilkins just stared ahead in silence.

"Deal?" Wendell repeated. "It's on the table for only five seconds. Four...three...two—"

"Okay. Deal."

"Right. Those in favour of the motion to take no action against D'Entremont say 'aye'."

Everyone at the table said 'aye', those on our side more vigorously and happily than those on the other.

"Motion carried! The chair will accept a motion to adjourn."

"So move," said Joan.

"Carried!"

At that moment a flustered Dana Edwards hurried into the room. "What's going on?"

"Dana, you're late," Wendell said. "We've just adjourned."

"But...but...what about D'Entremont?"

"The committee unanimously agreed to take no action."

"But...but—"

"Gotta go!" He grabbed his briefcase and rushed out, Joan, Angus, Angela and Chester in his wake.

I hung back to observe the aftermath. The Leader of the Opposition and his henchmen shuffled silently to the door, pausing only to scowl in my direction.

Edwards called after them, "Tell me what happened here?"

Receiving no answer, she floundered about until she spied me.

"You!" she spat. "I might have known you'd be at the bottom of this!"

She stalked out, dropping papers as she went, and leaving me somewhat bemused.

For a moment I thought about what had taken place, and did not know whether to be insulted or flattered that the reputation of the "The Enforcer" had spread as far as the enemy benches. For better or worse, I was stuck with the name and, it would seem, the role.

While part of me was pleased, another part felt ashamed, and I remember a famous speech given by Premier George Murray in 1923. He said that politics "drags many of our leading citizens down to the level of gangsters."

29

The next day I decided to see Kesegoo'e Sillyboy, the Minister of Social Services and Native Affairs. I had tried to get an appointment several days ago without success, and again failed on this occasion.

Since it was obvious that by now everyone in the caucus would know that Wendell had given me this task, I could not help wondering if the minister's unavailability was deliberate. If that was so, could the reason be that she harboured anti-Proctor sentiments which she did not want uncovered? I resolved to mention it to Wendell when next I saw him, because one call from the premier would soon make her available!

In light of my failure to connect with Sillyboy, I thought I would try to see at least some of the five MLAs in the Halifax area and, if I had time, get down to Chester to talk with Emma Mitchell. I looked at my list several times, asking myself if it would be a total waste of time trying to see Delia Parish, and decided that she had already made her position abundantly clear and was unlikely to change.

The closest to me on the list was Jenny Chan, who represented the downtown area, Halifax Citadel. She had been hostile at the caucus meeting when the library assistant affair was aired, but she might have had second thoughts since then.

I left the Bugatti at Province House and walked to her constituency office, which was a small store front on Barrington Street. Her assistant smiled when she first saw me, but scowled as soon as I told her my name. Not only did word travel fast among the politicians, I thought, but also among their staff.

"Jenny is very busy, today," she said acidly. She was a person of barely discernible gender, about twenty, wearing granny glasses and dressed, or rather draped, in a shapeless, earth-coloured garment.

"Please tell her I am here and would like to see her."

"I don't think that will be possible." She sniffed and tossed her head.

"Is she here?"

"Yes, but like I said, busy."

"I don't see anyone in the waiting area," I said, my patience exhausted.

"Sorry," she said in a tone which was anything but apologetic.

"Look," I said, deciding it was time for 'The Enforcer' to put in an appearance, "I've asked you nicely. Now get out of my way!"

I pushed past her, went down a short corridor and opened the only door. Jenny was standing in a corner like a deer in the headlights.

"Marc!" She tried to sound surprised.

"You need to teach your staff some manners," I said, taking a seat at her desk. I knew I should have been more diplomatic, but I was still annoyed by the assistant. "You know why I'm here?"

"I guess so."

"So, let's get to the point, Jenny. What advice would you give to the premier?"

"If he wanted it he could have asked me—"

"Please, just tell me what's on your mind."

She looked even smaller and thinner today than she had previously, and it crossed my mind that she might have been suffering from some serious illness. I guessed she weighed no more than ninety–five pounds, and the fact that she was dressed all in black did not help her appearance. I thought she could have looked quite attractive if she had not plastered her face with weird white makeup and violent purple eye shadow.

"Well, I would tell him that, for starters, he has to come clean about Frances Mullens."

For a split second, I did not recognize the name, then I realized, with some guilt, that we had all been referring to the poor woman only as 'the library assistant'.

"Come clean about what?"

"About how she was coerced into retracting her accusation."

"*She* never made the accusation in the first place! It was made by others without her consent or knowledge."

"I know she said that, but was it true?"

"Of course it was true. I was there when she told us; the Police

Chief and me."

"So you say."

"I do say! It was Denis MacNamara, her cousin, and Sammy Wong who did it in order to frame the premier."

She stared at me in silence for several minutes, all the while twisting her hands in her lap. Then she looked around the room as if looking for assistance or inspiration.

"McNamara and Wong?" she asked weakly.

"Yes."

"I don't know...."

"What don't you know, Jenny?"

"You could be making all this up."

"Why would I do that?"

"Because you men are all in it together."

I realized there was nothing to gain in pursuing this line any further: There was no point in trying to reason with a closed mind. The only other line open to me, I knew, was unlikely to be effectual, but I tried it anyway.

"The boss needs to know where you stand, Jenny, because he's contemplating another shuffle soon and needs to know who he could rely on."

"Hah!" she spat. "Bribery won't work with me. I know Proctor would never put me in his cabinet in a month of Sundays."

"You never know what's in the boss's mind, Jenny. You never can tell," I said unconvincingly, "but I've taken too much of your time. I'll see you when the House meets again in the fall."

Jeremy Reid, the MLA for Halifax Armdale, and Sean Leaman, the Member of Eastern Shore, were two members of the so-called 'wolf pack', the other being Cullum MacPhee from Pictou West. They sat together in the Members' lounge, socialized together after sittings, voted the same way in divisions, and often played off each other in debates.

I was fortunate to find MacPhee at Reid's house, the former being in the city for a committee meeting. I heard a loud discussion inside and, since the door was ajar, I pushed it open and went in.

"All hail! The Enforcer cometh!" shouted MacPhee as I came into the room.

They were sprawled on a large couch in their shirtsleeves, apparently in the middle of some card game. It was clear that both had been drinking, as a half-filled bottle of Famous Grouse sat on the table. They raised their glasses to salute me.

"Grab a seat, Marc," Reid said.

"And a drink," added MacPhee.

"No, thanks, it's too early for me." I said as I moved some files from a chair.

"We know why you're here," said Reid, "and you know we generally think alike."

"That's what people say. Like the three musketeers"

"Or Curly, Larry and Moe." McPhee hooted with laughter.

"It's broadly true. So I'm going to call Sean and put him on speaker phone."

This development took me by surprise, but I had no reason to object because it would save me a tiresome drive up to Sheet Harbour, where Leaman lived.

"Hi, Marc!" Leaman's voice came from the phone.

"Hello, Sean!"

"Now we are all here, let' start," said Reid. "What exactly is your mission, Enforcer?"

"Cut that out! My mission—as you call it—is to get your advice as to what you think the boss should do to improve the party's internal relations. Also, what he should do to improve our standings in the polls."

"I'll start," said Leaman. "As to the first, he should try to involve the brighter members of caucus—"

"That's us!" McPhee shouted.

"Yes, like ourselves, in more of the decisions. Too many decisions get fast-tracked at caucus, often before we even know what they are all about."

"Especially with large or complex bills," Reid added. "The minister stands up for a few minutes and gives us a potted version of the bill, but we don't really know what's in it, and especially not all of the provisions and what they might entail."

"Right," Leaman said, "and later we find out we've given the green light to a bunch of gobbledygook at best, and politically dangerous stuff at worst."

"I understand why the boss might not want to consult everyone in the caucus in detail—"

"Bunch of bozos," MacPhee shouted. "Half of them are as thick as a plank."

"But he could take some of us into his confidence more often."

"Okay, duly noted," I said. "Do you think the premier is too arrogant?"

"I guess if you're insecure, you might think so, but when you're the boss you can't hide your light under a bushel," Reid said.

"Yeah," said McPhee.

"I agree," said Leaman.

"Alright, guys. Now to the crunch. How far can the premier rely on your support?"

At this they fell uncharacteristically silent. I waited for several seconds.

"Come on, let's have it. If push came to shove, where would you stand?"

"I think," said Reid very slowly, "I can speak for all of us if I say we will support the leader as long as he is leader."

"Yes, that's right," Leaman said.

"But what the hell does that mean?" I was irritated by this turn of events. "What if there was another confidence motion? Where would you be?"

"If it was like the last one, no question we'd stand with the Boss," MacPhee said, and the others indicated their concurrence.

"What am I not getting here?" I asked. "You say if the motion was like the last one, but what it was about something else?"

"Ah. Then it might be different," Reid said.

"Different?"

Reid and McPhee nodded silently. No sound came from the phone.

"So, what I need to know is what kind of motion that might be. What are you talking about?"

"Look," said Reid, "If the boss's popularity with the voters were to drop below a certain point, we would have to consider our duty to the party—"

"To your own survival, you mean!"

"Everyone wants to survive, Marc. Except maybe you."

"Well, what would 'a certain point' be? Two points behind the opposition? Five points?"

"Certainly five," McPhee said, "and maybe two if there were other circumstances."

"Like what?"

"If there were a competent alternative available," said Leaman.

"And is there?"

"Is there what?"

"Is there, in your opinion, a competent alternative leader currently available?"

"Yes, we would have to say that there is."

"And who is it?"

"That's is as far as we are prepared to go at this point," said Reid. "We've been fair and open with you so far. And, it may never happen. The party may maintain its lead in the polls...or even improve it."

"Alright. Let me ask you this. If one or more of you were to be offered a cabinet post, would that change the water on the beans?"

"It might," said Leaman. "Certainly if all three of us were offered cabinet posts, it would definitely affect our position."

"You don't want much, do you?" I was incredulous at their outrageous audacity. "And if only one or two of you could be accommodated in the Executive Council?"

"We would have to decide that question if and when it happened," said McPhee.

From Armdale I drove over the bridge to Dartmouth to see the caucus chairman, Freeman Murphy.

For reasons unknown to me, his constituency office was closed, so I went to his house on Portland Hills Drive. There was no answer at the front door so I went around to the back and found him sitting in a deck chair on the lawn.

"Don't come any further!" he bawled at me. "I've got COVID! You sit on that little wall. You should be safe there."

"How long have you been like this, Freeman?"

"A couple of days. Had to close the office, because my assistant got it, too."

"It might be worth putting a note on the office door so your constituents don't think you're goofing off."

"A good idea!" Freeman said. "Thanks, Marc." He took out his phone, called somebody named Henrietta, and asked her to see that a sign was put up.

"I'm sorry to bother you at home, Freeman. I know I didn't have to talk to you, but I didn't want you to feel left out," I said, expecting him to cheerily agree that my visit was unnecessary. I was totally unprepared for his response.

"Why didn't you think you needed to talk to me?" He sounded angry and hurt.

"Well, you being caucus chairman, I figured you are one of the premier's staunchest supporters."

"Well, you figured wrong! I'm not anyone's staunchest supporter. As chairman, I gotta be neutral. Can't show favour to any side or faction."

"I understand that, but you have some influence in the party—"

"A lot of influence," he corrected me indignantly.

"Yes, quite, a lot of influence. So you might be able to sway people one way or another."

"No doubt I could."

"So, I'm asking you if the premier can rely on you to do the right thing."

"What's the right thing?"

"To lend him your support."

"Well, that's hard to say, isn't it?"

"Is it?"

"I'd say so."

"Look, Freeman, please can we stop this beating around the bush. Can the premier count on you when the chips are down?"

"My position requires neutrality," he said, folding his arms defiantly.

"Let me put it this way? If there were a tie in caucus on a question of confidence, would you vote for the premier or against him?"

"I refer you to my previous answer," he said pompously.

"Alright. Just for the record, if the premier were to offer you a cabinet post in the upcoming shuffle, would you decline on the grounds of neutrality?"

"Get off my property!" he roared. "Get the fuck out of here!"

"Gladly," I said, taking satisfaction that I had flushed out a traitor who was previously not even suspected.

30

The next morning, when I told Wendell about my encounter with Freeman Murphy, he exploded. I had never heard such a colourful string of invectives. He was so taken aback that, although he was ready to leave for work and his driver was honking the car horn outside, he sat back down and looked at me in a hapless manner.

"Holy moly! Murphy? I never would have suspected. What am I going to do, Marc?"

"Keep cool. My survey is not complete, but it looks as if we still have two-thirds of the caucus either in our camp or on the fence."

"Only two-thirds?"

"It's enough. They would need to swing at least a third of our people in order to pass a caucus vote asking for a confidence vote at a convention."

"God, are we already talking about that?"

"*Praemonitus, praemunitus.*"

"What the hell is that?"

"To be forewarned is to be forearmed. We're already thinking ahead so we can be prepared."

"Who's we? You and Tom?"

"No, Angus and me."

"Angus?"

"Yes. You needn't worry about him. He's with us to the end."

Although I had intimated to him before that MacKinnon was loyal and trustworthy, Wendell was surprised to hear this confirmed. In politics, I guess there were many like him who thought that once an enemy, always an enemy.

I was about to reinforce my point, by telling him how Angus had gone out of his way to be helpful, when my phone buzzed.

"Marc, this is Bamby."

My mind reeled, wondering if this was some kind of joke, and then I remembered Joe's nephew, my gardener.

"Oh, hi, Bamby, how's the garden shaping up?"

"Good, or it was good until a little while ago."

"Why what happened?"

"I thought that northwest corner would be ideal for asparagus so I was digging a deep trench to fork in some cow manure—"

"Cow manure?"

"Yeah, I got it from the farm up the road. I didn't think you'd mind."

"I don't, but what is all this about?"

"Yeah, well, when I was digging the trench I found a body."

"A *body*?"

"Yeah. I think you'd better come home. The cops are swarming all over the place."

"Holy crap! What kind of body? Is it recent?"

"Doesn't look like it. Just bones. The cops are putting up a kind of tent around it."

"Okay, Bamby, you just do whatever the police tell you. I'll be back before noon."

"What's that about a body?" Wendell asked as I ended the call.

"They found a skeleton in my garden. I have to go back."

"Shit! That means you can't go back to Cape Breton to see Nathanson and Walters."

"I wouldn't see Walters anyway, because she hates me. Why don't you call them?"

"Okay, if that's what you want."

"And ask Walters why she hates me."

"You got it."

"Now I must go up and tell Rosalie the bad news. She might not want to go back yet. Would Cynthia mind if she stayed on a few more days?"

"Hell, no. Tell her she can stay as long as she likes."

Rosalie was still asleep, so I shook her gently. She rolled over and glared at me, as if I was making a habit of doing this in the early mornings.

"What is it now? Do you have to go to Amherst or Timbuktu?"

"No, I have to go home."

"Already? Why?"

"You don't have to come if you don't want to. It's just that Bamby dug up a skeleton in our garden."

"What?" She was now sitting bolt upright.

"That's all I know. Bamby says the police are on the case and that I should go back."

"Jeepers! A skeleton! Man or woman?"

"I forgot to ask."

"Do you mind if I stay? Cynthia and I are having quite a good time."

"No, you stay. I'll be back as soon as I've sorted it out. Should be a few days at most."

"Okay, sweetheart. Drive safely." She said, curled up in the bedclothes, and promptly fell back to sleep.

"Danny Nathanson seems to be okay," said Wendell when I went back downstairs. "He didn't voice any problems or concerns. He said he was behind me, but didn't say it with unbounded enthusiasm."

"That's fairly good news. It more or less confirms what I had heard. How about Carol Walters?"

"She's one awkward cow. She won't say yes, and she won't say no. She doesn't know how she feels or what she might do."

"Sounds suspiciously like she's in the other camp."

"That's what I thought."

"Did you dangle the cabinet bait in front of her?"

"Sure did, but she said she's not interested in going into cabinet. Says she couldn't spare the time, anyway. Apparently, she and her husband run some kind of little greenhouse or garden centre."

"I didn't know that."

"Nor did I."

"What did she say about me?"

"Why would she say anything about you?"

"You said you would ask why she hates me."

"Oh, shit, I forgot! Next time."

"There! That's what will lose you support if you don't check it."

"What?"

"Thinking little people don't matter."

"How do I do that?"

"Idly making promises and then breaking them without a second thought. Wendell, I've got to tell you that, if push comes to shove, I'll bet it will have been small things like that which push people to the other side."

He stared at me as if I were mad, then looked away. I could tell he was recalling how many times he might have done this to people in the caucus.

"You're so used to getting your own way because you're the boss." I was determined to make the point stick. "You forget what effect your egocentric behaviour has on the folk below you. To some of them a thoughtless act, which you are not even aware you're committing, can rankle and fester for years. You, of all people, should know this. Think back to when you were on the way up. A black man getting to the top can't have been easy. Slights. Slurs. Racial comments. Remember?"

"Jesus! Even Tom doesn't talk to me this way."

"That's because he's as much dependent upon you as you are on him. I'm not dependent on you, and I don't want anything from you. That's why you know I'll always tell you the truth."

"Fair enough, Marc."

He stood up, knowing full well when to use his height to his advantage. He towered over me "Now you get down to Grand Pre and deal with your skeleton, and then you can get on with the job I gave you."

"Okay, but I want to leave you with this." I opened the side pocket of my suitcase and took out a card I had prepared last night. I handed it to Wendell.

"This is my preliminary assessment of where everybody stands. I suggest you put it up in Tom's office. If anyone changes their attitude, we can move them to the appropriate column."

"Wow. Hey, that's good, Marc. Thanks. I'll do as you say and get Tom to put it on the wall in his office." He studied it carefully. "You think both Dorion and Sillyboy are on the fence?"

"All signs indicate that, yes."

"I assume the column on the far left are solid, rock rib supporters?"

"Yes."

"And those in the next column? Does that mean their support is weak or might depend on some favour being granted?"

"Both, actually. In the cases of Reid, MacPhee, Leaman and D'Entremont, I think their continued support will depend upon some degree of recognition. With MacDonald, who knows? He says he's on board, but the man is such a liar. Franks, Sullivan Nathanson are okay

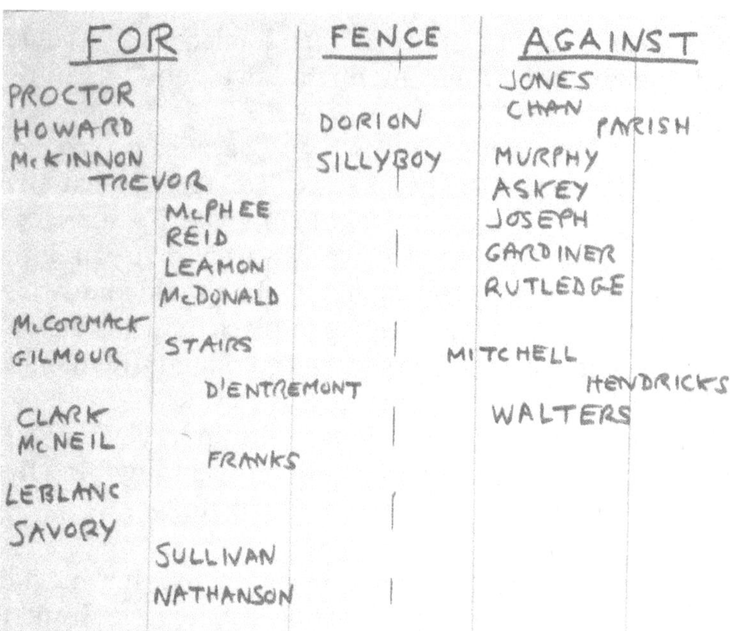

for now, but maybe not always."

"But I just promoted Sullivan!"

"Gratitude is the lively expectation of favours to come."

"What a job! Sometimes I wonder why I ever wanted it."

"You love it!"

"Yeah, I do." He grinned broadly. "So, right now, the other side has eleven, thirteen if Dorion and Sillyboy go over."

"Yes, but I think you will keep Dorion if you don't bring in redistribution. If you do, he's gone to the enemy."

"Hmm. How many do they need to be a real threat?"

"Twenty-two to get a non-confidence motion to the convention floor."

"That's a relief. We should be alright, if all goes well."

"Yes. *If* all goes well," I said firmly.

"Thank you for that, Mr. Sunshine."

31

The next day brought a strange mixture of events to engage my attention and cause concern, the most disturbing of which was a story on the local news. Apparently, a poll conducted in the province had found that support for the Proctor government had dropped to 43%, down 5 points from the election some months ago. The official opposition was now up to 39%, while Dana Edward's party was still at 18%.

The report carried a clip of Wendell saying the poll results were to be expected as the public had not had sufficient time to appreciate some of his "courageous but controversial measures". Privately, I wondered if inadvertently insulting the public's intelligence might not do more harm than good. What I was sure of was that this would undoubtedly cause some anguish within the party, and certainly in caucus.

I was unsure whether this was enough to cause me to adjust the 'score card' I had given to Wendell, but I recalled a famous quip of the late Tommy Douglas MP that the difference between a cactus and a caucus was that with a cactus all the pricks were on the outside.

I had arrived at Grand Pre before noon and at once had consulted with the RCMP officer in charge of the investigation. He told me the skeletal remains had already been removed and taken to a pathology laboratory for testing and examination.

When he and another constable took down their tent and I had a chance to look around, I was amazed at the progress Bamby had made with the garden. He had certainly earned his money, as the place was totally transformed from a dreary mess into a horticultural demi-paradise. Now, if I could, it was up to me to maintain it in this excellent condition.

After I digested the news about the party's drop in the polls, I had to go into Wolfville and attend to my constituents' problems. Cheryl was as bright and breezy as ever and, as usual, called me 'doctor.'

There were eight people in the waiting area, whose problems ranged from a complaint about Wendell's war on 'woke' not going far enough to an able bodied man who, on available evidence, seemed to have been unreasonably denied work on the highways. By the time I had dealt with the case work, it was mid-afternoon.

As I was heading for the car, my phone buzzed. It was the RCMP, informing me that there would not be a criminal investigation into the skeletal remains because the tests showed them to be of a 65-year-old male who had expired about 120 years ago. The officer said they could not determine at this distance in time if foul play had been involved in the man's death, but some of the cervical vertebrae were abnormally abraded. He said that, since dental records were not kept that long ago, there was no way to identify the deceased person.

This information caused me to wonder who had owned my property around 1910, so I walked down to Walter Bryson's office on Main Street. His large, ferocious secretary, Wanda, greeted me heartily and said that Walter had no client with him, so I could go right in.

"Hello, Marc. How was the session?"

"Not bad. I still haven't given my maiden speech."

"You've got three years to do that. When you do give it, make sure it's a good one. And memorable."

"I'll try"

"How's Rosalie?"

"She's well. She's still in Halifax, staying with Cynthia Proctor."

"Sounds like you've become very chummy with our premier."

"Yes, I guess I have."

"Not disillusioned yet? Your gods don't have feet of clay?"

"Not so much disillusioned as learning the ropes and realizing that there are many pressures on a man in his position."

"I understand. Look, if you're on your own, why don't you come over for dinner tonight?"

"I'd love to."

"Let me call Joyce and get her okay."

While Walter was calling, I wandered around the office, looking at the photos and maps on the walls, and observed that in many respects Walter had kept it pretty much as his father had it over twenty years ago.

"Right. That's settled. Joyce says she's making a huge pot of stew. You don't have to change or anything, so you can follow me home."

"Okay. Sounds fine to me."

"Marc, what brought you here today?"

"You've heard about my mysterious skeleton?"

"Skeleton? No. What skeleton?"

"My gardener found it the other day and the police dug it up. They say it's a 65-year-old man who croaked about 120 years ago."

"God Lord. So you want to know who owned your place around 1910."

"Exactly. I doubt if it will help us figure out who the corpse was, but you never know."

"Let's have a look."

Walter went to a large drawer containing charts and deeds, pulled one out and spread it on his desk. "Ah, yes. It was owned by a William Slocum."

"Do you know any more about him?"

"No, except that he sold the property in 1914 to Bernard Weather-all."

"Wasn't it the Weatherall family who sold it to the millionaire who went bust, just before I acquired it?"

"Yes, that's right."

"Why did he sell?"

"Why did who sell?"

"Slocum."

"No idea."

Walter turned the deed over and found a newspaper cutting attached to it. "Yes I do. Mr. Slocum sold the place because he was off to war. According to this, he was one of the first captains in the Royal Canadian Navy, which had been founded four years earlier."

"I guess he didn't think he'd be coming back."

"Apparently, he feared he might not, so he liquidated all his assets and distributed the proceeds among his family."

'Very generous of him."

"Indeed."

"Did he come back?"

"It doesn't say here, but I don't doubt the Navy records would show if he died in action."

"Thanks, Walter. It doesn't help me with my skeleton, but it was most interesting. Are you ready to go yet?"

"No, I have to clear up a few items. Give me half an hour."

"Okay I'll meet you back here. I'll run across the road and visit Gerald at the bookstore."

I have described Gerald and the circumstances under which he came to own the shop in a number of my books[6]. Suffice it to say here that he was a longtime associate of my family and a colourful character who possessed an extraordinary grab bag of information on a variety of unrelated subjects. If anyone could expand my knowledge of the skeleton, it was likely to be Gerald.

The, to me, unpleasant smell of incense greeted me as I pushed open the door. The place had changed out of all recognition in the six years since I had given the store to Gerald. Whereas before it was brown, sombre, musty and unbelievably overcrowded, now it was as cheerful and brightly dressed as Gerald himself, mostly in hues of violet and rose.

"Marc, my dear! What a lovely surprise! How's political life treating you?"

"Not too badly, Gerald. How's business?"

"Running at a small profit, which is all I need to keep body and soul together."

"I'm glad. You'll let me know if that changes. I'm always willing to help if needed."

"Oh, thank you very much. You're always so kind. Is this a social visit, or do you have something on your mind?"

"You've heard about my skeleton?"

"Oooh, yes! *Everyone's* talking about it. How delicious!"

"I was wondering if you knew anything about a William Slocum, who owned my place back in the early 1900s."

"Did he own your place? I wasn't aware."

"Yes. Do you know him?"

"Know *of* him, my dear. I'm not that old!"

"Of course."

"Yes, of course, he wrote the book. Well, a leaflet or pamphlet, really."

---

6   *Holy Grail, Sacred Gold; Unspeakable Evil; Best Served Cold;* and *My Brother's Keeper*

"What pamphlet?"

"*My Cousin and Me.*"

"That was the name of the pamphlet?"

"Yes."

"Who was his cousin?"

"Why, the famous Joshua Slocum of course! You must have heard of him."

"Sort of, yes."

"Well, sit you down and I'll give you chapter and verse."

"Can I come back tomorrow? I promised I'd meet Walter Bryson now."

"By all means, Marc. It'll give me a chance to dig out the pamphlet."

I crossed the street just as Walter emerged from his office, so we hopped into the Bugatti and drove the few blocks to the Bryson house. Joyce welcomed us at the door in her apron, which was always a good sign, indicating that tasty food was in the offing.

On my inquiring about their daughter, Jennifer, Joyce told me she was away, having secured a summer job, camping on an island and trying to protect the nests of roseate terns from the predations of rapacious gulls. I was fond of Jennifer, having been associated with several unfortunate events in which she had been involved, and was glad to hear she had recovered and was well.

"I guess you heard about the poll this morning?" Walter asked as we settled in his den with glasses of single malt.

"Yes. Not good, but it could be worse."

"Not for me. You know I'm on the other side?"

"How could I forget it?"

"Haha. How's my man, John Wilkins, doing?"

"He seems like a pretty decent guy to me. A goodish speaker who makes reasonable points most of the time."

"Sounds just like his father."

"Who was his father?"

"You may be a politician Marc, but you don't know much about Nova Scotia politics. M. H. Wilkins was an MLA back in the 1960s and 70s."

"Really? Same party?"

"Of course!" Walter looked horrified. "How could he be in a different party?"

"Why not?"

"My dear friend, don't you know the people around you in the House of Assembly?"

"Sure I do."

"I mean their *families*."

"What do you mean?"

"Okay, look at the Opposition front bench to start. Apart from Wilkins, you have Celia McArthur."

"So?"

"Granddaughter of Gordon McArthur, former Attorney General. Then you have Eugene Comeau, nephew of Gaston Comeau, longtime MLA for Yarmouth. Bill Jenkins—"

"I don't like him."

"—son of Gerard Jenkins, former MLA for Pictou Centre."

"You're kidding?"

"Kidding? Let's look at your side Stephanie Gilmour, granddaughter of cabinet minister and Senator Franklin Gimour. Chester McCormack, son of Christopher, former Minister of Highways. Angela Stairs, niece of Brandon Stairs, former Member of Parliament. Pierre Dorion, grandson of Benoit Dorion, MLA for Argyle for 32 years. I could go on."

"Is this true? I had no idea."

"And let me tell you that the power behind the public figures, the wheelers and dealers in the parties, are all descended from a dozen families who wielded influence before them."

"My God. So their adherence to a party really doesn't have anything to do with ideology, platform or policies?"

"Of course not! Their loyalty, which is passed down from generation to generation, is the same as it is to a hockey team or a football club."

"But you can't say that about Wendell."

"No, the first black man wasn't in the legislature until 1993—"

"Or Ms. Sillyboy."

"No, she is the first of her ilk, if I may use an ancient expression."

"Or Dan Nathanson."

"No, but theoretically he could be included. The first Jew, Ezekial Hart, was elected in 1807, although he couldn't take his seat due to religious restrictions at the time. But George Savory, young Reid and

Angus Mackinnon all followed in the footsteps of family members."

"I must confess this has been a revelation to me. I am starting to feel quite out of place in the House."

"Who's feeling out of place?" asked Joyce as she came into the den.

"Marc is. I'm giving him another lesson on Nova Scotia politics."

"Well, dinner's ready, so let's have no more political talk tonight. We'll give the poor man a rest."

32

It is a much-overused aphorism that bad news or misfortunes does not arrive alone. In *Hamlet,* Shakespeare wrote, "When sorrows come, they come not single spies, but in battalions!" I do not know if anyone has done a scientific study on this question, but life experience seems to bear it out.

The day after the poll was released showing the government to have dropped in public opinion, news came of a more tragic blow. I was eating breakfast when the radio news informed me of George Savoy's death, and that he had collapsed and expired while addressing a meeting of fishermen in Shelburne.

The report said that he was 75, which came as a great surprise to me because I had thought him younger in light of his always seeming to be bouncy and energetic. He was one of the first MLAs I got to know after I was elected, and I liked him immensely.

I was particularly pleased that I had a hand in Wendell's promotion of him to Minister of Fisheries, a post he had held and loved many years ago in another administration. He was fond of saying that everything "had gone to the dogs", and now I was inexpressibly sad that he had gone, not to the dogs, but to a better place.

I wondered whom Wendell would promote to fill the vacancy because no matter whom he chose, he would undoubtedly offend those not selected.

John Trevor had the most righteous claim, but if Wendell wanted to keep the "wolf pack"—Leaman, McPhee and Reid—in his camp, at least one of them would have to be elevated soon. And if Wendell picked one of them, how alienated would John become? If Trevor was Wendell's choice, who would he make the Chief Whip? Was it a post which would satisfy one of the "wolf pack" or would they consider it insufficient to keep them from kicking over the traces?

Then again, as ridiculous as it might seem, would Alaric D'Entremont expect to get the job on the basis of hints I had dangled in front of him when I had tracked him down in Cape Breton? I did not envy Wendell having to make decisions, which would inevitably make him new enemies.

I also wondered when Wendell would call a by-election in Shelburne and what our chances were of holding the seat. One would suppose that the contest should be held soon, so that the victor could take their seat in time for the fall sitting of the House of Assembly.

There was something else which troubled me, although only as a possible cloud on the horizon. In a recent conversation, George had told me that his constituency association had "gone to the dogs" because one family, the Wayberts, had "muscled in" and taken over the executive with an eye to the day when George retired.

"Now, there's still a bunch of my kind of folk," George had said, "They're dead set against the Wayberts. They're the stalwarts—you know, older, wiser people like myself."

"These Wayberts don't sound like a nice bunch."

"No, they 'ant, Mr. Man. The problem's made a whole lot worse by the fact that the Wayberts don't like the premier because"—and here George lowered his voice—"he's black."

"No!"

"This kind of prejudice was much more common when I was a young man, you understand, but it still hangs on in a very small section of the population."

If what George had said was true, it had serious possible ramifications. In the event we held the seat at a by-election, and our candidate was one of the Wayberts, it raised the unpleasant possibility of one vote having to be moved from the left side of my "scorecard" to the right side. The "antis" would still need to get another ten votes to force a leadership review, but anything which brought them closer to their objective was bad news.

In this depressed mood, I was not looking forward to hearing a lecture from Gerald, but since I had asked for the information on Joshua Slocum and promised to come to the store today, I had no option but to go.

"Well, now then," Gerald arranged himself delicately on the edge of the counter, "where shall I start?"

"I guess at the beginning would be logical."

"Right you are! "Joshua Slocum was born in 1844 in Annapolis County and was the first person to sail single-handedly around the world. He became an American and was a sailor, adventurer, and a famous writer. His *Sailing Alone around the World,* which he published in 1909, was an international best-seller. Are you with me?"

"Yes, please go on."

"There is a monument you can see down on Brier Island not far from where his family had a boot shop. There are all kinds of biographies about Slocum, although some of them, in my humble opinion, are rather hard going. The Slocum River in Dartmouth, Massachusetts was named after him, and a newly-discovered plant in Mauritius was named in his honour. And during World War II, a Liberty ship was named after Slocum.

"Now then, we come to the interesting bit. On November 14, 1909, Slocum set sail, again alone, in his sailboat *Spray* from Vineyard Haven, Massachusetts, allegedly for the West Indies on one of his usual winter voyages—"

"Why do you say 'allegedly'?"

"Ah! That's what people heard him say. However, he had also expressed interest in starting his next adventure, exploring the Orinoco, Rio Negro and Amazon Rivers. Apparently, Slocum was as great a talker as he was an explorer, so people were used to him—I wouldn't call it boasting—speculating on prospective adventures."

"Thus confusing people, whether deliberately or not?"

"Exactly. Anyway our Josh pushed his boat out into the water, sailed out of the harbour and was never heard from again."

"No ships saw him?"

"No, but then they were all looking in the seas south of Massachusetts. The next year, his wife informed the newspapers that she believed he was lost at sea."

"But he was an experienced mariner. Were there any particularly ferocious storms in November and December of that year?"

"Not *south* of Massachusetts."

"How about north?"

"Several really bad ones north of that coast." Gerald nodded slowly. "You're catching on aren't you?"

"I think I am."

"You see, what is especially interesting, Marc, is that Slocum never learned to swim. Several times he said that learning to swim was useless. Just like many of our fishermen today think swimming is only useful if the land is very near. In 1924, Joshua Slocum was declared legally dead."

"Hmm." Momentarily, at least, this had taken my mind off poor George's death. "Do you happen to know about how long it would take a small sailboat to get from Massachusetts to Nova Scotia?"

"Aha! I see where you are going, but I was there ahead of you."

"What's the answer?"

"Longer than you might think. A small sailboat journey from Massachusetts to Nova Scotia could take anywhere from 15 to 30 days, depending on the specific route, sailing conditions, and the boat's speed."

"Really?"

"I think I can guess your next question."

"Can you?"

"I can. You now want to know if there were any wrecks recorded nearby between November 31 1909 and the end of December."

"And were there?"

"Oh yes, my dear. I refer you to a rather informative if somewhat ponderous tome, Jerome Haliburton's *Wrecks of Nova Scotia*, published in 1935."

"And what does that informative, if somewhat ponderous, tome have to say which would be relevant to our purposes?"

"On December 9, the wreckage of a small vessel was washed up at Horton's Landing—that is less than two miles from here, as the crow flies. The boat was so badly damaged there were no means of identification."

"So, assuming it was the *Spray*, and assuming Joshua survived the wreck, it is just possible he somehow struggled over land and got to his cousin's place?"

"I would say it was eminently possible."

"He might have survived to see his cousin or he might have expired as soon as he got to Grand Pre."

"Indeed, he might."

"So the skeleton which Bamby dug up in my garden could very well be the remains of the famous Joshua Slocum."

"Absolutely. But, Marc..."

"What?"

"You will never ever know for sure."

~

As I was crossing Main Street heading for my constituency office I saw that one of the banks had a sign in the window saying:

Retirement Reality Check:
two-thirds (66%) of Canadians say
inflation and increased cost of living
have made them adjust their retirement plans

It reminded me of the two-thirds vote the anti-Wendell forces would need to force a leadership review at convention. And then I wondered where the two-thirds majority rule came from. Did the caucus follow similar rules to the House of Assembly? Or was it run by some other system of rules? I thought we should check to be sure.

There were seven constituents in the waiting area to my office, one of them wearing a wide-brimmed hat and hunched over in her chair. I told Cheryl to hold them until I had made a call to Sandy Fergusson at the caucus office.

"Sandy, it's Marc LeBlanc."

"Well, hello. The Enforcer himself."

"Knock that off, please."

"Okay, Marc. What can I do you for?

"Can you tell me if, when the caucus is meeting, it follows the same rules as those in the House?"

"Oh, no."

"No? Then what rules does it follow?"

"Roberts Rules of Order."

"Are you sure?"

"Of course I'm sure. I've been working here since Jesus was in kindergarten."

"I see. Do you recall the last time the caucus called for a leadership review?"

"A leadership review? What do you mean?"

"If the caucus passed a request asking the party to hold a vote of confidence in the leader at a convention or annual meeting of the party?"

"Oh. I've never heard of it happening, but if it did, it would've been long before my time."

"Thanks, Sandy."

I went to my computer and looked up Robert's Rules of Order and went to the "votes" section. This is what I saw:

> Amend (Annul, Repeal, or Rescind) any part of the Constitution, By-laws, or Rules of Order, previously adopted; it also requires previous notice
>
> Amend or Rescind a Standing Rule, a Program or Order of Business, or a Resolution, previously adopted, without notice being given at a previous meeting or in the call for the meeting
>
> Take up a Question out of its Proper Order
>
> Suspend the Rules
>
> Make a Special Order
>
> Discharge an Order of the Day before it is pending
>
> Refuse to Proceed to the Orders of the Day
>
> Sustain an Objection to the Consideration of a Question
>
> Previous Question
>
> Limit, or Extend the Limits, of Debate
>
> Extend the Time Appointed for Adjournment or for Taking a Recess
>
> Close Nominations [26] or the Polls
>
> Limit the Names to be Voted for
>
> Expel from Membership: it also requires previous notice and trial
>
> Depose from Office: it also requires previous notice
>
> Discharge a Committee when previous notice has not been given
>
> Reconsider in Committee when a member of the majority is absent and has not been notified of the proposed reconsideration

I read and re-read it, but the only item even to come close to requesting a leadership review was "Depose from Office", which was not the same thing at all. "Depose from office" clearly meant kicking somebody out lock, stock and barrel, not asking some other body to do it.

I was thunderstruck that we had been operating under a serious misapprehension and that what we feared could be accomplished on a simple majority vote. My trepidation was greatly increased by the presumption that the other side would also have this information.

I called Tom immediately.

"Fuck!" he exclaimed. "Where in the hell did we get the two-thirds idea from?"

"I don't know. We keep repeating it to each other so I guess we all thought that one of us actually knew."

"According to your scorecard on my wall, they have eleven votes now, so they would need only nine more."

"Assuming we know who all the antis really are."

"Hell! I don't relish telling Wendell. When are you coming up next?"

"Tomorrow or the day after. Good luck with the boss, Tom."

"I'm going to need it. He'll hit the roof!"

The constituents' problems ranged from unemployment cases (which were strictly the purview of the Member of Parliament), traffic problems in town (which were a municipal responsibility), and comments, both for and against, about Wendell's reforms.

The last person was the hunched woman in the wide hat. As soon as Cheryl had closed the door, the woman took off her hat.

"Hello, Marc."

"Ellie! Good God, what are you doing here?"

Ellie MacLeod was one of the Opposition MLAs who had befriended me in my early days in the legislature. Despite her being on the other side I found that I liked her enormously and that we agreed on a great deal.

"First, my condolences on poor old George. I always liked him."

"Thank you."

"Can we speak in absolute confidence?"

"I guess so. I hope this is not going to put me in a compromising position."

"So do I. Marc, I've heard whispers that the premier is in trouble."

"How could I possibly comment on something like that? Why would you want to know?"

"I'd like to help."

"Help? The premier?"

"You know I really like him and I agree with what he is trying to do with his reforms. You do know that?"

"Yes."

"Is it true? Is he in difficulties?"

I remembered an old trick which Walter Bryson had played with me when I had wanted him to discuss another of his clients.

"I'm putting this pen over on this side of the desk. That means you can assume the negative. If I move it to that side, you can draw your own conclusions."

"Okay. Is it true?"

I moved the pen.

"Ah. So it's true. Is it very serious?"

I couldn't do anything.

"Let me rephrase. Is it extremely serious?"

I moved the pen back.

"I see. So it is a problem, but not yet critical?"

I moved the pen again.

"Right. Now listen carefully, Marc."

"I'm all ears."

"If your lot would have me, I'm ready to cross the floor."

"Holy shit!"

"I like John Wilkins. He's not a bad sort and I don't wish him any harm, but it's getting very difficult to work alongside shits like McNamara, Wong, Jenkins, Wolf, Gallant, Winters and Hudson. They are really despicable creeps."

"There are creeps on our side too. Believe me"

"Yeah, I figured as much, but your leader is for the greater good. He's what the province needs. Wilkins is okay, but let's face it: as a premier he'd be a disaster because he'd be controlled by the rats. Guys like Cohen, Comeau and Downey are good people and so is my buddy Martha, but the rats are breeding and soon may be in the majority."

"Ellie, I don't know what to say."

"Do you think the premier would welcome me?"

I pointed to the pen but did not move it.

"Do you think the caucus would take me if he gave it the okay?"

I did not move the pen.

"Thanks. Why don't we leave things as they are until you have had a chance to think about it and maybe talk to the boss?"

"Alright."

"You can hold me in reserve if you want, then play me when I'm most needed."

"Ellie, that's a marvelous idea. Thank you very much."

33

Two days after Ellie's stealthy visit to my constituency office, the newspaper arrived as I was cooking some eggs, mushrooms and bacon for breakfast. There did not seem to be much news of importance on the first few pages, but an unusual editorial caught my attention:

PROCTOR, TIME TO MATCH THE WORDS WITH ACTION

This newspaper has had occasion to take issue with some of Premier Wendell Proctor's reforms, but one with which we are in hearty agreement is his pledge to effect redistribution of electoral districts. In a modern democracy, it is quite ludicrous to have some constituencies with 6,000 voters and others with 12,000.

We do not go as far as the premier in calling some of the present ridings "racist" but we feel that drawing boundaries on the basis of race, language and ethnicity is anachronistic. It reminds us of the days when constituencies had dual candidates for Catholic and Protestant denominations.

Thankfully, that nonsense is behind us and we have moved on to more enlightened measures. It is time for us to do likewise with regard to racial and linguistic considerations. It has been several months since the premier promised redistribution. The time has come to act.

Or is he afraid to do so because his MLAs in Argyle and Preston would lose their seats? Come on, Premier: where's your courage?

I had guessed this particular chicken would come home to roost sometime, but I had not expected it so soon. The newspaper was right, of course, that Wendell should get on with it and do what he promised to do. He had been postponing taking action in order to hold the threat over the heads of Pierre Dorion and Gloria Jones to keep them in line. The tactic had failed spectacularly with Jones, but so far had worked with Dorion.

If he moved now, as I was convinced he should, he would, in modern parlance, have to throw Dorion under the bus. And in turn that meant Dorion would move from the left side of the 'scoreboard' to the right, giving the 'antis' twelve votes.

After breakfast, I drove up to Halifax. I did not take the direct route up Highway 101, but instead cut across the province to Chester, where I hoped to see Emma Mitchell. She was not in her constituency office on King Street, but her assistant told me I would find her walking somewhere near the Yacht club.

I drove slowly along South Street until I saw her about to go on to Peninsula Road. I blew my horn to attract her attention and, when she turned and recognized me, the look of sheer disgust on her face compelled me to assess my visit as a failure.

She would not get in the car, so I parked it and walked back to where she had sat down on a stone marker near a monument to Norwegian sailors who had spent time in the town during World War II. I guessed I would be wasting my time, but I had to try to mend fences.

"Good morning, Emma."

"Marc. What do you want?"

"Nothing. I just wanted to say hello."

"Just hello? This is a bit out of your way, isn't it?"

"A bit."

"Don't tell me you made a detour just to see little old me."

"Yes, actually I did."

"So, what's on your mind?"

"Not to put too fine a point on it, the premier asked me to see you to see if you're going to cause any more trouble."

"Trouble?"

"Yes, like voting against the government in the House."

"What about abstaining?"

"That, too."

"You want me to promise that I won't do either?"

"That's about the size of it."

"Well, I can't do that. I'll have to wait and see what happens."

"With what?"

"With everything."

"You don't have a problem with any particular legislation, do you? I mean, a serious problem?"

"No, but…"

"But what?"

"I'm still not happy with the affair with the Mullens girl."

"Not that again? You've been told over and over that she did not make a complaint, that Denis McNamara did it without her consent or knowledge. So what is your problem?"

"I think you browbeat her into signing the retraction."

"What? You don't have a single shred of evidence to support that charge."

"And you don't have a shred of evidence to prove I'm wrong."

"I do, indeed. The word of Ms. Mullens herself. She would deny it in court if necessary."

"I know what I know, and I believe what I believe."

"Why don't you go and ask her yourself? She'll tell you."

"I don't have to ask her. She should be left alone to grieve."

"My God, you are an excessively stupid woman."

"You bastard!"

"Listen to me, Emma. If you repeat the accusation in public, I will sue the pants off you, and the Halifax Chief of Police will join me in the action."

"You wouldn't dare!"

"Just watch me. You tell that lie in public and we'll ruin you. You'll lose your house, your car and your seat in the legislature."

"Fuck you, LeBlanc!"

We already knew Emma was a hopeless case, and I should have left it alone, but I had to give it one last try. I was annoyed with myself for losing my temper, but I could not think of any other approach which would have produced a good result. When foolish people want to believe in something false and illogical, nothing on earth will induce them to surrender their idiotic notions.

It was good to see Rosalie again, and I was glad that she reported having had a wonderful time with Cynthia. Seemingly, there was not a store or place of interest in the city where Cynthia had not taken her, but she said she was now ready to go home.

Rosalie was fascinated by the story which Gerald and I (with as much imagination as fact) had woven around the skeleton in the garden, and she conceded that it may well have been that of Joshua Slocum. She wondered if a man over 60 would really have set out to sail alone to South America.

"Maybe he had a falling out with Mrs. Slocum and just wanted to disappear."

"And if that was the case," I said, "where else would he go but to his cousin Bill?"

"I wonder if William could have kept his cousin a secret from the community—you know, so Mrs. S wouldn't get wind of his where-abouts. Our place must have been more remote in those days than it is today."

"I guess it's possible. Do you think I should ask for it to be re-turned?"

"What?"

"The skeleton. They've done all their tests now. It belongs to us, doesn't it?"

"Are you insane?"

"Don't you think Joshua should be laid to rest where Bill originally put him, rather than in some hospital or police garbage dump?"

"No, I do not! That skeleton is not coming anywhere near our house!"

I was not really intent upon the skeleton's return, but I was sur-prised by Rosalie's vehemence, so I dropped the subject. She wanted us to leave early the next morning, so I had to get my business with Wendell and Tom done that afternoon.

Tom took the 'scorecard' down from his wall, carried it into Wendell's office and propped it up in a chair.

"Okay, what's first on the agenda?" asked Wendell.

"Emma Mitchell," I said. "I saw her this morning and her name has to be moved as far to the right as it can go."

"That bad, huh?"

"She is a lunatic and will go to her grave a Proctor hater."

"Well, it's not like we've lost her, because we never had her," Tom said.

"Alright, what's next?"

"Wendell, we must go to George Savory's funeral."

"Oh shit, yes. When is it?"

"I'll find out," said Tom. "I presume it'll be in Shelburne, Barrington or Clark's Harbour."

"We should go together, if that's okay with you."

"Yeah, sure," Wendell said. "What are our chances in a by-election?"

"Excellent," said Tom. "But that may not be a good thing."

"You mean those fucking Wayberts?"

"Precisely. It looks as if Norman Waybert may get the nomination."

"Shit! Who are we running against him?"

"George's son, Aubrey."

"What are his chances?"

"I'd said 50-50."

"Is there anything I can do to nudge things in the right direction?"

"For God's sake, Wendell, no! If you stick your fingers into the race, it'll do more harm than good. You know how constituency associations like to think of themselves as independent."

"Yeah, you're right. What else?"

"First we have to talk about today's editorial," I said.

"I agree," said Tom firmly.

"Hell! Have I *got* to?"

"Yes!" Tom and I spoke in unison.

"If it's got to be done, let's get moving." He clicked his intercom.

"Yes, Premier?"

"Susan, please call Pierre Dorion's office and have him come over right away."

"It's the right thing to do," Tom said.

"So, that leaves two vacancies in the cabinet. Suggestions, please. Marc?"

"I think you have to bring in John Trevor. He's been loyal as a dog, but has been waiting a long time for his reward."

"Tom, are you okay with that?"

"Sure."

"Say we move John to Municipal Affairs. Who do we move to Fisheries?"

"I think it has to be given to one of the 'wolf pack', if those guys are to be kept in line," I said.

"Which one?"

"Leaman seems to be the head wolf, so it should be him."

"How about we give John Trevor's job as Chief Whip to one of the other wolves?" Tom asked.

"No," said Wendell with a frown, "I've got someone else in mind for that. But tell you what—let's strip the caucus chairmanship from that prick Freeman Murphy and offer that to another wolf."

"Excellent!" Tom said. "Who should it be? Reid or McPhee?"

"Who has the seniority?"

"Reid was elected first."

"Then he gets it."

A knock on the door announced the arrival of Pierre Dorion. He looked nervous, and it was clear he already knew that his days were numbered.

"Premier." His voice was strangulated and weak.

"Pierre, you know why I called you over."

"I guessed when I read the paper."

"Exactly, I've decided to move ahead with redistribution. I can't put it off. I know it's tough on you and Gloria. And the Opposition is affected, too, with Joyce Babin in Clare—but I have to do it."

"I see."

"Under the circumstances, you will want to be free to vote against it in the House and that will be perfectly alright. I understand."

"Thank you."

"And, obviously, I cannot have a minister who is diametrically opposed to government policy, so all that remains is for me to thank you most sincerely for your service to the province."

"Uh...right...um...when?"

"Tomorrow will be fine. John Trevor is taking your place so I'll ask him to liaise with you. Very best of luck to you, Pierre."

Dorion backed out of the room, seemingly reluctant to leave it.

When he was gone, Tom turned to the premier. "After what you just told Dorion, you'd better get Trevor on the blower now. He can't get this news from Pierre."

"Okay, right." Wendell then asked Susan to track down Sean Leaman and John Trevor and ask them to call in immediately.

"Dorion seemed to take it pretty well, didn't he?"

"You didn't give him any room to manoeuvre," said Tom. "The poor bastard was under the bus before he even knew he'd been thrown."

"Had to be done. Marc, you may as well move Pierre's name over to the right of the 'scorecard'."

"Right." I crossed out Dorion in the centre 'fence' column and wrote him in the 'anti' column. "You can't blame him, but there's no question he'll be an enemy from now on"

"Premier," came from Susan's voice on the intercom. "I have Mr. Leaman for you."

"Sean! How the hell are you?...Good, good. How does Fisheries sound to you?...Can you handle it?...Of course, I mean as minister. What else would I mean? You accept?...Good. Welcome aboard. See Adrian MacIsaac at the Executive Council office and he'll arrange everything. Oh, Sean, will you ask your friend Jeremy Reid to call me right away?...Yes, I'm going to do something for him. Not as much as I did for you, but all I can manage right now. I'm sorry I couldn't also find a place for Cullum, but you know how things are. Very soon I hope to be able to fit him in....Right. 'Bye, Sean."

"That's one down. Ah, here's Susan."

"Yes, Susan?"

"Mr. Trevor on the line, Premier."

"John, my old buddy! How do you fancy becoming Minister of Municipal Affairs?...You would? That makes me very happy. Could you liaise with poor Pierre?...Yes, he had to move on because of this redistribution business. Any time after tomorrow you can occupy the office...Great. See you soon, John."

"Premier," said Susan's voice. "I have Mr. Reid waiting on line two."

"Jeremy! How's every little thing?...Good, glad to hear it. Look, I want you to do me a favour...Well, it's like this. Poor Freeman Murphy has had to relinquish the position of caucus chairman. I was wondering if you would do me the honour of stepping into his shoes...You would? Well done! Check in with Sandy Fergusson...Okay, Jeremy. See you."

"Who's going to tell Freeman he's out?" Tom asked.

"Ah, yes. That brings me to the other vacancy."

"The Chief Whip's job," I said. "Who's going to fill that?"

"You are, Marc."

"*What?*" Again Tom and I spoke together.

"Who better than The Enforcer as Chief Whip?"

"But I don't have enough experience."

"Get it fast! And your first duty will also be a pleasure."
"What is it?"
"Tell that bastard Murphy he's fired as caucus chair."

34

Rosalie and I arrived in Grand Pre around mid-morning, and the first thing she did was visit the site of the skeletal discovery.

"There's nothing here!" she cried.

"No, they took the skeleton away and then back-filled it," I said, pointing. "It was right here. We're going to have asparagus from this patch. You can see the little crowns Bamby has planted."

"From the dead comes good things?" she asked sweetly.

"Yes, but not this year. It won't be ready to harvest for at least another year."

"They take that long before we can eat them?"

"'Fraid so, but they should be good eventually. Bamby tells me he put a ton of manure under them."

"Charming. Marc, can we go away somewhere?"

"Away?"

"Yes, far away from here and your Wendell."

"He's not *my* Wendell."

"It feels like that. Almost as if you're more married to him and Tom than you are to me."

"I'm sorry, darling."

"So can we go?"

"Sure we can. Where would you like to go?"

"Can we go back to Wales?"

"I don't see why not. When do you want to go?"

"Soon. Tomorrow, or the next day."

"My new job requires me to tidy up a few things—"

"Your *new job*? What new job?"

"Oh, I didn't have a chance to tell you last night. I'm Wendell's new Chief Whip."

"I don't believe it! You must be joking. Wendell wouldn't be that stupid."

I had not sought the position, and knew I was not really qualified to fulfill it, but it hurt me beyond measure that anyone, let alone my own wife, would think me incapable of, at the least, being a moderate success. I did not need reminding that I was an amateur in politics who still did not know many of that pursuit's workings. I also knew, if I probed deep enough to admit it, that I had allowed my association with Wendell to go to my head, and to an extent had become insufferable as a result.

But my confidence started to return and I thought defiantly that if I was good enough for the premier of the province, I should certainly be good enough for my critics.

Hardly knowing how to respond to Rosalie without showing anger, I walked away and examined all the fine work Bamby had done for us. There were signs of vigorous green life everywhere, and in a few weeks the garden would be a riot of good things to eat. If we went to Wales, as Rosalie suggested, I would have to make another agreement with Bamby to maintain the garden in good order. I walked to the very corner of the garden and over the fence into the field.

I could hear Rosalie calling me, but I ignored her, waded deeper into the tall grass and called Bamby. We agreed on a price and he said he would start tomorrow and give the garden his attention for two hours a day until we returned.

"Marc, were you serious?" she demanded when I returned from the field.

"Yes. Crazy isn't it? There's never a dull moment with Wendell." I spoke in an offhand, jocular way, hoping she would leave the subject alone.

"I hope you told him it was impossible. You did, didn't you?"

"Rosalie, when the premier of the province asks you to do something for him, you don't immediately insult him by questioning his judgment."

"Hmm," she snorted, clearly suggesting that she did question the premier's judgment.

"There's not a lot involved. Just making sure all our people vote the right way on government motions."

"Oh, is that all?"

"Yes, that and generally trying to keep them out of trouble."

"How will you do that?"

"I read somewhere that a Chief Whip is like a children's nanny. He flatters and praises them, helps them with their problems, cajoles them when they are recalcitrant and, when necessary, disciplines them with an iron hand."

She stared at me as if I were a total stranger, slowly shook her head, and wandered away towards the house.

I sat down on a wheelbarrow which Bamby had upturned near the edge of a seed bed and took out my phone again. I got Freeman Murphy at his home.

"Good morning, Freeman, it's Marc LeBlanc."

"What the hell do you want, LeBlanc?"

"I called to let you know that the premier has appointed me Chief Whip."

"The hell he has! What happened to John Trevor?"

"He's joined the cabinet as Minister of Municipal Affairs."

"Jesus! So what?"

"The premier asked me if, as my first act as Whip, I would call you. Personally."

"What about?"

"He wants me to inform you that your services as Caucus Chair are no longer required."

"What the fuck!"

"Effective immediately, your functions will be assumed by Jeremy Reid."

"You little bastard!"

"Goodbye, Freeman."

Then I called Tom and asked him who appointed the regional whips.

"The Chief Whip does that. With the boss's okay, of course."

"Of course."

"What are you thinking?"

"John, Chester, Fred and I are the only MLAs we have in the Valley."

"Yeah?"

"So why do we need a regional whip?"

"Haha! You bugger. You want to fire Fred Askey, don't you?"

"Well, we know he's over in the 'anti' column and is likely to stay there, so why not?"

"Just let me check with Wendell."

He was gone for several minutes. When he came back on the line I could hear he was still laughing.

"Marc."

"Yes?"

"Wendell said he'd like to have the pleasure of doing it himself, but he'll let you do the honours."

"Thanks, Tom. Give the boss my thanks."

I was about to call Askey, but then decided to drive over to Kentville and deliver the message in person. Truth to tell, I needed to restore my self-respect after Rosalie had deflated it, and verbally wounding Askey would serve the purpose admirably.

I put my head around the door, told Rosalie I was going out for an hour.

"What for?"

"Whip's business."

"What kind of Whip's business?"

"I have to fire someone."

Her mouth dropped open and again she gaped at me as if she had never known me.

Before she could say anything, I ducked out and hopped into the Bugatti. I was outside Askey's office building twenty-two minutes later.

When I came off the elevator, the huge woman was behind her desk and immediately scowled at me. "He's busy. He can't see you."

Without acknowledging her presence in any way, I pushed past her and shoved the door open.

Askey was listening to something on his headphones and jumped up. "What do you want?" he said, dragging off the head-phones.

"'Morning, Fred. I'm here to tell you that we no longer need a regional whip for this area...effective immediately."

"Oh yeah? Does this come from John?"

"John now has a department. He's no longer Chief Whip."

"Then...who... is?"

"I am."

"*You?*"

"Yes. And, Fred?"

"What?"

"Fuck you!"

As I got down to the street and walked back to the Bugatti I was elated. Rosalie had reduced me to five cents, but telling Askey off made me feel like a million dollars.

When I got back, she was in a much better mood and gaily came out into the yard to meet me. "All done. First class all the way."

"You've booked our trip to Wales already?"

"No time like the present. Come in and I'll give you the details."

She had worked fast, but had managed to figure out a fairly good plan. I was particularly pleased that Rosalie had not hired some box of a car, but had secured an Audi RS 5 Coupe. It was no Bugatti, but was head and shoulders better than most rental vehicles.

She had arranged for us to stay the night at Heathrow on the day of our arrival, pick up our car the next morning, head west along the M4 and shoot off near Swindon to the Cotswolds. We would stay two nights at The Lords of The Manor Hotel in Upper Slaughter, then head for Ledbury, stopping at the lovely old town of Tewkesbury on the way. In Ledbury she had booked us in for two nights at the ancient, black-and-white-timbered Feathers Hotel.

After that we would be off to Wales, with stops at Hereford to see the cathedral, and Hay on Wye, where there are something like a hundred book shops. We would have two nights at Llangoed Hall in Llyswen on the river Wye; thereafter to The Lion in Llanbister, not far from where the infamous alchemist Dr. John Dee had come. Rosalie had done some research and had ordered a book, *In Search of Doctor Dee*[7], which outlined much of his strange career. An express order; with any luck it would arrive before we left.

After Llanbister we would head north to The Hand Hotel in a remote village called Llanarmon-Dyffryn-Ceiriog. From there we would drive almost due west to the Snowdonia National Park and stay for some days at Betws-y-Coed, from where we could explore the wonderful mountainous country surrounding Britain's second-highest mountain. Then further west still would take us to the Llyn Peninsula, where the famous Prime Minister David Lloyd George was born and practised law.

Rosalie had arranged for us to spend a few days in each of the

---

7 *In Search of Doctor Dee* by Jeremy Akerman, available from Moose House Publications

coastal communities of Aberystwyth, Cardigan and Saint Davids. Leaving the Irish Sea, we would then head east into Carmarthenshire and stay in an old pub in Rhandirmwyn, a small village on the old animal drovers' route to their ancient markets in the south. Then further east we would go to the beautiful Gwyer Peninsula, staying at Oxwich, a place noted for its miles-long beach and its incredible, protected sand dunes. Two days in Cardiff, the Welsh capital, would cap off our tour of this amazing country.

We had both been to Wales before and adored it. Most people have barely heard of this tiny land, which is less than 200 miles long and only 90 miles wide. There is nowhere in Wales from which you cannot get to the sea and back in the same day; and the topography changes every few miles, revealing hundreds of rivers, lakes, waterfalls, mountains, pastures and millions of sheep.

The more I thought about it, the more ready I was to leave behind the world of political wheeling and dealing, rewarding and punishing. It was time for The Enforcer to take a break.

35

If I had thought I could make a clean getaway, I was mistaken because, early one morning, a few days before we were due to leave for Britain, Tom called.

"What are you doing down there?" he asked.

"This is where I live. Rosalie and I are leaving for England in a day or two."

"Well, you'd better get up here. Can you be here by ten?"

"What for?"

"You don't want to miss your first cabinet meeting, do you?"

"What are you talking about?"

"Didn't you know that the Chief Whip is a minister without portfolio?"

"You're joking!"

"No, it's been that way since Brenton Granger was premier. I should know, I used to occupy the same position."

"Good grief! Rosalie will murder me. She already thinks I've let politics go to my head."

"Come up for cabinet. Wendell wants another strategy meeting with you and me afterwards. The day after tomorrow you can go back and take off for Europe with your beautiful wife."

"Why the day after tomorrow? Why not tomorrow?"

"George Savory's funeral. Had you forgotten?"

"Oh yes. All right, Tom. I'll be there before ten."

Rosalie was, as I had hoped, half asleep when I crept into the bedroom. I leaned down and whispered to her.

"Got to go to Halifax, darling. Be back in two days. Then I'm all yours until we get back from Wales."

"Mmmm." She murmured and rolled over. I took this to be assent, grabbed a few of my clothes and gently exited.

It still being early, there was very little traffic on the roads and the Bugatti pulled into Province House exactly forty-three minutes after leaving Grand Pre. The car was running beautifully, as steady as a rock even at the highest speeds. I wondered now, as I had often done so before. If there was anywhere, maybe some unknown abandoned airport, in the province where I could take the Bugatti to its 400 kph limit.

Only Adrian MacIsaac was in the cabinet room when I went in. He was laying out papers in front of each place. As Clerk and Secretary to the Executive Council he kept the minutes and coordinated action on any decisions made.

"Good morning, Marc. You'd better come next door with me."

"Hello, Adrian. Why?"

"I have to swear you in as a member of the Executive Council. Strictly speaking it should be done by the Lieutenant Governor, but he's out of town."

With this formality completed, we went back to the cabinet room, where ministers were filing in. Mark Gardiner gave me a glare of undisguised malice as he passed. Zandili Joseph's look was, first, of disbelief, then of defiance. Jill Rutledge backed away from me as though in fear of her life. Joan Howard, as beautiful as ever, Arthur Sullivan, Chester McCormack, Angus MacKinnon and Stephanie Gilmour all welcomed me. Hector MacNeil waved from across the table, but Angela Stairs and Harold MacDonald only nodded.

Wendell, the last to arrive, took his place. I looked around, wondering if I should sit at one of the chairs at the side of the room, but he beckoned to me and pointed to a seat directly opposite to himself.

"Sit down, Marc, you're holding up the proceedings."

After briefly explaining my presence to any who did not already know, he called for the first item of business.

I am ashamed to admit that I did not find my first cabinet meeting at all exciting. In fact, it was excessively boring, with some ministers, particularly Kessegoo'e Sillyboy, Joseph and Gardiner droning on and on, not very skilfully trying to relate every discussion to their own pet projects.

Kessegoo'e kept raising the matter of reparations to so-called "indigenous" people, prompting Chester to ask what per capita sum she had in mind. When she said she thought the minimum amount should be $10,000, Chester whipped out his calculator and asked her from where she would find the $550 million necessary to carry out her plan. When she was unable to identify a source, Wendell said they should move on.

However, Zandili jumped in, claiming that if reparations were on the table, she wanted them for black Nova Scotians, too. When Chester told us that the total for both would come close to one billions dollars, Wendell stepped in and said this was matter for a separate item for a future cabinet, adding, "a very future cabinet."

Cabinet lasted for about four hours, leading me to conclude that Wendell either was not a good chairman, or was not the dictator many made him out to be. He certainly did not take account of an old maxim the late Tommy Douglas often used that "the mind can absorb only what the ass can endure." I thought Wendell gave far too much latitude in debate, allowing ministers to take much more time than was either necessary or desirable.

Of course, I was in no position to compare Wendell's style with that of premiers who had preceded him. However, I had heard that, before cabinet met, Brenton Granger interviewed each minister with a proposed item on the agenda and grilled them mercilessly. Only when satisfied their proposal was sound would he let it go forward. Then, in cabinet itself, he would allow only those who had objections to speak, thus reducing the time consumed. Of the two styles, I would have chosen Granger's as the more efficient.

Tom was waiting for me outside the room and walked with me to Wendell's office.

"We are wondering if we should have a desert storm."

"What the hell is that?"

"Preemptive action. Clean out the rats now. Long before the next session of the House."

"It's an idea worth considering."

We went ahead of the premier, who was temporarily tied up discussing something with Susan, so we flopped down in the arm chairs.

"I guess you know, I could have been sitting there," said Tom, pointing to Wendell's high-backed chair.

"I'd heard something along those lines."

"When Granger drowned, the movers and shakers in the party— the establishment-- got together and took a vote on who should be their contender. Wendell came third."

"Then when why was he selected?"

"I was first, but turned it down because I was going through hell with Heidi at the time."

"Who was second?"

"Chester, but he declined on account of his age."

"Was that when Ernie Maddingly was premier pro tem?"

"Yes, that's right. He expected us to pick him! Good lord, can you imagine?"

"I remember interviewing him two years ago. He told me he had been denied the premiership by 'a jumped up cabal'."

"Poor old Ernie. Still, he's been an excellent Speaker. To put him in the Chair was an inspired move by the boss."

"Yes, from what I've seen I think it makes much more sense having the Speaker be someone of experience who is on the way out, rather than some newly elected bristling, young partisan who wants to impress the boss with his slanted rulings."

"I agree, but that's the way it was always done until Ernie."

"What are you two plotting?" Wendell came in, grinning from ear to ear. "Trying to wage a coup against me?"

"If we were," I said, "you'd already be gone."

He stared at me for a second, then burst into laughter.

"Right, let's get down to it. Marc, tell me about Zandili and Jill."

"I don't know what I can tell you that you don't already know."

"Would you say that their positions on the right side of the 'score-card' are immovable?"

"Zandili, for sure. With Jill, It's difficult to say, as she is such a wimp. If push came to shove and she was exposed to pressure from both sides, my guess is she would go with Hendricks, Jones, Parish and Mitchell."

"Yes, that's if push came to shove, but would promising to keep her in cabinet or even promoting her make her more susceptible to coming to our side?"

"My guess—and it's only a guess—is no. I think she's lost. You need to be more concerned about those on our side we could lose for lack of attention."

"Hmm. Who did you have in mind?"

"Nathanson. MacPhee, and D'Entremont."

"That little turd!" Tom broke in. "He should be grateful we didn't let him be expelled."

"I know, Tom, but he's an evil Walter Mitty type. He has grandiose visions of his own importance, and, in his own twisted mind, he can do wrong. If others criticize him, he thinks it's proof that he is right."

"So, basically, you're saying that no matter how much we reward him, we could never trust him?"

"Exactly. The minute he thought he could get more by switching sides, he'd be gone like a shot."

"Alright, let's set him aside. Should we move him to the middle of the 'scoreboard'?"

"Yes, I think it's be wise."

"Let me get this straight," said Wendell. "You told me that the 'wolf pack' were loyal to each other. If we got Nathanson to replace Rutledge and McPhee to replace Joseph, wouldn't Reid feel slighted, being left in a consolation position like caucus chair?"

"Maybe he would," said Tom. "We sort of told him putting him in as caucus chair was a temporary pause in his way up the ladder."

"Wendell," I said, getting an idea which so frightened me I wondered if I should keep it to myself. "Why not make a clean sweep? Fire the haters and the fence sitters. Sillyboy and Gardiner, too. Give Gardiner's job to Reid. You know he hates you, and if the crunch comes he will definitely be on the other side."

"Whoa!" Tom shouted. "Are you out of your mind? That would be like the Night of the Long Knives, don't you think, Wendell?"

"Hmm. That idea is not as crazy as it sounds. Let me think." He chewed his lip and looked thoughtful. "Alright, but not Sillyboy. I have to leave her there for the time being. Tom, has anything gone to the media about Marc yet?"

"Not yet."

"Okay, we'll announced a major cabinet shuffle. Gardiner, Rutledge and Joseph out. Reid to Tourism and Culture, McPhee to Lands and Forests, and Nathanson to Environment, LeBlanc to Chief Whip."

"Wow!" Tom exclaimed. "Then who will be caucus chair?"

"Shit! Marc?"

"Zila Franks," I offered, since there was nobody reliable left.

"I forgot about her," said Wendell. "I don't think I've even spoken to her more than twice. Is she alright, Marc?"

"I think so. She owes me big-time. I got her out of a real mess, and I think this will consolidate her support."

"Then, that's it. Tell Susan to get the unlucky ones on the blower and then the lucky ones."

"I'm on it."

"And, Tom, call George Savory's son. Tell him we'll be at the funeral tomorrow and that I'll be announcing a by-election in Shelburne for thirty-four days from today. That should give him time to get his ducks in a row."

The next day we drove down to Clark's Harbour for George's funeral and I was heartened to see that so many people felt the same way about him as I did. Hundreds turned out for the ceremony and his son, Aubrey, gave a marvellous speech telling us what a splendid father George had been. Of course, much attention was given to Wendell's presence, and after the service he was mobbed by people wanting to shake his hand.

I noticed a group of less-keen mourners over to one side and, on inquiring, learned that these were members of the Waybert clan, led by Norman, a tall, red-haired young fellow.

~

Predictably, the cabinet shuffle created a great stir. While there was much wailing and gnashing of teeth within the party, in the province generally the act was seen as that of a strong leader, and Wendell's stock rose somewhat.

Tom related to me by phone that, when told of her ousting, Rutledge had just whimpered that she had been expecting it. He said that Gardiner and Joseph had been viciously bitter when informed about their demotions, both blaming me for their misfortunes. On the other side of the coin, compensating for the abuse from Mark and Zandili, the 'wolf pack' gave me full credit for having recommended them to the premier. Tom said that Dan Nathanson had become fulsome in his expression of gratitude and had sworn life-long fealty to Wendell.

He also said that when he told Zila she was to be Caucus chair with an extra $11,000 a year, she had accused him of being a scam artist, and that it had taken several return calls before she believed what he was offering. She asked why she was being singled out for such an honour when she was only a freshman MLA and, when Tom told her that it was all my doing, she said, "Marc has been so kind to me. I guess it isn't true that he's a rat."

~

Rosalie and I were in central Wales when the Shelburne by-election was held. Our party won with a reduced majority of 891 votes, but, unfortunately, Norman Waybert became the party's candidate, defeating George's boy, Aubrey, by 124 votes to 113 at the nominating convention. In my absence, Tom wrote Waybert's name on the right hand side of the 'scorecard'.

36

For Rosalie and me the summer passed pleasantly, full of sunshine, surprisingly little rain, minor adventures on Welsh mountain tops and in deep valleys, and uneventful days back at Grand Pre. Our trip to Britain was even more delightful than we had anticipated, our only disappointment being that on three separate climbs to the top of Snowdon (Yr Wyddfa), the legendary magnificent view was denied us because of cloud cover.

We saw the remains of the homestead from which Owain ap Gruffydd Glyndwr set out on a fifteen-year mission to challenge the strength of the English King Henry IV. We saw dozens of incredibly-remote Iron-Age hillforts perched atop the pinnacles of every mountain range, the walls of Roman villas and, of course the myriad stone castles built by the mighty Edward I in his efforts to subdue the unruly Welsh.

Everywhere there was a pervasive lushness; a hundred shades of green wherever one looked, from the slightly brownish-green of the mountain slopes and the dark green of the oaks and elms which populated the valleys, to the bright lime-green carpets of the rolling fields, dotted with countless white sheep.

We were not surprised to learn that there are approximately nine million sheep in Wales, because we imagined we had seen at least half that number on our travels. They roam the countryside and mountain tops at will and, we were told by a farmer, whose name was Rhys, that they are rounded up twice a year for lambing and shearing. To avoid confusion at the time of the round-up, each animal is distinguished by means of yellow electronic identification tags or ear tags in blue, green, or orange (but not yellow, red or black, but we never found out why those colours were prohibited), or paint markings. Rhys said that all the farmers on a particular mountain range would gather with their dogs—mostly border collies—and bring in all the sheep they could find and then sort out who owned what from the animals' markings.

Wales has 1,680 miles of coastline, containing high, rugged cliffs; colonies of puffins, guillemots, razorbills and shearwaters; expansive sandy beaches; small islands inhabited by monks; precipitous promontories like fingers extending into the Irish Sea; and snug little harbours with curved wharves and brightly-painted fishing boats.

Our final stay in Wales was in Cardiff, where we saw the impressive castle, which has eleventh-century foundations, and the elegant civic centre built of white Portland stone. This latter includes government buildings, law courts and the National Museum of Wales. Building was started before World War One and completed in 1922.

Some people we talked to said that this magnificent civic centre, which only missed the Edwardian era by a few years, was somewhat out of place in a bustling city reinventing itself with incessant construction, but to us it was a much-needed oasis in a desert of crude modernity.

In the nineteenth century, Cardiff (Caerdydd) was transformed from a provincial town into a huge, dynamic seaport by the discovery and exploitation of vast amounts of coal in the many valleys which fan out to the north of the capital. The concomitant development of huge steel mills led to the docks becoming by 1896 an enormous port, the world's busiest for coal exports, dispatching seven million tons a year, which was more than New York. Just one of the docks, which covered 18 acres, could accommodate 300 ships simultaneously, with over a mile of wharves for loading.

This in turn led to a cosmopolitan dockland population which, in its notorious Tiger Bay area, produced riots, killings and Shirley Bassey, who became famous for singing the title songs for the James Bond movies. We spoke with one old man, Glynn Prosser, who told us that when he was a youngster the police (he called them "bobbies") used to patrol Tiger Bay in threes, truncheons at the ready, because it was so dangerous.

Rosalie and I had a wonderful time. As always, we were entranced by this wonderful, tiny country. I returned the Audi to the hire company in Cardiff and we caught the train to London, where we spent a day sight-seeing before flying home.

No sooner had we arrived back in Gran Pre than the phone buzzed and I returned to reality with a bump.

"Where the hell have you been?"

"Good day to you too, Tom. We've been away. I told you all about it."

"I guess you might have told me. Where've you been?"

"Wales, I told you that, too."

"Wales? That's the bit between England and Ireland isn't it?"

"Tom, you are such an ignoramus."

"Thanks. Seen the paper today?"

"How could I? We've only just this minute got through the door."

"Well, there's been a new poll. We're down again, this time to 41%."

"What was it last time? I forgot."

"43% and 39% to the Opposition. They stayed static, thank God."

"Where did the two points go? To the undecided?"

"No to Dana Edward's crowd. They are now at 20%."

"Much good may it do them. That's worth one more seat at best."

"Yeah, but it still doesn't look that good for the boss."

"If the Official Opposition had gone up at our expense, it would have been damaging, but as it is I don't think it'll do much harm."

"I hope you're right, but it's put Wendell in a gloomy mood."

"Any rumblings in the ranks?"

"Just the usual...from the usual suspects."

"No new rumblers?"

"Just young Waybert."

"How?"

"He's in here every second day demanding roads, culverts and wharves for his riding."

"Are they doable?"

"Bill Clark says we can do some of the secondary roadwork and the culverts, but we can't do wharves unless the Feds get involved. It costs over 100 million to build a new wharf."

"Is he setting us up deliberately to give himself a reason to openly challenge Wendell sometime in the future?"

"Wow! You're doing the long-term thinking. I never thought of that. Maybe, but I think for now he may want us to turn down his requests so he can rationalize being on the other side."

"Hmm. How are the new ministers doing?"

"Pretty well. John Trevor is a dynamo. I think he's already met with every mayor and warden in the province. The 'wolf pack' seems eager and competent, but Dan Nathanson seems to be struggling a bit."

"Remind me, what portfolio did he get?"

"For Christ's sake, Marc. You're a member of the freaking cabinet yourself now and you don't know who your colleagues are?"

"Sorry, Tom. But I've just come from another world. Better than this one."

"Alright for some, roaming around the world. Anyway, Dan is at Environment."

"Ah yes, now I remember. What's his problem?"

"He thinks his job is to save the earth."

"Isn't it, sort of?"

"Hell, no. The earth has looked after itself for 4.6 billion years, and it always will no matter what we do or don't do. Dan's job is to ride herd over a bunch of administrative minutiae dealing with rains, drains, and stains."

"That Wendell's view, too?"

"Very much so."

"What concerns me, Tom, is that after the shuffle, the gender balance of the cabinet is way off. Only four women left. We used to have twice that number."

"I know. Wendell brought that up with me the other day, but there's nothing we can do about it if the available women are all hostile."

"That's true, and it's much too early to consider Zila. We don't know yet if she's going to make a hash out of the caucus chair."

"We'll have to watch her closely. If she shows promise, we may bring her in. Don't forget that, under Robert's Rules of Order, the Chair can only vote to make or break a tie."

"Ah, that's interesting. I may have an answer to this problem, but I can't talk about it on the phone."

"Tell me."

"Not now. Later on, when Wendell is present."

"Don't be so fucking mysterious, Marc. Just for that I may not tell you my secret worry."

"You'll understand when the time is right. What's your secret?"

"It isn't a problem yet, but it has the potential to become one if we're not careful."

"What is it?"

"Unlikely as it may seem, the egomaniacal young D'Entremont has started an affair with one of our ladies."

"Good God, not with Zila, I hope. She's very vulnerable."

"No, not Zila."

"Stephanie?"

"No, she is too much of a lady for that creep."

"I can't quite see Kesegoo'e going for Alaric, but I guess stranger things have happened."

"Not her."

"Oh, you mean one of the many females in the hostile column. That would make sense."

"Wrong again."

I blinked and thought hard. Who on earth could he be referring to you? Then it hit me like a pile driver. "You don't mean Angela Stairs?"

"The Ice Queen herself, yes. Hard to imagine someone as controlled and cold as her falling for a rat like him."

"I'm flabbergasted. Tom, are you sure about this?"

"Documented late-night visits to her apartment on Brunswick Street, as well as highly unusual warmth shown in public."

"You've spied on them?"

"Had to. Security."

"Jesus, Tom. This goes too far."

"I would have had you do it but you weren't here."

"Does Wendell know?"

"Yes."

"And?"

"He had a quiet word with Ms. Stairs and asked her if she was sure she was doing the right thing."

"And what did she say?"

"She reminded Wendell how competent and faithful she had been all along, and coolly informed him that she was an adult and could make up her own mind."

"I'll bet that shut him up."

"It did. He said he didn't know what to say or do. Then he said that when she got up to leave, she suddenly turned round and said, "Wendell, for the first time in my life I'm in love!'"

"Holy shit!"

"My initial reaction too, but I have a suspicion the kind of shit will turn out to be very unholy."

~

The summer came to an end, and with the fall came a brief sitting of the legislature. The agenda was light except for the electoral redistribution bill, which was declared by both sides of the aisle to be a free vote.

The bill passed easily. As expected, Pierre Dorion, Gloria Jones and Joyce Babin spoke and voted against it and some, like Mitchell, Parish, Chan and Hendricks on our side and Dayle Doucet, Celia McArthur and Eugene Comeau on their side, abstained by leaving the chamber before the vote.

On none of the other votes did I have to impose discipline, and the background grumbling was kept to a low hum. Zila Franks, who was embarrassingly nice to me, performed extremely well as Caucus Chair, showing firmness and fairness. For once, Carol Walters did not express her contempt.

However, as anticipated, Gardiner and Joseph snarled at me when I was in their presence and Rutledge teared up and turned away.

I made a point of closely watching Angela Stairs and the wretched Alaric, and concluded that they were definitely deeply involved. However, I was very disturbed to note that when they thought they were unobserved, she was quite affectionate, but he seemed to be offhand, if not contemptuous. There was little question in my mind that no conceivable good could come of this liaison, but rather a great deal of mischief.

But on the whole I thought things could be a lot worse, and it looked as if we could have a decent Christmas and a relatively uneventful New Year.

37

Since neither of us had relatives in the province, Rosalie and I spent Christmas Day alone in Grand Pre. On Christmas Eve we went over to Joyce and Walter Bryson's house for drinks and were delighted to see Jennifer, whose demeanour suggested she had overcome the grief of losing her best friend, Tracey.

I have told the story of Tracey's murder elsewhere[8], but it would stay in our minds for years to come, not least because nobody had ever been charged with her killing. The four villains of the affair surrounding her unfortunate demise had all been sent to prison for many years, but the murder could not be pinned on any one of them, and officially stood unsolved.

The Brysons had told her about my being dubbed 'The Enforcer", and she teased me mercilessly during a long, interesting conversation about politics and her adventures at university. On one level I was envious, because I easily remembered the good times I had experienced at college, but back then a university education was more about learning then it was about abiding by moralistic regulations imposed by guilt-ridden western society.

Of course, the political correctness movement was well under way when I attended university, but its idiocy was not as far advanced it is now. I often wondered how the academics of the generations represented by Payne, Mill, Whitehead and Russell—or even Newton, Hobbes and Locke—would react if they could see what passed for a liberal education today. I am sure they would be horrified, and conclude that today's universities are the complete antithesis of places of learning as they had understood them. For them, no idea, no matter how absurd, was forbidden in discussion; all ideas were welcomed for

---

8 *My Brother's Keeper*, Moose House Publications

examination and dissection, all theses were invited to be put to the test of logical scrutiny.

I was depressed to learn from Jennifer that at her college a professor, of mathematics no less, was fundamentally misrepresenting the subject and its principles by claiming that math was racist, white and patriarchal. Other of her teachers, she told me, were insisting that portraits of the university's founder be taken off the walls because his wealth, which built the original college, had been accumulated in the nineteenth century and therefore had to have been indirectly obtained from slavery.

"Don't you corrupt my daughter," Walter said. "I expect her to vote the way I do, and the way my father did, and his father before him."

"Fat chance of that!" Jennifer said with a laugh.

"How sharper than a serpent's tooth it is to have a thankless child," Walter said. "In my day we obeyed our parents to the letter."

"Like you did when your mother told you not to date me," Joyce called from the kitchen.

"Ah, that was an exception caused by the rarity and preciousness of the prize I gained."

"You're not in court now, Walter Bryson," said Joyce, seating herself on the sofa with precision. "He does talk a lot of nonsense, you know, Marc."

"Not nearly as much as Marc does," said Rosalie. 'This politics business seems to have completely taken him over. I hardly know who he is any more."

The words struck me like a knife to the heart. Was it some kind of warning signal? I did not know what to think. I stared at her, clearly showing some alarm.

"Well, you know it's true," she said, "I've regretted it ever since I allowed Wendell to talk me into letting you be a candidate."

"In a real sense it was your decision that I should run," I said defensively. "I would never have done it if you hadn't encouraged me."

"Don't blame me for your own misdeeds!" Rosalie snapped.

I decided not to continue the discussion in front of the Brysons, and likely would not at any time. There was nothing to be gained from trying to convince someone who felt wronged that they had not been unjustly used.

I knew that politics had taken me away from home much more

than would normally have been the case, and I knew now—if I had not fully guessed before—that if matters continued as they were, my marriage might be in real danger. But I was committed to Wendell and his quest to consolidate his leadership of the party and the province.

Looking back, it seemed impossible that only a year ago I had been uninterested in and ignorant of politics and political life, but now it consumed most of my time and thoughts. In the early stages, I had said repeatedly that I was only in it for one term, but I noticed I had not said that within recent memory.

Now I knew it had to be that way. When this legislative term was over I had to get out and, if I could do so before then without letting Wendell down, I must.

On Christmas day, Rosalie and I roasted a duck, which we had with Brussels sprouts, roast potatoes and mushroom sauce. Because it was a special day, and we felt rather lonely, I brought up a bottle of *Romanee Conti* 1995 and let it breathe for about half an hour. It was exquisite, with penetrating aromas of red cherry, spices and oak, one of the most magnificent wines I have ever tasted. Sadly, I had only one more bottle left in my cellar.

On New Year's Day, we rambled around our huge field, which was swathed in snow, especially at the western end where it slopes sharply down to the small river. On our way down there, the snow was up to our waists and we stood on the small, sandy shore brushing ourselves off. We looked up the hill on the other side of the river, where the vines of John Dempster's vineyard were tiny black protrusions through a smooth white blanket.

That evening Rosalie decided she wanted chowder to warm her up, and, despite our having to use frozen fish and seafood, it was quite presentable, served with hot biscuits and rich, yellow butter from the farm up the road. With that we drank a bottle of Krug Champagne and had an early night.

If I felt a little bored with life, and expected the next month or so to be uneventful, I received a rude awakening in the form of a phone call from Zila Franks.

"Happy New Year, Marc. It's Zila."

"Same to you, Zila. How was your Christmas?"

"Quiet. Thank God my son and heir stayed away. I still owe you—"

"Zila, forget about it. Pay me back if you win the lottery."

"That's very generous, Marc. I'll never forget it."

"Why were you calling?"

"Oh, God, yes. I nearly forgot! I received a letter this morning and, seeing as how you're the Chief Whip, I thought you should know about it right away."

"Who's it from?"

"Delia Parish."

"Uh-oh. What did she say?"

"It's a notice of motion to be put at the next caucus meeting."

All my muscles tightened and my blood ran cold. My stomach turned over in the grip of fear.

"What's the motion?"

"'Resolved that caucus request the party executive to arrange for a leadership review at the earliest possible moment.'"

"Is there a seconder?"

"Yes, it's Emma Mitchell."

"Pair of bitches!"

"That's what I thought, too."

"Zila, please keep this to yourself for the time being. I'll get back to you after I've had a chance to talk to the premier."

"Okay, Marc. Will do."

I couldn't get Wendell at home and he was not in his office. I guessed he was attending some vast family gathering organized by his sister, Grace, and would be tied up there for some time, so I called Tom.

After some agreeable small talk with Heidi, Tom came on and I explained what had occurred.

"Fuck! This must mean that they think they have the numbers."

"You think?"

"Why else would they show their hand? How many votes would they need?"

"Sixteen."

"How many did they have the last time we checked?"

"Thirteen"

"How many do we have, including the ones we can't trust?"

"Eighteen."

"How many do we have that we can count on?"

"I'd say fifteen for sure, that's without Zila."

"Why're you counting her out?"

"She's in the Chair."

"Oh, right. Who do you think they have—or think they will get?"

"MacDonald, D'Entremont, Sillyboy would give them sixteen. You pays your money and you takes your choice. Do you know where Wendell is?"

"He's at his aunt's place in Harrietsfield."

"When's he coming back?"

"Tomorrow."

"If you can convene a meeting in the afternoon, I'll come up in the morning."

"Okay. I'll tell the boss."

I hesitated for about an hour before making my next move, not knowing if this was the right time. After puzzling Rosalie by walking up and down in the house like Felix the Cat, I finally called Ellie MacLeod.

"Ellie, it's Marc."

"Oh, hi, Marc. I was expecting to hear from you."

"You were? Why?"

"I was told there were rumblings in the other camp."

"Where did you hear that?"

"You know Martha McNaughton? Of course you do. Anyway, Martha is pally with Emma Mitchell's sister Andrea. Apparently, Emma was half in the bag two nights ago and said something to the effect that they had 'a nasty surprise for that fucker Proctor that would teach him a lesson.'"

"Really? In that case, I have to ask if you've changed your mind."

"No, not at all."

"Good. Get ready. Be prepared to move when I give the word."

"Right. I've had my statement to the media ready for some time."

"Have you told anyone?"

"No. Of course not."

"Well, please don't say anything until after the media has the story."

"I have to tell John Wilkins. I owe him that. You understand?"

"Yes, I do. You can call him the minute your announcement has been issued."

"Got it. Marc, how serious is the situation for the premier?"

"Might be touch and go, but it'll be a lot better if you're onside."

38

I had a good, clear run to Halifax, getting there before noon, about 45 minutes after I had left Grand Pre.

When I pulled the Bugatti into the Province House parking lot, I noticed a face in one of the windows that flank the main door. Normally, if one saw anybody in these windows it would be one of the commissionaires, but this person was blonde and wore sunglasses.

As I parked the car, I feared the worst, and, sure enough, it was Alaric D'Entremont lying in wait for me.

I tried to walk through to the west door very quickly, but he grabbed me by the arm. "Not so fast, my Acadian brother," he said in a strident tone. "I want a word with you."

"Oh, hello, Alaric, what is it? I'm due in a meeting."

"Come into the Uniacke Room and sit down for a minute."

"I don't think I have time."

"I think you'll make time. You might have noticed that things are changing around here."

Reluctantly I followed him into the side room where usually committees would meet, but this morning it was empty. He kicked a chair towards me and sprawled on the edge of a table.

"I think it's time to collect on your promises," he said.

"What promises?"

"The promises you made to me when you physically abducted me from Arichat last year."

"I did not abduct you. I rescued you from your own stupidity. And I certainly made you no promises."

"That's not the way I remember it."

"Then your memory is at fault, Alaric."

"Oh no. You said if I behaved myself and was a good boy I would get into cabinet—"

"That's a lie. *You* said you should go into cabinet, but I said that was a preposterous claim in view of your disgraceful behavior."

"Clearly our recollections are different." He sniffed. "Then you said that if I didn't get into the cabinet you would get me the whip's job—"

"Another lie!"

"Is it? You as good as promised it, but instead of getting it for me, you nabbed it for yourself."

"This is ridiculous. I'm leaving."

"Now you listen to me, LeBlanc. I know about the notice of motion. If you want my support in voting against it"—he paused with dramatic effect—"and the support of those close to me, you'll tell Proctor he better come up with the goods."

"The Whip's job?"

"Huh! That boat has sailed, LeBlanc. It's a cabinet post, or we vote for the motion."

"Who's 'we'?"

"You know what I mean. Don't play games with me."

I left him, rushed across the road and went to the seventh floor. As I came out of the elevator Susan told me to go straight into the premier's office.

Wendell was at his desk, surrounded by Tom, Joan, Chester, Angus, Stephanie, Bill Clark, John Trevor and Hector McNeil.

"Come in, Marc. Grab a seat, if you can find one. Anything new?"

"I was just collared by D'Entremont, who let me know, in no uncertain terms, that unless he gets a cabinet post he 'and those close to him' would vote for the motion."

"I've just had someone very close to him tell me the same thing."

"Angela? What did she say?

"She said that if I didn't put dear Alaric in the cabinet, she would have to consider her position."

"What did you say?"

"I told the silly cow I don't give in to blackmail and I'd accept her resignation any time."

"And what did she do?"

"She wrote it out and signed it there and then."

"My God! Amazing what the power of love will do."

"Love, huh! What else could I do? Having the pair of them in cabinet would be insufferable. How many have they got on their side now,

Marc?"

"Fifteen."

"And how many do we have?"

"Sixteen, including Harold and Kessegoo'e and excluding Zila, because she'll be in the chair."

"What do you think, Chester?" asked Wendell.

"Premier...I...er..."

"Chester?"

We all turned to look at McCormack who seemed to be lost for words, clutching at his throat and turning a purple-grey colour.

"Chester," Stephanie said, "are you alright?"

He reached towards her and, as he did, crashed to the floor.

"Tom, call an ambulance quickly." Wendell barked. "Give him some space!"

We all backed away from the crumpled figure on the carpet and waited for the paramedics to arrive. They came a lot quicker than I expected, strapped Chester on their stretcher and took him away.

"How bad do you think he is?" Bill Clark asked.

"Hard to say," Wendell said, "Tom, go after them. Stay with him and call us when you know something."

"I'm on it," Tom said, and was gone.

"If Chester is in a really bad way," said Angus, "or, God forbid, he dies, that will leave us with the same number of votes as the other side."

"Jesus!'" said Wendell. "Can we delay the vote?"

"Only by delaying the session of the House," I said. "If the House sits there has to be a caucus meeting beforehand."

"That's right," said Bill Clark. "How long could you delay meeting the Legislature?"

"If necessary until May, but it would cause such a commotion, the media would soon get wind of why we're doing it."

"That won't work," Trevor said. "We just have to go ahead as usual and hope for the best."

"You're right," Wendell said. "So the question which now has to be answered is this: what do I do if Harold or Kessegoo'ee try to blackmail me?"

"What would they want that you could give them?" Angus asked.

"Chester's portfolio, for starters, and yours, too, Angus."

"If that's what it takes, Wendell," said Angus, "I'm willing to step aside. Of course, I can't speak for Chester."

"I guess I could replace him due to the condition of his health." Wendell said. "But neither one of them would be right for those port-folios."

"Wendell," Joan said quietly, "you've already refused to be black-mailed once. You can't depart from that course now. If they try it on, you have to say 'no.'"

There was a long silence during which Wendell stared at the car-pet, deep in thought.

At length he looked up and sighed. "Yes, Joan, you're right. Dammit!"

"What if one of them goes over to the other side?" Stephanie asked.

"We would scrape in by the skin of our teeth," I said.

"And if we lost both of them...?" Clark asked.

"We'd lose," I said.

"Fuck!" Stephanie cursed and we all gaped at her. Prior to this, none of us had ever heard her swear. She was always so proper and classy.

"On that note, we'd better disperse," Wendell said. "As of now, we still have the numbers. I think I'll have a word with Harold and Kese-goo'e and see if there is some bribe I can offer them without giving them the key to the vault."

"Be very careful, Wendell," said Joan. "Very careful indeed."

"I will." He pressed his intercom button. "Susan, will you get Ms. Sillyboy and Mr. MacDonald over here right away, please?"

As the others filed out of the office, I hung back.

"Wendell, after you've seen them, I need to have a word with you."

"Okay. Why don't you stay? You're the Chief Whip, and I need a wit-ness."

We walked to the window and stood side by side, watching the traffic below. It was at moments like this that I realized what a big man Wendell was. He towered above my six feet, and I noticed that he had to bend slightly so that his eyeline would clear the head of the window.

There was a knock on the door. It was Harold.

"Come in, Harold. Sit down. There's no point beating around the bush. You know I'm in a bit of a pickle. I need to know where you stand."

"I thought you might," MacDonald said in his broad Cape Breton accent. Then he grinned. "I brought my shopping list with me."

"No, I won't have that. One favour in return for your support. And it can't be a different portfolio, at least not yet."

"Hmm. In that case, I want a new coal mine opened in Glace Bay."

"You're joking?"

"No, b'y. Unemployment is too high in my constituency. I need a new industry which'll employ a lot of men."

"But, even if it were viable—and that's a huge 'if'—you're talking hundreds of millions of dollars, which we don't have. Opening a new mine would be like turning the clock back twenty years."

"You heard my offer."

"There must be something more reasonable."

"Alright, make my brother, Lauchie, Deputy Minister of Highways and Public Works."

"But your brother is…"

"Is what?"

"Nothing."

"You were going to say that my brother's a fool, weren't you?"

Wendell said nothing.

"Weren't you?"

"Something like that, yeah. Let's face it, Harold, Lauchie's not up to the job. You know that."

"After insulting my family, you can take it or leave it!" He jumped up and made for the door.

"That's your final offer?"

"Yeah! You better believe it is."

"Then, I have to say no."

"Fucking jigaboo!"

"Why you—"

Like lightning I managed to get between them, and with great difficulty held Wendell back while MacDonald got away. Wendell was so fit and strong that in another minute he would have overpowered me and there would have been bloodshed.

Breathing hard, we both collapsed into the nearest armchairs.

"Thanks, Marc. If I'd got my hands on him, God knows what would have happened."

"It would have ended your premiership, that's for sure."

"Maybe it's ended anyway."

"Maybe not. I might be able to find a way out of this."

At that moment there was a knock on the door and Kesegoo'e Silly-boy poked in her head.

"I didn't know you were busy, premier. I can come back later."

"No, please come in and have a seat."

"I understood you wanted to speak in private," she said, nodding towards me.

"These are difficult times and I want to be sure there are no misunderstandings. Marc is here as a witness."

"Oh. Well, I have nothing to hide and I don't care who knows what I say."

"That's good. Exactly what I want."

I was amazed how quickly Wendell had switched from towering rage to soft-spoken gentility. He was kindness itself in dealing with Sillyboy; all smiles and deference. In contrast, she looked and sounded aggrieved and combative.

"Would you like a cup of coffee...or tea?" He half rose from his seat to show his eagerness to accommodate her.

"No, thank you, premier. I think we should get down to business."

"Exactly. You know about the notice of motion?"

She nodded.

"Not to put too fine a point on it, I wonder if I can count on your support."

"I appreciate your directness. I shall be equally direct. You want to know what you could do to make sure I vote against this motion."

"In a nutshell, yes."

"I don't think there is anything you would be prepared to consider. You know my views on reparations. Apart from that, what I would like most are a thousand new, modern, equipped houses, but you wouldn't do that either, would you?"

"Keegoo'e, you know my opinion on identity politics. I don't believe in it. I think it is divisive, corrosive and racist. I think you know that, as a black man I have never, ever played the race card.

"That aside, even if I believed in reparations, we don't have the money and I wouldn't raise taxes to a level which would provide the necessary sum. As for houses, I recognize the desperate need for new housing on reserves, but even if I wanted to provide them, I can't because they're within federal jurisdiction."

"I knew you'd say that."

They just sat there looking at each other in a kind of staring match.

Finally, Wendell shifted in his seat and leant across the desk. "So, what will you do about the motion?"

"I've been a loyal member of your cabinet and have great respect for you and your achievements, especially considering the prejudice you had to overcome. But I have to consider my options. You and I both know that whichever way this goes, and whoever is premier, I'll be in the cabinet because I'm the only indigenous woman."

"You're right about that," Wendell said with a laugh.

"So I have to decide what happens if you go. Should I try to be leader and premier?"

I could see that this took Wendell as much by surprise as it did me. Sillyboy for premier! Was it a feasible proposition? I knew that in Dana Edwards' party they would elect her leader in a shot *because* of her ethnic identity, but I wasn't nearly so sure about our party. With some of our people there was, if not actual prejudice, a lingering suspicion of what used to be called "Indians."

"So you'll keep us in suspense until the moment of decision?"

"Yes, that's when I'll make up my mind."

"Well," said Wendell, standing up, "thank you for being honest. I wish you well, whatever you decide. The respect you say you have for me is reciprocated."

"Thank you, premier. Goodbye, Marc."

She rose very slowly and drifted out of the office.

When she was gone, Wendell thumped the desk. "Damn! That woman's got balls."

"Yes, but I think we have to assume she is now in the other column."

"You're right."

"We have to adjust our plans accordingly."

"What was all that about before, Marc?" Wendell stared hard at me. "You said you might be able to find a way out of this."

"Oh, yes. If we had another MLA, Zila could create a tie."

"Could she do that?",

"Yes. Under the rules, the chair can vote to break, or *make,* a toe.

And, if there is a tie it would mean the motion would be lost."

"But we don't have another fucking MLA, you clown!"

"Yes, we do."

"What are you talking about?"

"Ellie MacLeod."

"Who the hell is…? Oh, isn't that the nice-looking one who sits behind Wilkins on the opposition benches?"

"It is."

"What about her?"

"She wants to cross the floor."

"No!"

"Yes. If you will have her."

"Will I have her? You bet I will." The grin disappeared from his face. "Are you sure she'd be with us on the vote?"

"Absolutely."

"Marc, I could kiss you."

"Please don't. A simple 'thank you' is sufficient."

"What's her constituency?"

"Queens."

"How soon could she get up here?"

"She's in the city. I can have her here in half an hour."

"Well, go get her, Marc. What are you waiting for?"

Ellie and the premier got on like a house on fire. I just sat back and listened to them swapping jokes and stories as if they had been bosom friends for years.

I hated to interrupt, but there was an important point which needed clearing up. "Excuse me please, but, Ellie, I have to ask if you are a member."

"A member of what?"

"Of this party."

"No. Should I be?"

"You sure should," said Wendell, reaching into a drawer, fishing out a form and pushing it across the desk. "Sign here and give me twenty dollars."

"I've only been here five minutes and already you're trying to fleece me," said Ellie, laughing.

"Sign it E. MacLeod," I said.

"Why?"

"So we can process it quickly without any questions being asked or any measures taken to foil it."

"All very cloak and dagger, but if you think so…"

She signed the form and found the money from her purse. "Is that it?"

"No," I said. "If you have a membership card in your former party, you must destroy it."

"Yeah," Wendell said. "You can't be a member of two parties."

She rummaged in her bag and found the card. Wendell solemnly handed her a pair of scissors, which she used to cut the card into small pieces.

"Wonderful!" I said. "Ellie, you don't know how happy you've made us."

"So when's this vote?" she asked.

"I'm waiting to hear about Chester. He was taken ill earlier. As soon as I know he's going to be alright, I'll have the Speaker summon the House. The caucus meeting would be a day or two days before that."

As if right on cue, Tom came bustling into the office. "Boss, I've just come from the hospital…oh, hello, Ellie. What are you doing here?"

"Ellie's our newest caucus member," said Wendell.

"No kidding? That's great. How…?"

"Marc found her out on the wild ocean and brought her to safe haven."

"Amazing. Look, about Chester. They say he had a stroke. They don't yet know how serious it is."

"Is he conscious?" I asked.

"No. And they say he could be in this state for weeks. They told me that sometimes the patient is out for years."

"*Years?*" Wendell was aghast.

"Yes, they said this could develop into a coma. The doctor said something about a Glasgow scale, but I didn't really understand it."

"So, there's no hope for an early recovery?"

"No chance."

"Poor old Chester."

Wendell looked inexpressibly sad. I may have been mistaken, but I thought I saw a tear in his eye.

He sniffed and came round to sit on the edge of desk. "I guess there's no point in delaying. I'll get Zila to call a meeting next week. We may as well get it over with."

"And a session of the House?"

"Better leave that in abeyance for the time being. I may not be in charge by then."

"Let's not give up hope yet," said Tom. "Marc, you'd better do a new scorecard so we can clearly see where we are."

AGAINST THE MOTION		FOR THE MOTION
PROCTOR		JONES
HOWARD		CHAN
McKINNON		PARISH
TREVOR		MURPHY
LEAMAN		ASKEY
REID		JOSEPH
MacPHEE	SILLYBOY?	GARDINER
GILMOUR		RUTLEDGE
CLARK		MITCHELL
McNEIL		HENDRICKS
MacLEOD		WALTERS
LEBLANC		WAYBRET
SULLIVAN	CHAIR ZILA FRANKS	DORION
NATHANSON		D'ENTREMONT
		STAIRS
		McDONALD
14		16

They watched me as I took out a fresh sheet of Bristol board and hastily penned in the names and where everyone stood. We stood back and surveyed what was, now, a gloomily discouraging display. I could tell that Wendell was considering how many things he had done wrongly to bring him to this point.

Wendell and Tom stayed behind to deal with a question concerning a government loan to a company which had defaulted, so I left.

After dropping Ellie off, I drove back to the Proctors' house and put the Bugatti in the second bay of their garage. When I got in, Cynthia was sitting at the kitchen table, a glass of what looked like scotch in front of her.

"Hi, Marc," she said, "would you like a drink?"

"I would, thanks. It's been a hell of a day."

She got up, walked over to the counter and returned with the bottle and a glass. She poured me a generous measure and slumped in her chair. "Where are we now?" she asked wearily.

"I'm afraid that, as of today, we have fourteen sure votes and they have sixteen. Kessegoo'e Sillyboy is still on the fence."

"That figures. She's a calculating lady."

"I saw that today. She thinks she could become premier."

"That doesn't surprise me in the least." She took a sip of whisky. "You know, Marc, I won't mind if he loses. For his sake as well as mine."

"You can't mean that."

"Yes, I can. You've no idea what a strain this has been on us—on our health and our marriage."

"I can understand why you would feel like that, but Wendell seems to be taking it all in his stride."

"You're quite wrong about that, Marc. Wendell is such a proud man, the thought of being defeated is crushing him."

"I guess I haven't seen that side of him."

"Worse than being defeated for him is the thought that so many people are against him because they don't like him,"

"I've certainly not seen that side of him. He seems so self-assured, and almost indifferent to what people think of him."

"It's his size which helps to give that impression. Underneath he's more sensitive than me. You know, sometimes when we're alone at night, he cries."

"Cynthia," I said, horrified by these intimate confessions, "I don't think you should be telling me stuff like this."

"Well, we both love him, each in our own way, don't we?"

I had not considered my relationship with Wendell in that way, but when I thought about why my journey in political life had come so far so quickly, I had to admit that my feelings for him were not unlike those towards a brother.

"Yes, I guess we do." I said. "But we won't have long to wait. One way or another, it'll be over next Tuesday."

"That's four days from now." She drained her glass. "It will be good to have him home more often and not coming in after midnight every day."

I nodded my agreement, but secretly I thought of the old saying from *Aesop's Fables*: "Be careful what you wish for, lest it come true!"

39

Waiting for the caucus meeting was excruciating. Everything hung on whatever decision Kesegoo'e made.

Of secondary interest to me, but it was tweaking my curiosity, was the reasoning behind her decision. If she had conducted soundings and found that she had widespread support as a candidate for leadership, then I supposed we were finished. I was totally committed to Wendell; he was the entire *raison d'être* for my being in politics. But the notion of Kesegoo'e as premier was an appealing one in the abstract, but only in the abstract. While I admired her courage, I hoped our colleagues would give her no encouragement in her aspirations so we could get her vote.

It was, I knew, a cowardly and unworthy wish, but we were in a life or death situation and could not afford to allow sentiment to get in our way.

This is why, without telling any of the others, I went to see Kesegoo'e that night. On the pretext of wanting to get some documents to her by courier, I found out from Sandy Ferguson at the caucus office where Kesegoo'e lived.

I do not know what I expected. I am ashamed to admit that I half anticipated her to be living in a kind of commune with a shaman and a lot of sweet grass and smoke blowing. I was amazed to discover that her address was one of the ritziest, most expensive in the city.

It was a very different woman who answered the door from the one I had last seen in Wendell's office. It had never occurred to me that she would wear makeup, that her brown complexion would need any artificial assistance. Clearly, that was not the case, and the person standing before me appeared to be very small, very thin, very plain, and almost white.

"Marc. It's you."

"Kesegoo'e, I'm sorry to bother you."

"It's gone ten o'clock."

"I know, but I had to come."

"I understand."

"May I come in?"

"Yes, but I warn you I have my panic button at the ready." She laughed, showing brilliant white teeth. "If you lay a hand on me the police will be here in minutes."

"Thanks for letting me know." I said as I walked into the most luxurious apartment I had ever seen. The carpets were so lush one's feet almost sank into them. There was a strange smell in the air and I could see wisps of fine smoke.

"Are you burning sweet grass?"

"The term is smudging. But no, that's incense. Like it?"

"Not particularly."

"Sit down, Marc."

I have difficulties with our own arm chairs and couch at home in Grand Pre being so sumptuous as to be too comfortable, but Kesegoo'e's were opulent to the extent that you almost disappeared into them.

"Wow! Bit of a change from the old tepee," I said.

"Marc!"

"Sorry, I couldn't resist."

"I'll remember that and use it myself sometime. It'd be alright for me." She settled herself and was so enveloped by the chair that she looked like a tiny, frightened kitten.

She knew why I had come, and we rehashed what had been said in Wendell's office. Then she veered off into the story of her life.

It was a tale of both incredible success and good luck, and of horrendously painful and difficult experiences. That she had chosen a political life in the 'white' world outside the reserve was a decision she said she couldn't rationally explain except to say that she thought she might serve her people better.

She told me about her great triumph in securing the party's nomination in Truro-Bible Hill and having been elected three times since then. The first time she was voted in was when an old party supporter, ignorantly wanting to show respect, called her "little mother."

"I don't know where he got that from!" She shrieked with laughter.

"Sounds like something out of Tolstoy."

"I like him, although by all accounts he wasn't a very nice man."

"But Wendell is."

"Yes."

"Kesegoo'e, can I ask you if you've taken any soundings about support for the leadership...should the job ever be vacant."

"Yes. I have."

"And?"

"Fifty-fifty."

"Not very helpful in making your decision."

"No." She seemed sad and tired.

"I won't burden you anymore," I said, doing my best to get out of the chair.

"It is late. And we have a big day tomorrow."

"The biggest."

"I'm sorry I couldn't be more help, Marc. I don't even know myself what I'm going to do. You'll know when everybody else does."

"Thank you anyway."

"I'm sorry about my name."

"Your name? What do you mean?"

"The votes will be called alphabetically. You'll have to wait until something like twenty-five other people have voted before you know mine."

40

When we gathered in the caucus room at noon the next day, you could cut the atmosphere with the proverbial knife. While there were coffee urns, plates of sandwiches, and baskets of cakes and cookies on the tables around the walls, nobody was under any illusion that this was a party. There was no waving, laughing with or even nodding to those who once had been friends, but now were in opposite camps.

Normally caucus members sat in assigned positions based upon seniority, but today most of those in favour of the motion had crowded together around the table on the right side of the room. As I watched them, I could see that their leaders were thrilled to have Harold MacDonald with them, and were absolutely ecstatic to see Stairs and D'Entremont on their side.

It appeared to me that quite a few of them had not been aware of the strength of their own numbers until today, and seemed a little nervous with that knowledge. Now that they knew they might win, I wondered how many were regretting their positions, maybe thinking they had gone too far. After all, some of them representing marginal constituencies had been elected on Wendell's coattails, and if they replaced him, who could say what, if any, magnetic appeal the new leader might have?

I noticed Waybert and Gardiner, in particular, looking extremely uncomfortable and grim. Were they thinking they had chosen the wrong side? And, I wondered how they would vote if the ballot were secret. Instantly, I realized that we had not settled whether it should be open or secret, and quickly tried to figure out which method would best serve our purposes. If I had been able to decide that, I was prepared to make an issue out of it.

In the event, it did not matter, because as soon as Zila had called the meeting to order, Kesegoo'e moved that the ballot be secret.

Whether that was a good sign or bad, I could not make up my mind.

Waybert seconded the motion. Zila ruled that the motion was procedural and could not be debated. When she asked for the "Ayes", there were only seven votes in favour. I tried to see whose hands had gone up but could only see Waybert's. On the call for the "nays" Zila announced that twenty-three had voted against. She did not reveal who had been the lone abstention.

"Order, please!" Zila shouted for silence. "We will now proceed to the only item of business. In the interests of brevity"—there were some laughs at this—"including the mover of the motion, I will ask each side to name six speakers, each of whom may have a maximum of fifteen minutes. The mover will have an additional ten minutes to close the debate. Please consult with your colleagues and come up with your chosen speakers."

I could see that some in the room were minded to challenge these rules, but changed their minds because they realized there would be no chance of the chair being overruled.

On a sheet of note paper, Joan hastily scribbled six names. She showed it to Wendell, who nodded, then passed it down the line. Nobody objected to her list, although some eyebrows were raised when they saw Ellie's name there.

I could see the commotion on the other side and could only guess who was on their list. I could see Joseph asking Gardiner, but he shook his head. The same happened with Angela Stairs, Pierre Dorion, and my old nemesis, Carol Walters.

After further consultation and apparent argument, Jones finally passed their list to Zila.

"The names submitted to the Chair are as follows: For the mover's side Gloria Jones, Delia Parish, Leila Hendricks, Freeman Murphy, Emma Mitchell, and Jenny Chan. For the opposers' side, Angus MacKinnon, Sean Leman, John Trevor, Joan Howard, Ellie MacLeod and Wendell Proctor."

There was a general murmuring and shuffling as the choices were considered, approved or disapproved according to each person's taste and prejudices. I was surprised that they had left off Askey and MacDonald, both of whom were powerful orators.

As the other side examined our list, there seemed to be a degree of consternation among them.

"Madam Chair." It was Delia. "Point of information."

"There's no such thing as a point of information," Zila said. So far, I thought she was conducting herself admirably. "If the member would like to raise a point of order she may do so, but it is not strictly proper while a vote is taking place."

"This Ellie MacLeod is a member of the Opposition! She's got no right to be here. She's a member of another party!"

"No, I have examined her membership card and it is quite in order. Ms. McLeod crossed the floor and became a member of our caucus last week."

The defection of a member of the opposition would normally be treated as a pleasant surprise worthy of celebration, but on this occasion Jones's side seemed to regard it as a piece of Wendell's trickery.

"The motion before the meeting is as follows: *Resolved that the caucus ask the party to hold a leadership review as soon as possible*. The motion is moved by Gloria Jones and seconded by Delia Parish. I call upon Ms. Jones to state her case."

Whatever their case amounted to, we had heard it all before. There were recitations of Wendell's arrogance, his lack of communication, lack of consultation, lack of sensitivity, lack of consideration, lack of understanding, and lack of respect; but almost all of it was conveyed in generalities with few allusions to specifics.

Delia and Gloria both used bitter language claiming that Wendell had "deserted his own people."

Freeman Murphy seemed to forget what the motion was all about and spent most of his time ranting about "an ungrateful public."

If any mind other than Kesegoo'e's was available to be changed, it would certainly have been adversely affected by Jennie Chan's speech, which seethed with the most bitter of poisonous invective.

Leila Hendricks broke down and descended into an embarrassing display of whimpering before Chan pushed her back into her seat.

To my amazement the best speech, but the most dishonest, on their side came from Emma Mitchell, who was remarkably cool and collected, and presented a well-marshalled array of facts, which by themselves were nothing, but when put together sounded like a damning indictment.

I was immensely proud of the performance of our side. Angus, of course, was magnificent, his stentorian tones rang throughout the room as he waved his finger at the opposition asking, "Which of you can say you have not benefited from Wendell Proctor's leadership and kindness, not in one way, but in many, many ways?"

Joan spoke of her glitzy career in Hollywood, and how none of the fame, the glamour, the awards, the adulation of the paparazzi meant as much to her as working alongside "this wonderful man, this great human being."

Leaman surprised me by delivering a dynamic, if unduly pointed, attack on some of our opponents, summing up by saying, not very diplomatically, that Wendell was "better than ten of you put together."

John Trevor simply got up and said, "Wendell is the best, and I want the best. I don't know where you expect to find anyone as good as him, but good luck with that."

The second-best speech of the afternoon came from Ellie MacLeod. She used no histrionics, but made an irrefutable, logical case. She had been drawn to the party by Premier Proctor. She had been moved to cross the floor, not by Ms. Jones, or Ms. Parish, or Mr, Murphy or Ms. Mitchell, but by Wendell Proctor. If the party wanted to attract others as it had her, they had better keep in place their best asset.

Jones, as the mover, had the last word, but it must have been the greatest anticlimax in history because the desperate repetition of her opening arguments was lost in the tumult caused by Wendell's speech which immediately preceded hers. I do not know where I got the words from—likely the Bible—but I later told Rosalie that Wendell "arose in his wrath like an avenging angel."

"Madame Chair," he began quietly, almost inaudibly. Those who leaned forward to catch what he was saying were soon sent reeling back by his next words.

"Now listen to me!" he thundered. "I am a black man. I am the equal of every one of you. No better and no worse. I will not bow. I will not scrape. I will not crawl. And I will not beg. I fought for this job. I have earned this job. I am owed this job. You want me to fawn, to apologize, and to simper?" At this point his voice was almost deafening. "You want me to kiss your feet? I will not. I will not kiss your feet! I will not fawn and simper! I will not apologize for having won two elections for you. I will not beg for my job! I will not beg!"

It was the shortest and most powerful address I had ever heard, more for the way it was delivered than for its content, although that too stirred the blood. Our side went wild, cheering and pounding the table. I saw Joan and Angus put their arms around Wendell. I could see that Joan was crying.

"Order, please!" Zila shouted above the hubbub. "We will now proceed to the vote. A secret ballot having been rejected, this will be conducted by roll call in alphabetical order. Those in favour of asking the party for a leadership review will say, 'aye'; those opposed will say, 'nay'.

"Fred Askey."
"Aye."
"Jennie Chan."
"Aye."
"Bill Clark."
"Nay."
"Alaric D'Entremont."
"Aye."
"Pierre Dorion."
"Aye."
"Mark Gardiner."
"Aye."
"Stephanie Gilmour."
"Nay."
"Leila Hendricks."
"Aye."
"Joan Howard."
"Nay."
"Gloria Jones."
"Aye."
"Zandili Joseph."
"Aye"
"Sean Leaman."
"Nay."
"Marc LeBlanc."
"Nay."
"Harold MacDonald."
"Aye."
"Ellie MacLeod."

"Nay."

"Angus McKinnon."

"Nay."

"Hector McNeil."

"Nay."

"Cullum McPhee."

"Nay."

"Emma Mitchell."

"Aye"

"Freeman Murphy."

"Aye."

"Dan Nathanson."

"Nay."

"Delia Parish."

"Aye."

"Wendell Proctor."

"Nay!"

"Jeremy Reid."

"Nay."

"Jill Rutledge."

"Aye."

"Kesegoo'e Sillyboy."

There was a silence of about five seconds, during which I almost chewed my tongue off. I held my breath and prayed.

"Ms. Sillyboy, are you going to vote?"

"Yes. I vote nay."

The relief was immense on our side, and it was not at all clear if the other side appreciated the significance of Kesegoo'e's vote.

"Angela Stairs."

"Aye."

"Arthur Sullivan."

"Nay."

"John Trevor."

"Nay."

"Carol Walters."

"Aye."

"Norman Waybert."

"Aye."

That concludes the vote. I declare those in favour of the motion to be sixteen votes and those opposed to be 15...Order please!"

The other side was cheering and thumping the table.

"Order please. In accordance with the rules, where there is one more vote in the *affirmative* than in the negative, the chair can create a tie by voting in the negative to cause the motion to fail. I therefore cast my vote in the negative, so the motion is los—"

"Excuse me," came a voice from thee doorway. It was an old voice. A voice thinned by much usage over many years. But today, it was a clear voice.

We all turned to look.

"Why, Mr, Speaker," said Zilia hesitantly.

"Madame Chair, I have been a member of this party for almost half a century. I am also a member of this caucus, I demand to know why my name was not called."

"Why, I didn't know—"

"Call it now, if you please!"

"Er...all right...Ernest Maddingly."

"I vote Aye."

The room broke into an uproar, their side jubilant with having overcome our tactics and our side enraged by Maddingly's unexpected appearance. He had never attended caucus since he was made Speaker, never attended a party meeting of any kind, but that did not extinguish his rights.

There was no reason at all why Wendell and the others should have thought of this eventuality. But I should have. The words he had spoken to me two years earlier should have resonated with me long before this moment. He had told me he had been forced out of the premiership by a 'jumped up cabal', and, of course, Wendell had been a member of the 'cabal' and had been the primary beneficiary of their actions.

After nurturing his grievance to keep it warm for all these years, Ernest Maddingly finally had his revenge.

Epilogue

"Do you think Wendell could have fought the leadership review?" Rosalie asked me one summer several years later.

"In theory," I said. We were sitting on our deck in the declining afternoon sun, sipping our preprandial drinks. "But he would have been so damaged. Personally and politically."

"Would the convention have backed him?"

"I'm not sure. Maybe, but the delegates would have known that he didn't have the majority of the caucus with him. That would have discouraged many many from voting for him."

"I'll bet he wanted to fight."

"Oh, yes. When we went back to his office he was all for fighting. So were most of the rest of us."

"Including you?"

"At that moment, yes."

"What turned the tide?"

"Joan. She told him the game was up. That if he went on he would lose everything—his leadership, his self-respect and his marriage. She said that if he went to the convention, she would vote against him because she could not subject him to that indignity."

"Really? There's not much he could do after that. Do you think Joan was in love with Wendell?"

"I don't think she was *in* love with him. She loved him as we all did, but not in that way."

"And you don't think she had an ulterior motive in getting him to quit?"

"No. Not at all."

"Well, she did succeed him as leader."

"I was out of it by time. A good thing, too. I wouldn't have been able to choose between Joan and Kesegoo'e."

"It was close wasn't it?"

"Five votes. A squeaker. But then, Joan lost the next election."

"You think it was inevitable?"

"Yes. It was on the cards. The party had been in office for almost twenty years. It was time for a change."

"Now we have Premier Wilkins. What's he like?"

"Not bad, I guess. I never knew him that well."

"Do you regret not having friends in high places anymore?"

"If I'm honest, I do. I regret it. But, you know what is the oddest thing?"

"What?"

"What I regret most is that I never did find out why Carol Walters hated me."

Jeremy Akerman

Acknowledgements

I should like to record grateful thanks to my wife, Caroll Anne, for having read and approved each chapter as it was written.

I also want to acknowledge the debt I owe to the late C. P. Snow, the author of many fine novels which have sustained me all my life. One of his greatest stories, *The Masters,* is in part the inspiration for this book.

In 1964 C.P. Snow became Lord Snow of Leicester, and it was a few years later that I established contact with him. He told me that nearly all of his many characters were based upon real people whom he had known, and advised me to do the same. He said that the more closely the fictional people were based on the actual, the more true they would seem to the reader. I have never forgotten that, although I have not stuck to it as assiduously as he did. He died in 1980 aged only 74. He wrote 17 books during his life. Had he lived another ten years we might have had another half dozen wonderful works from him.

About the author

Jeremy Akerman is an adoptive Nova Scotian who has lived in the province since 1964. In that time he has been an archaeologist, a radio announcer, a politician, a senior civil servant, a newspaper editor and a film actor.

He is painter of landscapes and portraits, a singer of Irish folk songs, a lover of wine, and a devotee of history, especially of the British Labour Party.

Jeremy's first novel, *Black Around the Eyes,* was published in 1981. Other projects required his intention until recently, when he was able to take up fiction again. From the start of 2023 to the spring of 2025, he wrote and published ten novels.

See: moosehousepress.com/authors/jeremy-akerman